Ramona crossed the street to  a convenience store. From t clerk in the bulletproof booth, at i Were they just what they seemed curiosity failed to get the best of i she did, however, a shift in the _____ _____ brought her up short. A faint, vaguely familiar scent caught her attention. Her flaring nostrils held onto it for only a moment before it was gone.

I know that smell, she told herself, but from where, and what was it?

She stood and sniffed at the air, but the briefly teasing breeze on that sticky summer night was dead.

She knew that scent. *What is it?* she tried to recall.

Suddenly, Ramona turned to her right, upwind, and dashed in that direction. If the wind wouldn't cooperate, she'd find the source of that smell herself.

One block then another fell behind her. She scanned the street and kept alert for the odor she was tracking. The mortals driving past probably didn't see her. She moved with a speed that only recently had ceased to surprise her.

After six blocks, she stopped and again sniffed at the air. The scent was gone, or else it was masked by the rich, layered stink of the city. Ramona felt sure that she could pick it out if it was still there.

She stood for several minutes half-heartedly sniffing. Nothing.

Maybe, she began to think, she was just overreacting to her surroundings. New York offered hundreds of new odors every night, and the potency of her sense of smell still caught her off guard at times, even after two years.

VAMPIRE

THE MASQUERADE

CLAN NOVEL

GANGREL

BY Gherbod Fleming

WHITE WOLF

part one

stone

Wednesday, 7 July 1999, 12:34 AM
A tenement in Harlem
New York City, New York

Quiet. Or as close to quiet as Zhavon was ever likely to hear. True silence was something she wouldn't have recognized. Even in the middle of the night, there were cars in the distance. And maybe gunshots, but they didn't bother her unless they were really close. She could even block out the sounds from the street below: a drunk, or a prostitute, sometimes one and the same—a faceless, skanky woman who might once have been beautiful (it was hard to imagine), but the drugs and the never-ending game of musical pricks had worn her out, until she was not much more than a skinny collection of gaudy colors and harsh angles—tits and elbows, lipstick and high heels.

Those noises were background, the undercurrent of life. Zhavon would've missed them if they were gone.

She almost didn't hear anymore the stomping and screaming of the Hernandez children downstairs. They were in bed now, and the late-night almost-calm had reluctantly settled over the apartment building.

The particular sounds that Zhavon strained to hear were not in evidence. The next room was quiet. Mama had gone to bed. Half an hour later, just like every night, she'd gotten up for a glass of water and then gone back to bed. That had been an hour ago. If this were going to be one of the sleepless nights, the TV would have come on by now. Not loud, because Mama wouldn't want to wake Zhavon, but with walls thin enough that she could hear someone on the other side scratch an itch, each commercial came through clear as day. But not tonight. Mama was asleep. She had to get up early in the morning and catch the subway to work.

Zhavon dressed silently. Mama might be willing to sleep her nights away, but her little girl wasn't.

Little girl, hell, Zhavon thought.

She was fifteen, a grown woman. She had friends who already had little babies. But that wasn't the life for her. No how. No way. She'd seen what her friends went through, lugging around screaming children or dumping them off with an aunt or cousin just to get away once in a while. Nothing wrong with babies, but they were a lot of work and a lot of money.

At least Mama had a job. She wasn't about to sit back and rot on welfare, and neither was Zhavon. She was going to finish school. Someday she'd have a job and a baby, but not yet.

Of course, that didn't mean boys were off limits.

The window was open and beckoning. The beat-up air conditioner they'd had didn't work anymore. Sure, it rattled and dripped, but that was about it. Didn't condition much air. Next paycheck, Mama was going to buy a fan, but for now, Zhavon slipped easily enough through the window, after checking the fire escape to make sure that Mr. Hernandez wasn't sitting out below.

Some nights, especially when it was really hot, he would sit out there and drink beer. When he did, Zhavon could smell the cigarette smoke and hear the clink of bottle caps as they bounced through the iron ladders down to the street. He wasn't there tonight, but blue TV light flickered from inside his apartment.

Zhavon cautiously climbed down to the Hernandezes' window and peeked between the worn curtains that hung lifelessly in the still air. Mr. Hernandez was asleep on the couch. His wife sat next to him and stared at the TV. Mrs. Hernandez, like Mama, was pretty, but it was a tired pretty. Four babies had taken it out of the Puerto Rican woman, had drained the life from her, but despite the sunken eyes, her face was still attractive and thin—small nose, high cheekbones. She was lucky not to have any scars from the times that Mr. Hernandez drank too much and hit her. It didn't happen often, but when it did, Zhavon and Mama heard it like they were right there.

Hell, the whole block hears it, Zhavon thought.

Last time had been the worst. So loud Zhavon had thought she could feel his fist. Mama'd had enough. Zhavon tried to stop her, but Mama went down there and said if he was going to hit his wife again, he'd have to hit Mama first. All the yelling back and forth, Zhavon had been afraid he'd do it, but after a while, he stomped out cursing and slammed the door. Pretty quiet since then.

Squatting there on the fire escape outside the window, Zhavon noticed the almost-empty beer bottles by her feet. She picked one up. There was no cigarette butt inside, so she took a swig. She tried not to grimace—*Tastes like piss!*—but couldn't help it. Her friends always teased her about that whenever Alvina stole a six-pack from her daddy.

Still wondering how anybody could like the stuff, Zhavon put the bottle back down, but the glass knocked against the metal fire escape. The hollow clink, as it echoed through the still night, sounded to Zhavon as loud as the garbage truck rumbling down the alley at 6:00 in the morning. She jerked back from the window and held her breath. Her heart pounded furiously. Zhavon waited for what seemed like forever, holding so still that she thought she'd pee her pants.

Nothing happened. The chatter from the TV continued unabated. The blue light still flickered from inside. There was no sign that anyone had heard the bottle, but Zhavon still wasn't sure. She edged toward the window again and peeked in.

Mr. Hernandez hadn't budged. He was still dead to the world with his head lolled back against the couch. Mrs. Hernandez, however, seemed more alert than before. She'd tilted her head to the side and was listening more closely.

She heard! Zhavon realized. She went completely rigid—afraid to move, afraid to breathe.

Eventually Mrs. Hernandez, probably satisfied that whatever she might've heard was not one of her children, returned her attention to the quietly droning TV. Mr. Hernandez stirred in his sleep, and she lovingly stroked a curl on his forehead.

Zhavon breathed a long, silent sigh. Just to be safe, she waited a few more minutes—it seemed like hours—then snuck one more look in the window to satisfy herself that Mrs. Hernandez wasn't on to her. The older woman sat oblivious as before.

Four babies in a one-bedroom apartment, thought Zhavon, shaking her head in disbelief. The same size apartment was small for just her and Mama, and that with Mama giving Zhavon the bedroom and sleeping on a pullout sofa. Zhavon shook her head again. But that was Mrs. Hernandez's life, and Zhavon had her own to lead.

The last two turns of the fire escape passed only blank wall and ended ten or twelve feet above the alley. Lowering the last length of ladder would make too much noise, so Zhavon instead dangled from the bottom step and dropped. Later, she would climb the drain pipe to get back to the steps. She was fairly athletic and coordinated, but this time she landed hard and had to catch herself to keep from falling on her butt. A sharp, stinging pain shot through her right hand.

"Ow! Shit!" she half whispered, half blurted out.

She raised her hand to find a beer-bottle cap stuck into her palm. It must have been lying on the ground with the jagged edge pointed up. Zhavon plucked it from her hand and blood welled up from the tiny but deep ring of holes. She was more angry than hurt as she threw the bottle cap against the wall and glared up at the Hernandezes' window.

Stinkin' Rican drunk.

There was nobody in the alley. No one to have seen her or to have heard her call out when she hurt her hand. Even so, Zhavon remained crouching low and looked carefully around. Sometimes, even when she was alone in her own room, she had the feeling that someone was watching her. For a moment just then, she'd felt that way again. But, she knew now, there was no one there.

Zhavon turned her thoughts to what had brought her out tonight:

Adrien.

Just thinking about him sent shivers down her spine. He was tall and fine, and he didn't wear his pants falling down off his ass. Sure, she'd smacked him the other day when he felt her up, but that was because she wanted respect from the man.

Not because she didn't want him. Zhavon wasn't about to let him crawl down her pants that easy, not yet. She knew the ratty club where he hung out. He wasn't old enough to get in either, but his brother worked the door, and as long as no cops were around and nobody was starting fights, who really cared anyway?

Zhavon turned right, away from the main street, and headed deeper down the alley. She had about twenty blocks to go, and she didn't want to draw the attention of anybody that would be driving around at this hour—policeman or pimp. There were plenty of alleys criss-crossing the middles of the blocks, and she was quiet enough and fast enough to scoot by anybody that might be trouble. She'd be gone—past or doubled back the way she came—before they even knew she was there.

She tried to think of what she was going to say to Adrien when she saw him. She didn't want him to get big-headed and think that she was desperate for him, because she wasn't. But why was she tracking across half the city to see him? No way he was going to believe that she just happened to be out and stopped in to get her under-aged ass a beer. She had to think of something. She could see him laughing, and the way his eyes shone. Zhavon had seen the way he looked at other girls. She wanted him to look at her that way, but she didn't want him to be a man who was on her, off her, and then out of her life. That's what had happened to her friends. The boys swarmed around like a bitch was in heat, but once they got what they wanted, they were gone until the next time they got an itch to scratch. Zhavon didn't want it that way.

She paused and hugged the wall as the alley opened into a larger street. An old, beat-up car was cruising along. Zhavon could make out the silhouettes of two people and the glowing ash of a cigarette hanging from the mouth of one. They didn't seem to take any notice of her as they drove by. She looked again, then ran across the street and partway down the block to the next alley. Seven or eight blocks down. Almost halfway.

One time a few weeks ago, Zhavon had mentioned Adrien to Mama, and Mama had gone off on the "car-stealin', dope-smokin' gangsta wannabe." Mama said that she knew his mama, and that he might as well be growing up in a crackhouse. She said not even the good Lord could make that apple fall far from the tree.

"But you don't even know him!" Zhavon had insisted. "You're always saying we should act charitable to people."

"I know him," Mama'd snapped. "I know his *type*. Why you think your daddy ain't 'round anymore? I'll be charitable to Adrien, all right. I'll be charitable when he brings hisself to church instead of sellin' drugs and chasin' girls."

But Mama was wrong. Zhavon winced at the thought of them yelling at each other. They'd never fought much. Never used to, anyway. Lately there seemed to be more to fight about every day. But that was only because Mama was as stubborn as she was wrong.

"If you're so smart, how come you work yourself to death and we're poor and live here in this stinkin' place?" That's what Zhavon had said, and she'd wished she hadn't the second the words were out of her mouth.

Mama had exploded. "You get your poor self to bed right now! Not another word! Not another word, or so help me...!" But that night Zhavon had heard Mama crying, even over the sound of the TV.

But she's wrong! Zhavon still held onto that. Mama couldn't always know what was right for Zhavon. She knew what she was doing. That's what she was thinking as she turned the corner and bumped right into a scraggly man out of nowhere.

Zhavon yelped in surprise. The man, she realized as he grabbed her, wasn't surprised at all. His dirty hand clamped down over her mouth flat and hard enough that she couldn't bite him. He lifted her almost off the ground—only the tips of her shoes brushed the pavement—and dragged her farther back into the dark alley. With the hand that wasn't over her mouth, he was grabbing at her chest, pressing and squeezing her breasts. She tried to bite again. Too tight against him to grab his balls, she reached up with her free hand, the arm that wasn't pinned, to scratch at his eyes.

Then she heard another noise—the sound of a switchblade clicking open. But the man pawing at her wasn't holding a knife. She saw movement in the shadows to her right. There was someone else.

For an instant, Zhavon thought that maybe someone was going to help her, to jab that knife into the dirty-handed bastard who had hold of her, but then she saw the twisted grin of the squint-eyed man who stepped out of the shadows. "Well, well, well. Whatcha got here, Reggie?" Light glinted on the blade of his knife.

Reggie didn't answer but guffawed and groped even harder as Zhavon stopped struggling. She could feel his hard-on pressed up against her ass.

"That's more like it," said squint-eye. "Don't want no trouble, do we?"

He moved the knife to her face and with the tip of the blade lightly traced a line from her chin down her neck. Zhavon's heart pounded until she thought it was going to explode out her ears. The stink and taste of Reggie's filthy hand overwhelmed her senses. As Reggie reached under her shirt and squint-eye fumbled with her belt, she began to feel sick to her stomach. Maybe that would make him let go of her mouth—if she threw up. Or maybe he wouldn't, and she'd choke on her own puke.

The knife pricked her skin at the collarbone. Squint-eye was getting excited, careless. His hand was down her pants, probing, but her knees were squeezed together. Frustrated by her resistance, he punched her in the eye. Lights danced in the darkness, and the strength drained out of Zhavon's legs. As squint-eye tugged at her pants, the knife dug more deeply into her shoulder.

The lights cleared and Zhavon twisted. The sudden move caught them off guard, but not so much so that Reggie lost his grip. Squint-eye cursed and hit her again in the face. The darkness closed in. She only faintly realized that he had her pants down to her knees. Reggie had ripped apart her bra and was bruising her nipple between his fingers. His stale breath and dripping spit were hot on her neck.

Don't kill me, she prayed as the lights danced for her. *Don't kill me.* But why should they rape her and leave her alive to call the cops?

"Mama..." Zhavon heard her own voice. Reggie had let go of her mouth and was grabbing at her crotch as squint-eye worked at his own fly.

Suddenly, in a snarling flash of motion, squint-eye was gone. The knife fell to the ground. Squint-eye cried out in pain and fear.

"What the...?" Reggie loosened his grip just enough that Zhavon was able to squirm out of his grasp. She spun as she dropped to her knees and, as hard as she could, swung her fist up into his crotch.

Reggie doubled over and crashed to the ground, where he lay wheezing. Zhavon fell back away from him. Her vision flickered as again the dancing lights smothered her.

Dear God...dear God...dear God...

The pavement was rough beneath her bare hip. She lay in a ball and clutched her ripped shirt to her chest. A few feet away, squint-eye no longer struggled. The night was full of savage growling and the sound of tearing—clothes? Skin? A rabid dog. Zhavon thought she saw the flash of canines. It pounced on Reggie. He started to scream, but the sound was cut off, lost to the snarling and rending.

Zhavon knew that she should get up and run. The dog would be on her any second. But she couldn't move. Her will had retreated deep within her. She could do nothing but hug her knees and rock back and forth and call for Mama. The alley was spinning. The taste of Reggie's hand was in her mouth, on her tongue. She flinched as his blood splattered across her face from several feet away. Lingering moans... The seconds and minutes ran together. She felt hands on her. Squint-eye was tugging at her pants. Reggie was grabbing at her chest, lifting her off the ground. But weren't they gone?

Don't kill me.... Dear God... "Don't kill me."

Dancing lights. Darkness. Spinning.

Zhavon's eyes fluttered open. Rusty iron. Ladder. Fire escape. And she saw a face, a girl not much older than herself—*Is that blood on her face?*—kneeling over her in the darkness. The girl held Zhavon's hand... was kissing it—no, *licking* her palm.

Darkness again.

But then Zhavon opened her eyes, and it was morning. The first pink light of sunrise was visible, and the city was already hot, sticky.

Zhavon hurt all over—her head, her shoulder, her chest, her legs. But she was home, lying outside her window. She was alive.

Lifting her right hand from her chest, she remembered the first and by far the least serious injury from the night, but the ring of tiny punctures from the bottle cap was gone.

Wednesday, 7 July 1999, 9:39 PM
The Bronx
New York City, New York

Water. Dripping. Ramona opened her eyes, but the darkness within mirrored the darkness without. Which way was up, which down? A sharp pain in her neck told her that she had been knotted into a ball for too many hours, but she didn't move. She listened to the water dripping. A distant plink. Eventually another would follow. The interval between them stretched out toward infinity. How long had she been lying there? Ramona's ears pricked up. She would pluck the sound of the next drop from the vacant hours. She was the ultimate predator. Patience would bend time to her will. She imagined, somewhere miles of rock and ice above her, the rays of the sun breaking through thick clouds to play on the blinding surface of a glacier. Even beneath the biting wind, a single droplet of water formed and, a prisoner of gravity, worked its way through cracks and crevices. Down, down. Hours? Days? It clung to the underside of a boulder above the void, elongated, contracted, began to fall, drew back to the rock. Finally, it broke free. Falling, falling…

There. The distant plink of water dripping.

Ramona pressed a button on her watch, and a wan, greenish light illuminated her little space. Water dripping. Or maybe antifreeze. She read the digital numbers. Twenty-eight seconds.

"Shit." Ultimate predator, indeed.

She drew her knees up to her chin—only a few inches—and a sharp, double kick popped open the trunk. Ramona's junked car was near the bottom of the stack, so she didn't have far to drop to reach the ground.

Towers of dented and twisted metal surrounded her on nearly every side. Narrow paths wound like canyons in several directions. As Ramona stretched and yawned, dried blood cracked and fell away from her mouth.

Almost as soon as her feet touched the ground, the barking began from somewhere on the other side of the yard. The sound came rapidly closer through the maze of scrap, until the two Rottweilers, teeth bared, frothing at the mouth, barreled around the turn closest to Ramona.

"Evenin', boys."

Instantly, they quieted and lay down, shaking and licking the foam from their jowls. Ramona scratched Rex behind the ear. Rover, who she'd noticed before had a bad case of earmites, grunted appreciatively as she knelt down and licked out his pink ear. Rex and Rover. Ramona had named them after the attributes of a hooker she'd once known whose "twin, pink-nosed dogs" had always been happy to greet a customer.

Ramona was tempted to curl up with the boys and spend a quiet evening. Her belly was full, so she wouldn't need to feed for several nights. After last night, though, a vague restlessness tugged at her. She should probably check in with Jen and Darnell at some point, but the thought didn't really excite her. Still not sure what she wanted to do, she patted the boys one more time and then wandered away through the automotive heaps.

She let her feet take whatever path fell before her, and with an easy leap over the barbed wire atop the fence, she entered the greater wilderness that lay beyond. Ramona knew little of New York, and she didn't care to learn. How differently she looked at the city than she would have just two years ago. This borough or that, the names of streets and neighborhoods—all were meaningless distinctions of the daylight world. The single, essential lesson she had learned long before setting foot in New York: *Beware.* Its permutations were many.

Beware the sun; it burns flesh.

Beware lack of blood; the hunger will take control.

Beware too much blood, the sight and smell; the hunger, again, will take control.

Beware your own kind; they are everywhere.

Even in her wandering, Ramona was alert. She knew enough to be wary, if little more. As she walked the nameless streets, the mortals going about their lives did not concern her. But which ones were, like they seemed, really mortals, and which were like her? With no way to tell, Ramona tried to stay away from them all. She remembered the gang in Los Angeles that she had assumed to be mortal, and how they had laughed when they should have run away. She remembered the *thing* out in the mesquite thickets in Texas, and her close escape.

Ramona crossed the street to avoid the light and activity of a convenience store. From that distance, she stared at the clerk in the bulletproof booth, at the black man at the payphone. Were they just what they seemed or something more? Ramona's curiosity failed to get the best of her, and she continued on. As she did, however, a shift in the slight breeze brought her up short. A faint, vaguely familiar scent caught her attention. Her flaring nostrils held onto it for only a moment before it was gone.

I know that smell, she told herself, but from where, and what was it?

She stood and sniffed at the air, but the briefly teasing breeze on that sticky summer night was dead.

She knew that scent. *What is it?* she tried to recall.

Suddenly, Ramona turned to her right, upwind, and dashed in that direction. If the wind wouldn't cooperate, she'd find the source of that smell herself.

One block then another fell behind her. She scanned the street and kept alert for the odor she was tracking. The mortals driving past probably didn't see her. She moved with a speed that only recently had ceased to surprise her.

After six blocks, she stopped and again sniffed at the air. The scent was gone, or else it was masked by the rich, layered stink of the city. Ramona felt sure that she could pick it out if it was still there.

She stood for several minutes half-heartedly sniffing. Nothing.

Maybe, she began to think, she was just overreacting to her surroundings. New York offered hundreds of new odors every night, and the potency of her sense of smell still caught her off guard at times, even after two years.

Putting the enigmatic and possibly imaginary smell behind her, Ramona realized that she was in a familiar neighborhood. The route of her wandering was unintentional but didn't surprise her. Last night. Tonight. Many nights before. She had passed over these particular streets numerous times since her arrival in the city.

From two blocks away she smelled the blood. It didn't bring the hunger screaming to the surface, because she was full, and the blood was not fresh. But with each step she smelled it more clearly. No one had bothered to spray off the pavement. Ramona heard the buzzing flies even before she turned the corner and ducked under the police tape. Those two men would not be mourned. Bloody footprints betrayed the carelessness and indifference of the police.

She had not planned to save the girl. In fact, Ramona had followed at a distance and found herself, disconcertingly, drawn into the mindset of the hunt. She'd stalked silently and waited for the perfect moment to strike. Never mind that she wasn't hungry, that she didn't need to feed. Her instinct for the hunt had grown so strong—almost too strong to be denied.

Last night was the closest Ramona had come to losing control, but it wasn't the first time that she'd watched Zhavon after dark, or listened from outside while the girl joked or argued with her mother.

She does argue, Ramona had to admit.

In fact, the first time she'd noticed the girl, just past dusk one night several weeks ago, Zhavon had been involved in a minor altercation. She'd been on a corner near her home with a few friends, talking to a boy about her own age. Ramona had watched unnoticed from a rooftop across the street. The boy had been goofing around, putting his arm around Zhavon, then he'd reached a little farther and copped a feel. The smack of her hand across his face had split the still night like a gunshot. Ramona had laughed and watched the embarrassed boy slink away. She could still see the fire in the Zhavon's eyes, the raw defiance.

Before that night, Zhavon had been like any other of the

millions of people in the city, but from that point on, Ramona had paid close attention to her, had come back night after night. How many times—ten, twenty? Ramona could only guess. She had come wanting to see that flash of bravado in Zhavon's eyes, the sound of it in her voice. Even in her hours of sleep, the steady rise and fall of her chest seemed a challenge to anyone or anything that would oppose her. She stood against all that was out there in the world.

The difference last night was that Zhavon had gotten a taste of what actually was out there.

Ramona had a bit more of an idea than Zhavon did about what was out there—she herself was part of it, after all—but she too had questions, questions about the hunter instinct, about the bloodlust that had all but taken over as she'd followed Zhavon through the dark alleys. It had been while she struggled with these predatory urges, to hunt, to feed, that the other predators had struck.

Zhavon had stumbled right into the trap where they had lain in wait for her, and as Ramona had watched her prey taken by others, a wave of rage—not hunger, but welling up from the same place—had washed over her, and she'd found herself pouncing on them. Her fangs ripped into the neck of the one with the knife—not just searching for blood, but rending flesh, leaving a gaping wound. And then the second one.

Their blood had appeased her, soothed her rage, the frenzy that was almost as strong as the hunger could be. All the while, Zhavon had huddled on the ground and cried. Ramona had lifted the hysterical girl in her arms and had seen her once-defiant face twisted with fear and desperation. Her invulnerability was chipped away to expose the victim beneath. Ramona had seen, and had understood.

Ramona breathed deeply of the blood-aroma from the pavement. She thought for a moment that she could see the two men lying there before her with their eyes staring blankly, but it was only the false memory of the blood within her, like the phantom itch of an amputated limb.

For the second time that evening, Ramona turned and ran, almost before realizing that she was doing so. Her legs carried her forward with long strides, more powerful than she would have appeared capable of.

She retraced her steps of the night before, this time unencumbered. A very few minutes found her leaping and effortlessly reaching the familiar fire escape, scrambling up the steps.

Ramona squatted at the open window. Her eyes sifted through the darkness inside, and her gaze fell upon Zhavon, asleep in her bed. The low sound of a TV in another room hung in the air. The girl rested quietly. The already dark skin of her face was bruised and puffy around the mouth and eyes. A wet towel lay on the floor beside the bed. Despite the heat and humidity, Zhavon clutched a sheet up to her neck as if the thin cotton would protect her from harm.

Stay inside at night if you want to be safe, Ramona thought, but she of all people knew only too well that there was no real protection.

Thursday, 8 July 1999, 2:15 AM
A tenement in Harlem
New York City, New York

Zhavon's eyes opened but were still full of sleep. She'd been dreaming again of the girl—about Zhavon's age, maybe a little older; skinny but muscular; smooth skin several shades lighter than Zhavon's; short hair, curly, messy. And could Zhavon be remembering correctly that sometimes the girl had blood on her face? But not tonight.

Mama was still up. Zhavon could hear the TV. She thought sleepily that if she hadn't been hurt and scared so badly, Mama probably would've beaten her senseless for sneaking out. As it was, they had spent most of the day at the hospital and then with the police. She started to roll over but was too sore. Face, neck, shoulders, arms, chest, pelvis, thighs—bruises everywhere.

Zhavon pulled the sheet more tightly about her and squinted through her swollen black eyes. Everything was as it had been when she went to sleep, except the ice in the towel had all melted. She tried to shake off the unsettling feeling that someone was watching her. The room was empty. The fire escape out the window was empty. Zhavon laid her head back and listened to the comforting sound of the TV on the other side of the wall until she again fell asleep and dreamed of the girl.

Thursday, 15 July 1999, 1:21 AM
Chantry of the Five Boroughs
New York City, New York

The sensation of his pen's brass nib scratching across the paper eased Johnston Foley's tension somewhat. The nib grabbed satisfyingly, even at this fairly modern grain of paper. Though the experience was far inferior to that of using his favored ritual pens and quills on actual parchment—there was no comparison, really—it did provide the comforting familiarity of discipline. In fact, the list to which Johnston was currently adding items was purely an exercise in discipline, for he did not *need* a list. His memory was infallible. Yet he had become a creature of lists over the years. Lists, for him, had initially provided a means of establishing order amidst a world where entropy was only too willing to rush in at the slightest lapse in vigilance and fill the void. Even after his faculties had progressed beyond the point to which the lists *per se* were a necessity in his intricate and exacting studies, he'd continued and actually redoubled his efforts to impose order—that perfect order that is a reflection of the truly disciplined mind and spirit. And his unwavering perseverance had not been lost upon his superiors.

Johnston paused at the conclusion of the next entry to his list—lifting nib from paper, so that ink could not collect and produce an imperfect character—and congratulated himself on his steadfastness of purpose. This was a minor vanity, he conceded, but indulging it was a conscious allowance that he made, and by that very awareness of his own nature he disarmed this foible, one of few, and relegated it to its harmless niche in his ordered psyche.

Johnston took great pride, though not to an excessive degree, in his attention to detail and organization (he'd been a good Presbyterian in his mortal days). His writing table was clear except for the inkwell and paper he was using, and his entire, compact study, though crammed to capacity with bookshelves, beakers, alchemical equipment and the like, was nonetheless distinctly uncluttered. Each book, each vial, each arcane scroll had its place, from which it was removed only when Johnston required its use, and to which it was promptly returned.

A sharp knock sounded at Johnston's door.

"Enter," he said, allowing the displeasure to be readily apparent in his voice. The knock should have come ten minutes earlier.

Jacqueline, Apprentice Tertius of Clan Tremere, stepped demurely into the small room. She was a mature woman, a former academician whose features continuously betrayed the torment of one accustomed in her mortal life to speaking authoritatively to students, yet who now took orders from practically every other member of the vampire clan that had chosen her. The abrupt disjuncture obviously did not sit well with her. Her contentment or lack thereof, however, did not concern Johnston.

"You are late," he said curtly.

"I was assisting Aaron with a task," she responded, eyes downcast.

"Did I request an explanation?"

"No."

Johnston narrowed his eyes. "And that is how you address your superior?"

Jacqueline stiffened, realizing her breach of etiquette. "No, Regent Secundus."

Johnston paused, laid his pen across the inkwell, allowed her time to ponder her error. She seemed adequately contrite, though an Apprentice Initiate of the Third Circle should have been beyond such lapses of decorum. It was a difficult situation, when an apprentice's capabilities exceeded her understanding of her station—for Jacqueline had proven beyond doubt her boundless potential—but the Tremere could ill afford chinks in the armor of discipline that had allowed the clan to survive this long despite the best efforts of countless enemies. Johnston made a mental note to have her flogged at a later time, and if the problem persisted to advise Regent Quintus Sturbridge that Jacqueline should be terminated.

"I will not abide familiarity in a subordinate," he said at last, then paused again significantly.

"Yes, Regent Secundus."

When Johnston was satisfied that she had suffered an appropriate amount of mental anguish, he handed her the piece of paper from his desk.

"Here is the list of materials I require for a certain ritual next week," he said. "See that they are assembled in my laboratory by dawn the 22nd."

Jacqueline studied the list. After a moment, Johnston held out his hand and, realizing his meaning, she reluctantly returned the paper to him.

"That is all." Johnston watched as she backed out of the chamber. He was gratified by the brief glint of alarm he'd seen in her eyes as she'd handed back the list. He had allowed her ample time in which to commit the items to memory. If she'd failed to do so, that was her shortcoming, and she would be held accountable. Of course, Johnston wasn't about to let her potential incompetence interfere with his upcoming ritual—dawn the 22nd would allow him more than sufficient time to inspect her work and make any necessary adjustments. The knowledge that ultimately he would be held responsible for the failings of underlings was not lost upon Johnston.

He rose with the list in his hand and moved into his laboratory, an adjoining room that also was rather cramped with tables, shelves, several scales for various types of materials, more books, and a host of other tightly-packed paraphernalia. The compressed nature of his chambers—including his sanctum, which was little more than a closet—was a point of some irritation for Johnston. He realized that his accommodations constituted no slight against himself, but still the matter was galling. Thus was unlife at the Chantry of the Five Boroughs. So hotly contested between Camarilla and Sabbat was the city of New York, that the energy of every Tremere present was required for defense, and little time was spared for expansion or material comfort. So it had been for many years.

Johnston supposed he should let the matter of his chambers drop. After all, his appointment at the chantry was not inconsequential. It was the turmoil that had necessitated him being here. Never mind that he would be leading any other chantry to which he might be assigned. Five Boroughs was one of the few chantries that sustained two regents: himself as the junior regent and his superior, Aisling Sturbridge. It was not normal clan policy, but with the immediate Sabbat presence, this was no normal chantry. After all, Sturbridge had been a junior regent before her superior had been caught unawares by Sabbat beyond the chantry defenses. Aisling had inherited the chantry leadership. That the same fortune, and a greatly deserved promotion, might fall into Johnston's lap was not beyond the realm of possibility.

So he tried, with some if not complete success, to tuck his resentment into its appropriate niche in the back of his mind. Probably Sturbridge's quarters were no more spacious than his own, though he had never been invited within her chambers. Another aspect of the square footage problem was population pressure. Because of the Sabbat danger outside the chantry, and beyond the boundaries of Manhattan especially, more apprentices resided on the premises than was normally the case. That led to working and existing at closer quarters than Johnston appreciated with neophytes like Jacqueline, Aaron, and the others.

The chantry, tucked beneath the Camarilla fraction of the city as it was, made up in strategic value what it lacked in acreage. "There's only so much space between Barnard College and the Harlem River," Sturbridge had told him the one time he'd ventured to mention his cramped quarters to her. Her summary dismissal of his comment had dissuaded him from asking why the chantry didn't expand in other directions.

In his laboratory, Johnston turned to the modest wooden chest—no larger than a jewelry box—which held the subject of the ritual for which he'd assigned preparations to Jacqueline.

The only adornment on the chest, a mother-of-pearl, *fleur-de-lis* inlay on the lid's exterior, glowed faintly. Johnston held his hand over the ornamentation and felt the slight warmth that it emitted.

Good, he thought. *It's still active.*

With a practiced, steady hand, he opened the lid of the chest and looked upon the contents, which had kept him so busy of late. Nestled in the box's felt-lined interior was a semi-precious stone no larger than a marble. It was finely polished quartz, a deep, cloudy red except for two black circles on opposite sides. Johnston thought of the black spots as poles, as on a globe. The black surface on top, the north pole as he saw it, was smooth and flawless. The red all around and down the sides was grooved in a perfectly descending spiral. The black south pole, unlike the rest of the stone, was slightly jagged, the raised areas making no special pattern that Johnston could discern. He had never expected the gem to prove so intriguing.

Sturbridge had presented the gem to Johnston several years earlier with the expectation that he would perform experiments on it, but the stone had not been deemed a high or even medium priority. It radiated a magical aura of some type, but then again so did an amazing number of trinkets and faux-artifacts that found their way into the possession of Clan Tremere. Johnston had done some preliminary experimentation, but to little effect, and with Sturbridge's blessing he'd set aside the gem. He'd thought of it seldom since, and then mostly in derogatory terms—a semi-precious stone taking up precious shelf-space.

All that had changed three weeks ago.

After disciplining one of the apprentices, Johnston had entered his laboratory and found not only the seal, which he'd placed on the chest as a precautionary measure, broken but the lid cast open as well. The gem was practically seething with preternatural energies— *amazing* energies! Johnston had never imagined that such potential lay within the gem. And when he'd gotten over his surprise and set about examining the stone…it had grown dormant again. There were trace amounts of residual energies, of course, but nothing as compared to what he'd perceived moments before.

So he'd been forced into a pattern of watchful waiting. He'd checked the gem several times nightly, resealing it in the chest following each inspection. For weeks, nothing changed, except the residual energies grew weaker. Then last night, the gem had suddenly come to life again and tonight, as indicated by the glowing mother of pearl, it still burned with power. To the naked eye there was no such indication, but Johnston fancied that he could fairly smell the churning energies.

He took the list he'd shown to Jacqueline, placed it in a brazier on his work table, and struck a match to the paper. Its edges curled and blackened. Johnston needed the list no longer; he'd taken it back from Jacqueline merely on principle. Before the paper was completely consumed, he took a long purple candle from a nearby shelf and held the wick to the fire. Once the candle caught, Johnston turned back to the chest and began the proper incantation. Slowly, he passed the fingers of his left hand through the candle's flame. It did not burn him, and he felt not the slightest discomfort.

Having prepared the candle, he began slowly and steadily to move it toward the chest. While the candle was still a foot away from the gem, the flame flickered and went out, as if snuffed by a sudden gust of wind. But there was no wind, nor even the slightest breeze.

Johnston repeated the minor ritual, and again an unseen force extinguished the candle at the same distance from the chest. He nodded with bewildered satisfaction.

An inch and three quarters farther away than last night, he thought. *It's growing even stronger!* If it continued to increase potency at such a rate, he'd have to move his ritual up by several nights—and wouldn't that drive Jacqueline to distraction?

But that was the type of decision he shouldn't make until Sturbridge returned to the chantry. She'd been called away to attend a council meeting in Baltimore—something to do with the recent Sabbat unpleasantness to the south. As if the Chantry of the Five Boroughs didn't have enough of its own difficulties without the rest of the Camarilla coming begging for help. Besides, the other clans would only turn on the Tremere again after the trouble was past.

Johnston laid the candle back in its place, then closed the chest. He would continue to monitor the gem. This was the type of breakthrough that could lead his superiors in the clan to grant him a chantry of his own. One where he'd have sufficient working space.

Thursday, 15 July 1999, 11:44 PM
A subterranean grotto

The constant flickering of the desk lamp's bulb cast a strobe effect over the tiny oasis of light. The seated figure drummed his taloned fingers, then finally raised a hand to strike the recalcitrant lamp. Steady, if not bright, illumination replaced the flickering just before the blow fell. The hand lowered slowly.

The figure turned back to the aged, manual typewriter that it was hunched over and impatiently ripped the paper from the machine. Before the gritty whirring of the typewriter wheel had fallen completely silent, a red pen scratched quickly and unhesitatingly across the page.

Insert Image 1

15 July 1999
Re: Eye of Hazimel

Atlanta——Resha's courier confirmed
among dead from (raid) Rolph reports——
no sign of Eye in city. Has it fallen
to Sabbat? Not according to info via
Vykos's pet assassin/ghoul.

the blasted Eye. *Where IS*

↳ HELL of a 'raid': Atlanta,
Savañah, Columbia, Charleston,
Raleigh, Wilmington, Norfolk,
Richmond, D.C. ...

Note: file action update:
Pieterzoon, Jan, to arrive in
Baltimore tonight.

Friday, 16 July 1999, 11:03 PM
Piedmont Avenue
Atlanta, Georgia

"Hold still, my dearest." *Damn you, bitch!*
Even with the benefit of his newfound vision, the muse flitted in and then out of Leopold's line of sight. He held his right eye closed with his hand and with great trepidation cast his glance after her.

At first he had swung around trying to follow her, but he'd quickly discovered that the world, once set in motion, did not soon willingly stop. His studio listed like a drunken sot. Up and down, left and right, other and self—such distinctions blurred with the Sight. Too much so in the beginning. Dull blackness had taken him, and he had cracked his head on the concrete slab floor.

Now he moved more carefully, but still the ripples of motion, of Sight and unSight, blurred at the edges, ran together. Or was that the muse teasing him again?

"Come where I can see you, dearest." But she ignored his kindest entreaties. *Bitch! Whore!*

She taunted him. *Capture me, Leopold.*

The studio shifted. Leopold stumbled and fell against—a table, an easel? It gave way beneath him and he crashed to the floor. Her foot passed within inches of his face. Her slender, naked ankle flashed before him as an epiphany. In the back of his mind, something else demanded attention—a finger bent and doubled back in the fall, bone stressed and cracked. He shunted aside the distant pain as images of the muse blossomed—the sharp angle of her ankle, the inviting curve of her calf.

She was gone again, but her seductive laughter echoed throughout the studio, grew from the tinkling of tiny bells to the crashing of timpani and cymbals. The world shuddered. It rolled Leopold along the floor—or was it ceiling now? Yet onward he crawled with the vision ever before him. His artist's mind locked onto the detail that he would render. Though the muse proved elusive, the Sight would not be denied.

Everything had changed for Leopold the night of Victoria's party. Had it only been three and a half weeks? Sometimes it seemed as if a lifetime had passed with every minute, so much progress had he made. So much had been revealed to him. Never again would Victoria or any of the other high-society Toreador, so smug in their shallow little appreciations, laugh at Leopold, for a great truth had been revealed to him, was still being revealed to him.

From the moment he had seen that vision of beauty, the human form stripped of the preconceived limitations of self-awareness—and staring up from the midst of it, the Eye—Leopold had known that he must reproduce the effect. The inherent truth of his discovery would be apparent to all. None would deny his skill, the immensity of his vision. So he had reached down and taken the orb, for it was the heart of his vision.

And the moment of clarity had faded.

Gone was the long-awaited vista of lustrous beauty. With the Eye resting in his open palm, Leopold had stood above a heap of torn flesh and broken bone, the mangled body of Vegel.

Panicked, he'd returned the Eye to its perch, but the orb outshone its surroundings as if the sun appeared in the night sky. The image that had captivated him was no more.

But no matter.

Leopold possessed the soul of an artist, and there it was that he carried the vision. Once it had touched him, he was incapable of forgetting. He snatched up the Eye again and left behind the transient mass that ever so briefly had been a part of ephemeral beauty.

Almost immediately, Leopold had taken stock of the ways that the vision had changed him. Returning to his studio, he found himself surrounded by the flotsam of his previous, unenlightened, artistic endeavors. Just to be in the same room with the pieces that had once engendered in him such great pride was painful. He saw clearly each work's failure.

No wonder Victoria and the others had scoffed at his pretensions.

Victoria. Her name tugged at his memory. He had wanted to find out something...had visited the Tremere witch. But that was a concern from before. Just as the pitiful attempts at sculpture arrayed for his review were from before—and they he could not tolerate.

Plaster molds he smashed to bits. Models he swept into a box that was then hidden away beneath a work bench. And thus the period of Leopold's enlightenment began with the destruction of what had gone before.

A table brushed free of its clutter became the wooden pedestal for the Eye. He placed it there lovingly, reverently. Even after setting it down, he could still feel its moist touch where it had filled his palm. Resting on the table, the heavily veined eyelid slowly opened and then receded from around nearly the entire pulsating sphere, until the protective flesh was nothing more than a tiny base beneath the Eye. Leopold marveled at it.

For weeks, he worked before its unblinking gaze. For weeks the beauty that he had beheld, that he expected to be evident, did not reveal itself in the fruits of his labor. The Eye watched impassively Leopold's embarrassment at his unsatisfactory first model. The Eye watched as he set aside the second attempt halfway through, as he smashed in frustration the third, and the fourth, and the fifth....

Nights passed. More and more often he flew into a rage as desperation took hold of him. With his eyes, within his soul, he had seen the vision. Truth and beauty had been revealed to him. But over and again, his hands failed him. Did he lack the skill to render that which he'd beheld? Had he merely imagined that talent resided within the sinews of his fingers?

Only once during that time did Leopold falter in his quest. *Victoria.* Her name came to him unbidden on that second night after his wondrous discovery. He moved toward the stairs of his basement studio. He would go to her. She might need him. But then his gaze, as it inevitably did these nights, fell upon the orb of his passion, and merely the sight of the Eye, waiting patiently amidst its burbling and fizzing secretion, returned him to his senses. Victoria was no more than any other of the unenlightened. Why would he interrupt his labors for the likes of her?

And then the muse had spoken to him. *Trust,* she said, her sensual voice massaging the muscles and tendons that failed him. *Trust.*

All thoughts save those of his art were banished from Leopold's mind.

Trust.

He set aside his precision tools and modeling clay. Stripped of process and regimen, he stepped as a naked child to the marble block. He set chisel to stone and reached within his soul for the angle and pressure that would set free the perfection he had witnessed, which he knew resided as well within the stone. Each tap of the hammer chipped away marble from the veil that concealed truth. He would find it and show it to the world.

And his greatness would be revealed.

All the while, the Eye watched.

Night after night, Leopold worked. He rose at sunset and went straight to his art untroubled by thoughts of feeding or any other distraction. The vision was his sustenance; the task before him, his only consideration. As more stone fell away, a form began take shape, but Leopold would not allow himself the luxury of stepping back and viewing the larger picture. He would not allow himself the slightest respite or reward until the representation of his vision was complete. Over the tiniest details, he labored hour upon hour. From top to bottom, head to toe, the piece began to take shape. Leopold relentlessly chipped away at every granule of marble that did not belong until, finally, he was done.

Leopold laid down his chisel. He had viewed the Eye, tangible memento of the most perfect of forms, and then looked upon his own accomplishment. The hollowness in his stomach took him as if in a deathgrip, for he realized that his work was a crude mockery of the beauty he had envisioned. Not a hint of truth could he find in the curve of its limbs, and not the faintest trace of perfection. His child was stillborn. A deformed, freakish abomination.

That was when he had first heard the laughter of the muse—cruel, mocking laughter. She did not recognize the expenditure of will, the great effort he had put into the work. She recognized only failure. Her laughter filled Leopold's heart like acid, for he could not defend the shortcomings of his failed masterpiece. With an anguished cry, he took his largest hammer and set upon his work. Within the hour, the labor of weeks was transformed to rubble, but even the rubble offended Leopold, mocked his pain. He continued with the hammer, smashing each piece of marble, no matter how small, until in the end only fine powder remained. Still his failure was not purged, and the muse's laughter taunted him. Leopold saw Victoria laughing at him as well. She stood before him in her lavish evening gown, garishly begemmed, and his failure was her entertainment. He had set out to prove his worth to her, and he feared that his failure had done just that. He determined to erase the sneer from her lips. He took his chisel and laid it upon the cleft of her bosom and swung his hammer with a fierce and defiant scream. But she was gone, and he merely fell to the floor sobbing.

And all the while, the Eye watched from the center of its simmering pool of juices.

Again, the muse spoke to him. Leopold hung on her every word. He could not begrudge her the rejection of his masterpiece, because she was right. He had failed badly.

What is the essence of life? Of beauty? she asked. Her question floated to the highest, most remote corner of the studio.

The essence of life. The essence of beauty.

She had told him to trust, and he had trusted.

But that was not enough.

The essence of life. The essence of beauty.

For hours, Leopold lay on the floor in earnest contemplation. A fine dust of pulverized marble settled on him until he could have passed for one of his own creations. As the sun rose and he skulked down to the cellar, the muse's words rang in his ears.

The essence of life. The essence of beauty.

A day and a night and a day he lay pondering. When he rose again, he gently wrapped the Eye in a clean cloth and gathered together the chisels and tools he would need. Thus equipped, he ventured out of the studio.

Leopold had practically forgotten about the Atlanta skyline, about the bohemian hubbub of Little Five Points toward which he naturally gravitated. He noted the outside world only briefly, however. The grungy clubs and sex shops, the punks and hippies, unwashed vagrants old and young—he had seen them all before, and though in the past this scene had sparked in him impulses of the avant-garde, now he was absorbed by the life of the mind and of the spirit.

The essence of life. The essence of beauty.

Leopold ignored the buzz of humanity as he moved along Moreland Avenue. He slipped away from that thoroughfare, past an apartment building, beyond a dilapidated Victorian house, and wound his way through a deep wooded lot. Night after night he returned to the thick oak tree that he found. Night after night he carefully unwrapped the cloth and set the Eye on the ground so that he could watch it, so that it could watch him. Leopold lost track of how many sunsets brought him to the oak—a week's worth, two weeks'?

At last he was finished, and he gazed upon his work—a failure as complete and utter as that which had come before it.

The muse's laughter sounded throughout the meandering copse of trees. Every leaf danced with the weight of her disdainful mirth. The vaguely human figure carved into the trunk of the oak seemed to laugh at Leopold as well. He laid his hands upon its face and dug his fingers deep into the wood, which crumbled beneath his touch. Splinters pierced his flesh, shot beneath his fingernails, but Leopold had no room for mercy, neither for himself nor for the tree-figure. He ripped and clawed and shredded until the laughter died away.

Suddenly overcome by exhaustion—how many nights had it been since he had fed?—Leopold fell to the ground. His most valiant efforts had been for naught. He clasped his hands, gory with sap, over his face. As he lay and mourned his incessant failure, his gaze fell upon the Eye, and as surely as Saul was blinded on the road to Damascus so that he might become Paul and truly see, an epiphany was visited upon Leopold. Firm in the conviction that his entire existence, both kine and Kindred, had been spent in preparation for this moment, he reached out.

For the three nights since then, epiphanies had followed one after another. Scarcely two or three hours had passed when Leopold hadn't caught sight of the muse. She led him toward the eternal, the undeniable aesthetic, and with his newfound vision, he followed.

Leopold crawled to his current project, but the studio turned upward like a crazed gyroscope. He lurched to the side, grasped for a table leg, but was closer than he had realized and smashed his face into it. Paralyzing fear shot through him.

Gone for the moment was any thought of his glimpse of the muse's ankle and the well-toned curve that led upward to fleshy thigh. Leopold closed tightly his eyes, his left eyelid stretching taut and unable to protect its new charge completely. Fingers quivering with trepidation, he inspected by touch his face and breathed a sigh of relief to discover no damage. He hadn't hit the table so hard. The Eye was safe. The Sight was still his.

Leopold turned again to his project. Behind him, the muse's high-pitched giggling tempted him, but he did not turn. He would not be distracted until he had performed the proper stroke, until he had been true to his vision. Then he would be free to pursue the muse further.

He crawled through the gelatinous ichor that seeped from the Eye and dripped to the floor before him. Finally, the feet loomed close. Leopold did not look up at the full figure, at the young man tied naked to the post, his raised hands swollen and blue above the rope. The sculptor was too intent on that which must follow. He reached around blindly, never taking his gaze from the ankle mere inches from his face, and pulled toward him the chisel and hammer that were never far away.

Imprinted on Leopold's soul was each glimpse of the muse—the perfection of line and form that he would have been forever blind to, were it not for the Sight.

He raised the chisel to the upper curve of the bone and with a delicate stroke, despite the fact that this was not his medium of training and experience, he carved away that which did not fit his vision. He was not daunted by the sliding of flesh over bone. Each tap of the hammer was precision incarnate, the pressure of his grip upon the chisel steadfast. He worked with the diligence of a master sculptor spurred to ever greater heights by the compelling force and beauty of his vision.

A tiny flow of stale blood dribbled from the incision. Though Leopold had feasted the first night of his transformation, almost each cut managed to draw forth a tiny reserve of blood hidden in the tissue. He caressed the wound, brought his fingers to his lips, tasted the gritty mixture of marble dust and blood.

How resilient is the human body, Leopold thought, *how full of potential.*

Just then, he noticed the heavy silence that had enveloped the studio. The air did not stir, no sound from outside intruded, and most telling, the laughter of the muse was not to be heard.

Have I done it? Leopold wondered hopefully as he gazed at his work, though he did not feel that he could be finished. Surely he would know when the momentous occasion arrived.

Ever so slowly, so as not to imbalance the precarious world, he turned from the naked, carved form. He squinted shut his right eye to eliminate the overlapping perspectives of Sight and unSight. The studio walls grew faint, pale, as if they were half-finished set pieces on a minimalist stage. Columns took on a translucent sheen. Everywhere Leopold looked, the periphery of his vision was a dancing swirl of colors, a swarm of multi-hued locusts. He continued carefully to turn, and his restraint was rewarded.

For a split second, she stood revealed to him in her glory, yet even though he could now, with the Eye, see her, her ineffable visage was beyond his ability to comprehend. The Eye saw, but the Sight could not encompass. Again the world shifted. Leopold fell to his knees. The studio shimmered and swam before him.

But he could see the displeasure on her face. The disappointment.

So fragile, she said as she gently shook her head.

Leopold, his reality gyrating wildly, turned back to his

work. The carved nude hung as if from the ceiling, but his hands were tied below him. Leopold fell to his elbows with a jolt, and the studio righted itself somewhat, though its bearing continued to fluctuate like the needle of a scale swinging from heavy to light to heavy, on and on, and only slowly closing in on the true weight.

The nude hung lifeless, its posture stiff, while at the same time its limbs were limp. Here and there, chunks of flesh and bone were gouged away—the brow, shoulder, belly, hip, knees, ankle. Only now did Leopold perceive the flies that amassed around the sweet smell of carrion.

So fragile.

Leopold threw the hammer away from him. It sailed into the distance, miles and miles to the other end of the studio.

Lying whore! he wanted to shout at her.

But, again and inevitably, she was right. He could look upon his folly no longer. With an anguished roar, Leopold slammed the chisel into the body. Ribs snapped as he embedded the tool in the chest cavity. The nude recoiled with all the emotion of a sack of flour. Neither did it object as Leopold wept on its bruised and bloodied feet.

"Why?" he cried. So much work, and for no purpose. Leopold strove to convey the perfection he perceived, but again he'd failed. He would go mad with failure. He must succeed.

Away from here, she teased, her playful nature having quickly returned. *Away from here.*

Away? Her words latched onto Leopold. He slowly cast his hybrid gaze around the studio.

Away from here. Away from this place, his thoughts echoed her words.

The hard concrete, the plain, wooden interior—they were unremarkable to his Sight, almost immaterial. How could he hope to express truth among such drab environs? His spirits rose at the implication that the failing had not been completely of his skills. Of course he would succeed. Why else would the muse have chosen him?

Patience, he chided himself. *Patience.* But he wanted this so badly!

Mmmm, she purred very close to him. She breathed deeply of his confidence. *The tools, Leopold... I will take you to them.*

Yes, the tools. The hammer in some dark, far-off corner, the chisel embedded in the abomination— these were the primitive tools of his failure, and like this studio, this city, they were contaminated by his unenlightened hands of yesterday.

I will take you to them.

To the proper instruments. To a place of enlightenment. She would entrust to him the relics of perfection, and he would wield them in a shrine to beauty. She was his muse, his goddess, and with the Eye he would learn her mysteries and become high priest of the hidden truth. The unenlightened masses would beg to drink from his hands.

Come.

"Yes, dearest." The world swirled sickeningly with his every step, but still Leopold followed.

Saturday, 17 July 1999, 3:00 AM
George Washington Bridge
New York City, New York

More than a hundred feet below, the river passed beneath Ramona, but the motion was difficult to detect except in the scattered patches of illumination. There the surface of the water shimmered and appeared to move quickly through the light from one black nothingness to another black nothingness. This was the nightface of the river—the only face that Ramona would ever see. She clung to the underside of the George Washington Bridge as she shimmied along one girder to another. Above her, every few moments, a car rumbled across.

She could be the troll under the bridge, she thought, and make out a hell of a lot better than three ornery goats. Hunting, she decided, was governed by the same three golden rules as real estate, which her shuckster uncle, Kenny, had so often recited: location, location, and location. Thanks to Ramona, Kenny didn't sell much real estate anymore.

Ramona paused in her crossing and hung her head back to look at the river below. It really did look like a wide paved street at night. Maybe that was what gave so many jumpers second thoughts when they stepped over the railing and saw where they were about to go. Jumping into a river didn't sound so bad, as far as suicide went. It was almost like being a kid again and going swimming, jumping into a pond or a pool. But when the jumper stood on the edge and saw what, with the force of impact, might as well be rock-hard pavement...

One then the other, Ramona eased her feet off the girder. The lower half of her body swung down and dangled beneath the bridge. She was neither large nor heavy and barely felt the added weight her arms were bearing.

What would happen to me? she wondered. *What would happen to this thing that used to be my body?*

She had thought herself invincible for a while after becoming what she was now, but as she and the others had traveled east across the country, they had been attacked by that...monster, for lack of a better name—a giant blur of teeth and claws and death. What happened to Eddie proved that Ramona's kind were *not* invincible. Far from it. Just when she thought she had everything figured out, it seemed something new always came along to throw her off.

She let go of the bridge with her right hand and let that arm hang loose at her side.

What would happen to me?

Would that sudden impact be the end? Would she crawl from the water broken in body but only needing more blood to be good as new?

Hanging by one hand, Ramona gazed down at the patches of dancing light that broke up the black pavement of the river. Her world had become that black river, and she was a tiny patch of the familiar surrounded by darkness and unknown.

She hadn't asked for this. Imperfect as her old life had been, she would've made her way. Never would she have chosen to enter this world where so much was deceptively familiar, but scratch the surface and nothing was the same.

She lifted one of the fingers of her left hand from bridge, and then a second finger. She raised a third finger, her thumb. One finger held her aloft. It was more than strong enough. The strength of her body, this collection of muscle and bone and tendon that she used to know, constantly amazed her. She felt a claw—where her fingernail used to be—dig into the steel girder.

What would happen to me?

What, she wondered, had already happened to her?

Reluctantly, Ramona raised her right hand and again took hold of the bridge. Like the patches of light on the river, she was not alone, and though whatever responsibilities she took on herself were of her own making, they served to keep her, like the water beneath the bridge, moving forward.

With uncanny ease, she lifted her feet back to the girder and continued her commando crawl across.

Closer to shore, she dropped to the bank, twenty, maybe thirty feet below. She landed on all fours in a cat-like crouch. Scrambling up the incline, she paused to tug at her shoe. The old sneaker felt odd, like the side had busted out, but there didn't seem to be any damage. Probably the drop from the bridge had ripped the insole or something. Ramona hopped over the crest of the bank and tapped her foot to straighten whatever had gotten askew.

"Hey, sweetcakes. Nice acrobatics."

Ramona dropped to a defensive crouch. The guy facing her, however, sat unconcerned on his motorcycle, hands clasped behind his head, feet propped up on the handlebars. He sneered out of one side of his mouth and took obvious pleasure that he'd surprised her.

"Good night for a swan dive?" He started a high-pitched whistle, the sound of a bomb falling to the earth, and ended with an imitation of a splash.

Ramona eyed him warily. Very few people got the jump on her anymore, and those who did very likely meant trouble. His short hair and sharp eyebrows were very dark, a striking contrast to his incredibly pale skin. Blue veins bulged from his biceps, his forearms, his neck.

Like me? Ramona wondered.

She had been more darkly complected before... before the change, and had paled considerably since. But nothing like this guy. His skin seemed to hug each and every muscle and collapsed to fill every hollow space. His tight features reminded Ramona of what she noticed when she looked in a mirror.

"Sooo..." He drew the word out, and his crooked smile vanished.

Before Ramona could even react to his movement, he was standing before her. From semi-reclined atop the bike to fully upright had taken him barely a second.

At least his display mostly confirmed Ramona's suspicions. He had to be like her. Or worse.

"Are you ready to play with the big boys?" he asked.

Ramona surprised herself with the deep, menacing growl that erupted from within her. The biker inched back almost imperceptibly but immediately tried to shrug off his retreat.

"Who the hell are you?" Ramona demanded.

"The question," he said, "is who the hell are you, and what the hell do you think you're doing here? Last time I checked, this was Sabbat turf, and you ain't part of the club."

Sabbat.

It was a name Ramona had heard occasionally over the past two years, mostly before she and the others had left L.A., but what was it? Some kind of gang, but on the West Coast and the East Coast?

She held her ground and watched for any move the biker might make. Ramona had an idea of her own capabilities, but who was to say whether this guy was equally fast and strong, or faster and stronger?

"Not much of a talker, are you, sweetcakes?" he said and began to ease back toward his motorcycle. "I'll tell you what. Since I'm such a nice guy..." he threw one leg over the bike and turned the key, "I'm gonna give you a chance. I'll be back. You be ready to come with me. Otherwise, beat meat now." He kickstarted the bike, revved the engine to a prolonged, deafening roar, and then with a snide wink screeched off down the street and over the bridge.

Ramona relaxed, but not much.

Sabbat.

She and the others had left L.A. because there were so many creatures like them roaming the streets at night. Was New York going to turn out to be the same way?

Cities are where the food is, she reminded herself.

Food. *Blood.*

How quickly she had grown accustomed to this new diet, so much so that she thought of cities in much the same way that she used to think about restaurants. Los Angeles or New York? McDonald's or Burger King?

Satisfying herself that the biker was actually gone—the sound of his engine had faded across the river—Ramona made her way the last few blocks to a relatively small aluminum building. A chain was wrapped several times around the door handle and a bracket on the wall, but when she pulled the door open as far as it would go, there was enough room for her to squeeze through.

"Hey," Ramona called as her eyes began to adjust to the darkness. A light illuminated the center of the open room, ruining her night vision.

"Ramona?" came a small voice from one of the large holes in the floor, also the source of the light.

"Yeah."

Jenny's head rose into view, then her shoulders, then torso, as she climbed the steps from one of the twin grease pits. She carried the type of light on a hook that a mechanic would hang above an engine he was working on. A cord ran from the light back down the steps.

"Is Darnell with you?" asked Jenny.

"No."

Jen was taller than Ramona, and blonde. She must've been a looker before, Ramona had always thought, but now she was a bit too gaunt and pale to be pretty. Like Ramona, Jenny wore ripped jeans— torn not to be stylish, but after months and months of wear and tear. But while Ramona sported a ratty T-shirt, Jen huddled beneath not one but two oversized sweatshirts, despite the summer heat.

"It's cold in here," said Jen. She crossed her arms and hugged them to her body. "Are you cold?"

"No."

"Where've you been?"

"Out." Ramona glanced around the abandoned garage. Both bay doors were still chained from the inside. Other than that, she couldn't really see much beyond the small area the light penetrated. Probably, she thought, they could both see better if Jenny just turned off the damned light. Potent night vision was another side effect Ramona had noticed since the change. But Jen clung to her old ways.

Like a jumper to that rail, thought Ramona, remembering the bridge. "Any trouble?" she asked. She didn't see any sign of the biker, or anyone else, having bothered the place.

"No. You?"

"Not really."

"What do you mean, 'not really'?" Jenny was instantly agitated. It didn't take much.

Ramona wished she hadn't said anything. "I mean not really. Some biker acting tough. That's all."

They both jumped when the door banged against the chain. To their relief, Darnell slipped in. "Turn off the fuckin' light."

"Fuck you," Jen snapped.

"Fuck *you*," he shot back. "You can see the light outside through the cracks around the door. Keep it in the pit if you're afraid of the dark."

Ramona sighed. This was why she stayed away. She didn't need the headache. She'd be better off without them. Or she might be dead without them. "Who cares if anybody sees it?"

"You don't sleep here during the day," Darnell pointed out.

Ramona sighed again. He was right. There was no point taking stupid chances. She nodded to Jen, and the light went out. They stood in the darkness for a while. Ramona could hear Jen grinding her teeth, and Darnell shifting his weight from one foot to the other, crossing and uncrossing his arms. Very shortly, they could see fairly well. Not as much detail as with the light, but more range.

"There are others here too," said Darnell finally. Ramona nodded.

"Others? Where?" Jen looked around frantically as if they were on Darnell's heels and going to break down the door any second.

"Here in the city," said Darnell. "I followed 'em. Watched 'em feedin'."

"Followed them?" The idea upset Jen. "Did they see you?"

"They didn't see me."

"They might've followed you!"

"They didn't follow me."

Ramona looked on as Darnell glared at Jenny. He constantly discounted her fears, but he couldn't seem to ignore her hysteria. He forgot how much they'd each helped one another. They all tended to forget that, Ramona realized, when the danger wasn't right at hand.

"Eddie didn't think nobody was followin' us," said Ramona quietly. A heavy silence fell over them. Darnell shot her a hard glance.

"That was different," he said. "That was a werewolf."

"Werewolf, ha!" Jen snorted.

Darnell turned his ire again to her. "Why the fuck not? It wasn't a bear, and it sure as hell wasn't a wild dog." Jenny's rolling her eyes served only to spur him on. "You've seen what *we* can do, what we *are*. Why the fuck not a werewolf?"

"Doesn't matter what it was," said Ramona. "We got away."

"Tell that to Eddie," said Darnell.

Again, silence enveloped them. Jen set the extinguished light on the floor then sat, feet dangling over the edge of the pit. Ramona watched Jen and knew that they probably never would've met had they not become what they were. They certainly wouldn't have become friends. Jen came from a life of privilege, and this new sort of life had cost her the most. She could be infuriatingly difficult at times, but she'd been one of the few people Ramona had known—ever, before or after the change—to offer kindness when Ramona had needed it. That, Ramona realized, was why she came back to be with this woman who was more troubled by everything that was happening than was Ramona herself.

Darnell was a different story. Unlike Jenny, he could make it on his own. At least he could if any of them could. Ramona watched him as he pulled over a large box to sit on. Like herself, he didn't talk much about before. She knew he'd lived in Compton and that he came from a big family. He'd talked once about his mother dragging him and all his brothers and sisters to church. That was about all that Ramona knew about his old life, and they didn't know much more about hers. The strange thing was that it didn't matter really. Those old lives were dead and gone, and here were the three of them with people they never would've hung with if it weren't for—

"Where did you see them?" Jenny's voice broke the silence. She was shivering in the darkness.

"Farther in the city." Darnell sat on the box, but he wasn't at ease. He was never at ease, Ramona thought, unless he was in motion. Sitting still made him nervous. "I could tell they were huntin'," he said, "so I hung back, stayed out of sight, followed 'em. It was weird. Even before they caught somebody, I could tell they were vampires."

"Vampires..." Jen shook her head and let her voice trail off.

Instantly, Darnell was on his feet. "Fuck you! You don't think we're vampires?"

Ramona sighed to herself. They'd had this argument maybe a hundred times. "If you're gonna yell, we might as well turn the light back on so everybody'll know we're here."

Darnell took a step back from Jen, lowered his voice a little. "We drink blood." He bared his fangs at Jen and pointed to his mouth. "These look familiar? And I don't see you lyin' out in the sun to tan your lily-white ass. What else you think we are?"

"I don't know," said Jen, and then added under her breath, "but I'm not a vampire."

"You sure they didn't see you?" Ramona asked.

Darnell shot her another dirty look but then decided it was an honest question. "I'm sure."

"I saw one too," said Ramona. Darnell sat back down. He didn't seem surprised.

Jen sat up straight, her eyes wide. "The biker?"

"Mm-hm." Ramona looked over at Darnell. "Said he was with the Sabbat, that he'd be back."

Jenny fidgeted nervously, but Darnell met Ramona's gaze. "Let him come back," he said.

A loud crash filled the garage—the explosive echoing of the heavy door slamming shut. They all three jumped at once. Darnell was down from his box. Ramona dropped into her crouch and was ready to spring in any direction. Jen was halfway down the steps into the pit. She peered up over the edge.

"You leave that open?" Ramona asked Darnell, nodding toward the door.

"Must have."

Ramona didn't see anyone else in the room. She edged

toward the door, ready to attack or retreat if either were
necessary. At the door, she sniffed the air. A faint scent lingered
just below that of old motor oil and cigarette butts. It was a smell
she recognized. She'd noticed it several times recently, but she
still couldn't place it. Now it was gone again, and she was left
standing by the door.

"What is it?" Jen asked from the pit.

"Don't know." Ramona stood perfectly still. She listened for
any movement from the other side of the metal door. Nothing.
Could the door, only able to open a few inches because of the
chain on the outside, have slammed that hard from the wind?
She didn't remember feeling any breeze.

Darnell was at her shoulder now. He moved almost as
silently as she did.

Slowly, Ramona reached for the handle. With one quick
motion, she turned it and pushed the door open. It caught
against the chain. She waited. Nothing.

Satisfied that no one was coming in, Ramona counted to
three in her head, then shot out the opening. As quickly as she
moved and as narrow as the crack was, she barely brushed
against the door as she slid out. Darnell followed her.

Again she thought she noticed the strange, lingering odor,
but then it was gone, drowned by all the smells of the city and
the familiar scent of Darnell beside her.

"I guess we're alone," he said.

Ramona stared into the night, shook her head. "We should
be so lucky."

Saturday, 17 July 1999, 11:38 PM
A tenement in Harlem
New York City, New York

"She *can* send me there, and she's gonna," Zhavon said into the phone with an urgency that almost defeated the purpose of her whispering.

"Girl, you tell her you just not going," said Alvina.

"*You* wanna tell that to my mama?" Zhavon asked. Silence answered her question. Alvina had been around enough to know better than to mess with

Mama. "That's what I thought."

"Well, what you gonna do?"

"I don't know." How was Zhavon supposed to know what to do? That's why she'd called Alvina in the first place, but so far, Alvina hadn't been much help. "I guess I'll go."

"It's your own damn fault," Alvina said.

"I *know* it's my own damn fault," Zhavon said. How many times had Mama drilled those same words into Zhavon's head? Except Mama didn't swear, of course. "I don't need you to tell me that." Zhavon lay back on the bed. With her free hand, she lightly tested the swelling that was almost completely gone from her face now. No permanent scars. Most of the bruises were already gone. As soon as a few scratches finished healing over, she'd be as good as new. So what, she wondered sometimes, was everybody making such a big fuss about?

"If you'd just stayed away from Adrien—"

"I wasn't goin' to see Adrien!" The lie came quickly to Zhavon but wasn't convincing.

"Uh-huh."

"What you mean, 'uh-huh'?"

"I mean, uh-huh, sure you wasn't goin' to see Adrien," said Alvina.

"I'm not that stupid," Zhavon said, realizing fully, as she spoke the words, how stupid she'd been—but that didn't mean she wanted to be constantly reminded of the fact. "Look," she said, "I don't need you bitchin' at me and tellin' me I'm stupid. I can talk to Mama for that."

Another long silence hung between the two girls. "I know...." Alvina said at last. "But sometimes you're just so stupid."

Zhavon laughed despite herself. Everything had been so serious for the past week and a half since she'd been beaten and almost raped. This might've been the first she'd laughed since then. She couldn't remember for sure. Zhavon smothered her laughter so she wouldn't bother Mama—not that Mama didn't already know that her daughter was on the phone. "Hayesburg probably has better schools anyway," Zhavon said, not so much because she cared, but because she could think of nothing else hopeful to hold on to. The last thing she wanted was to be trundled off upstate to Aunt Irma's, but Zhavon didn't seem to have a lot of say in the matter.

"Better schools, but no Adrien," Alvina said.

"Forget you, girl!" Zhavon clamped her hand over her mouth. She really didn't need to piss off Mama again. "Listen," said Zhavon, "I'm leavin' day after tomorrow. So how 'bout tomorrow night, you bring your sorry ass over here with my *stupid* ass—"

"And we'll call Angelique's *fat* ass..." said Alvina. They broke into giggling again.

"And we'll call Angelique's fat ass," Zhavon agreed, "and..." but suddenly the words caught in her throat. The laughter turned into a big lump in the pit of her stomach. She couldn't force out the rest. "And..." And then they wouldn't see each other again.

"And we'll have a good time," Alvina said.

"Yeah," said Zhavon, though they both knew that wasn't what she'd wanted to say. "Look, I gotta go. I'll call you tomorrow."

After she hung up the phone, Zhavon heard the quiet sound of the TV on the other side of the wall. Probably Mama wouldn't sleep tonight. Just like most of the nights the past week and a half.

Sunday, 18 July 1999, 12:34 AM
A tenement in Harlem
New York City, New York

Ramona perched on the top rail of the fire escape and watched Zhavon sleeping peacefully. The first nights after the attack, the girl had tossed and called out, trying to escape whatever hoodlums haunted her dreams.

There's worse out there, Ramona silently warned her.

From several blocks away, car tires screeched. Ramona cringed and waited for the crash, which never came. Almost as a second thought, she glanced back and made sure that the noise hadn't awakened Zhavon. The girl still slept quietly. Over the past few weeks of watching, Ramona had developed an uncanny sense of when the sleeper would awake—the slight turn of the head and stretching of the neck just before the telltale fluttering eyelids. Ramona was sure that, aside from the night of the attack, Zhavon had never seen her, and even that night was easily explained away as hysteria or trauma. Even so, there were times when Zhavon was awake, times when Ramona knew beyond a doubt that she was out of sight, that the dark-skinned girl seemed to know that someone—or something—was watching her.

I remember that feeling, Ramona thought.

She was distracted for a moment by the sound of movement from the shadows below, but there was nothing there.

You're jumpy tonight, girl. Probably because of that biker last night, she decided—the thought of which reminded her that she shouldn't leave Jen alone so much. Darnell didn't spend any more time with her than he had to, and what if the biker did come back?

But Ramona's gaze drifted back to the sleeping Zhavon. Ramona understood Jen's fears, and even shared a few, but with Zhavon, a strange affinity ran more deeply. Jen was the monster that Ramona had become, and there was a connection there, but Zhavon was the human Ramona had once been. The mortal girl looked so peaceful lying there beneath the sheet. When she was awake, however, she possessed a certain defiance, a naïveté coupled with a wrong-headed sense of invulnerability.

I remember that feeling too, thought Ramona. She had once felt almost exactly that way. Now she knew better. She knew better than to think everything would turn out all right. She knew better than to expect nothing too bad to happen to her. Zhavon, though, continued sleeping, oblivious to the worst fears the night had to offer.

After a few minutes, Ramona realized that she'd been staring at the mortal—and that's what normal people passed for these days: mortal, meat, blood. Above the line of the white sheet, Zhavon's hand rested limply on her chest, and above her hand was her bare neck. Ramona imagined that she could see the pulse of the jugular—or could she really? The surrounding sounds of the city faded away beneath the thump-thump, thump-thump of a single human heart, beneath the intermittent swish of blood forced through arteries and veins.

Ramona was halfway through the window—licking her lips—before she caught herself. She retreated back to the fire escape and shook her head forcefully.

"I *hate* that!" Ramona growled under her breath as she sat and hugged her knees to her chest. Losing control like that, even momentarily, brought memories of the change flooding back, of the first night she'd tasted blood at her lips and lost herself to the undeniable hunger.

Sitting there, Ramona wanted to look over the window sill at Zhavon but was afraid to let herself.

What if it happens again? What if I can't stop? Why'd I even bother to save her? Ramona wondered, though she knew that ripping those two men apart had been less an act of heroism, and more the predatory impulse of a hunter whose prey was being stolen away.

Hell, if those bastards hadn't stepped in the way, she fully realized for the first time, *I might've killed Zhavon myself.*

The instinct for the hunt had taken over, as it had so many times. Who was to say when it would happen again? Ramona knew better than to think it wouldn't. For all her newly found powers, it was another way she was helpless.

Angry with herself and seeking distraction, Ramona pointedly did not look at Zhavon, but instead tugged at her own shoes. They'd been bothering her for some time, and she was in no mood, at the moment, to take crap from inanimate objects. She yanked at the tongues of her leather sneakers as if they were the source of all her problems, and when she pulled her feet free, the cause of her physical discomfort was readily apparent.

The shoes were fine. But Ramona stared in horror at her feet. From the heel to the ball of each foot was mashed together and only about half as long as it should've been. Her gnarled toes, however, were abnormally elongated. They stretched almost like tiny fingers, tipped with thick, curved nails.

Claws, Ramona thought, aghast.

She'd watched before as her fingers transformed into razor-sharp claws, but that had only happened when she'd been angry or upset, and it hadn't lasted long. She continued to stare at what couldn't be her feet and waited for the illusion to fade, or, at the worst, for them to change back.

But they *were* her feet, and they didn't change to suit her.

Oh my God.

Ramona tentatively reached out and was actually surprised that she felt the sensation in her foot of her own fingertips brushing across wrinkled and twisted skin.

"You gave in to the Beast," said a voice from below.

Ramona jumped to her deformed feet. A level below her on the fire escape stood, not the Puerto Rican man from the downstairs apartment she'd expected to see but, instead, a complete stranger.

The hair on the back of her neck shot up straight.

The stranger neither retreated nor advanced. He stood there with a blank, unfriendly expression. Dark sunglasses and his long, tangled hair partially obscured his face. The shades of the torn, wrinkled clothes he wore blended almost perfectly into the night-time cityscape.

Ramona's initial shock quickly gave way to the low growl that rose up from her gut, but the stranger raised a finger to his lips. "Shh." He nodded toward Zhavon's window.

He was right, Ramona knew. She didn't want to risk waking Zhavon. Even so, Ramona bristled. Who was he to tell her what to do? She swallowed the growl, but her anger demanded an outlet, and before realizing that she was going to, she leapt down the steps at the stranger.

He seemed less surprised by her actions than she was. With one fluid motion, he placed a hand on the top rail and vaulted off the fire escape.

As Ramona's knees uncoiled from the impact of her landing, she sprang after him without the slightest pause. Her shift in momentum carried her over the rail, and she landed crouched and ready to attack in the alley only feet away from the stranger.

"Hold still, you bastard," she growled, now that she was safely away from the window.

The stranger cocked his head as if he heard a distant sound and then gazed up toward Zhavon's window. "Who will you leave unwatched?" he asked.

The question froze Ramona. *He knows about her,* she thought with alarm, and in the instant she followed his gaze to the window, he was gone. Ramona stood alone in the deserted alley.

The stranger was gone, but his scent lingered—a faint yet distinctive smell that Ramona had noticed other times, but never before had she been able to connect the odor to its source. At once, she began in the direction her nose told her the stranger had gone, but she stopped after only a few steps.

Who will you leave unwatched? His words of just moments before came back to her.

She glanced again up at the window. Was there a threat to Zhavon?

Who will you leave unwatched?

He obviously knew about the girl, although not even Ramona understood what drew her here almost every night. *The smell.* Ramona forced herself to think. Her instincts had swung instantly from aggression toward the stranger to protectiveness of Zhavon, but Ramona needed to think. She'd noticed the smell last night at the garage. Did that mean he also knew about Jen and Darnell and of their resting place?

I'll be back, the biker had said—like a bad rerun of a Schwarzenegger flick. Was this stranger part of the Sabbat as well?

Ramona glanced up at the window again.

Or is he luring me away so he can come back? she wondered.

Like so many nights over the past few weeks, she found herself torn between staying and watching over the sleeping mortal and going to those of her own kind. Without consciously resolving the dilemma, Ramona found herself following the scent, and though it soon faded away to nothing, the first steps had set her on a path to the George Washington Bridge.

After half a mile, Ramona realized that she'd left her shoes behind on the fire escape, but she had dithered long enough. Besides, her malformed feet moved easily over the pavement. Neither gravel nor broken glass pained her tough, leathery soles, and the rhythmic tap of claws on asphalt lulled her into a loping trance.

Who will you leave unwatched?

The blocks and miles fell away behind her until she was crossing the bridge, passing a car that swerved away from the shadow flashing, only for an instant, through the driver's peripheral vision. Then the bridge, too, was receding in the distance. Ramona passed the spot where she'd faced the biker the night before. She pressed onward frantically, urged ahead by the great dread building within her. What if she was too late reaching her friends? What if she'd made the wrong decision, and something terrible happened to Zhavon?

As the garage came into view, Ramona felt not relief but an instant of inexplicable terror. All seemed dark and quiet from without.

Normal quiet or too quiet?

The question had scarcely flashed through her mind before she was at the door. She ripped it open. The chain on the handle shattered as the links were met with a force they couldn't resist. The clinking of the chain fragments scattered across the parking lot was lost to the explosion of the metal door slammed open against the aluminum wall of the building. Ramona charged in ready to attack.

Darnell jumped up from where he sat and spun to face her. Ramona caught only a brief glimpse of Jen as she scuttled down into the nearest pit.

"Mother...!" Darnell started to yell, but his curse trailed off as recognition slowly replaced shock on his face. "What the *hell* you doin'?"

Ramona quickly scanned the darkened interior of the building. "Has he been here?" she blurted out.

"What...? Who?" Darnell, already angry and more than a little embarrassed at having been caught off—guard, was not calmed by Ramona's near—frantic manner.

The biker, she started to say but then realized that wasn't who she was most worried about. *The stranger.* "Anyone."

"Nobody but your crazy ass breakin' down the damn door!" Darnell said.

A light flickered to life in the pit where Jen had fled. She poked her head into view and lifted up her mechanic's lamp. "Ramona? That you?"

"Turn off the damn light!" responded Ramona and Darnell in unison as they shielded their eyes.

As the light went out and all three were bathed in total darkness, Ramona heard, for the second time that night, the screeching of car tires. Earlier, she'd expected a crash. This time her expectations were fulfilled.

A roaring engine burst into a sudden crescendo of destruction, twisted and torn metal, as a car barreled through the garage's left bay door. A headlight shattered into a blinding spray of glass and sparks. The car ripped the tall door from its track and slid to a stop near the pits.

Ramona dove away from both car and falling door. Darnell wasn't so lucky. The sliding car struck him squarely on the right side and flung him into the air through the darkness.

Ramona rolled and jumped to her feet. The remaining

headlight cast an eerie light through the garage as the dented old car jerked to a halt amidst the smell of burnt rubber. Almost instantly, three of the four doors opened, and out stepped the biker and two others wearing similar, unofficial uniforms— ratty T-shirt, faded, tight jeans, black boots.

"Hiya, sweetmeat," the biker called out to the darkness. His companions flanked him on either side. "Ready to play with the big boys, or do you wanna practice that swan dive for real?"

Ramona felt around and found a large crescent wrench on top of a stack of boxes. The tool's weight was solid and comforting in her grasp. The crack along the handle was not a problem for Ramona. With a quick, axe-like motion, she launched the wrench at the biker.

It struck him on the temple and snapped his head to the side. He staggered back a step but didn't fall, and when he regained his balance, to Ramona's dismay, an evil grin spread across his features.

"Come to papa, baby," he said, as he licked his lips and stepped forward into the darkness, retracing the path the wrench had followed. He seemed oblivious to the trickle of blood that ran down his face, and to the blow that would've killed a mortal.

Ramona looked around for any other weapon at hand as she backed away from the advancing biker. Could this, she wondered, be the same person who, last night, had shied away from a confrontation with her? It was, but tonight he had numbers on his side.

Or so he thought.

Suddenly, a bestial roar erupted over the hum of the idling car. From the darkness across the way, Darnell came hurtling through the air like a demonic bird of prey. He crashed onto the two Sabbat behind the biker, driving them to the floor beneath his furious attack.

As the biker whirled about at the commotion, Ramona leapt for his throat. He sensed her attack at the last second, but only enough to deflect, not to evade, her blow. Ramona's force carried him to the ground.

For a moment, five vampires writhed in a mass on the

floor like maggots on carrion. Pale bodies flailed, struggling for leverage. Ramona and the biker were the first to untangle themselves. Each rolled away and sprang up.

Darnell climbed onto one of his two foes and clawed and bit his opponent's face. The unfortunate creature struggled to defend himself, but had little success against Darnell's savagery. Behind Darnell, however, the other Sabbat stood and took from his belt a .38 special, which he aimed at the back of Darnell's head.

Ramona moved to save her friend, but the biker, taking advantage of her distraction, struck her across the back of the head with his iron-hard fist. Ramona stumbled to her knees as time seemed to freeze before her very eyes.

Suddenly, Jen rose from the pit immediately behind the Sabbat holding the revolver. She held in each hand the clamp of a set of jumper cables, and at once she hooked them onto the unsuspecting gunman.

The cables must've been hooked to a battery in the pit, because sparks shot out of the clamps, and out of the Sabbat vampire. The revolver fell from his hand as he contorted into an unnaturally rigid pose. Crackling electricity danced around his body as he jerked spasmodically and his eyes rolled up into his head. Acrid smoke and the smell of seared flesh seemed to fill all the garage at once. In slow motion, he fell to one knee, then, mouth agape and drooling, he toppled to the floor.

Jen, horror etched on her face, stood back away from her victim. The other Sabbat vampire took full advantage of his friend's demise and scurried away from Darnell and, holding his bleeding face, continued out of the garage.

None of this was lost on the biker. For the briefest moment, he froze in indecision, caught between staying to fight and running with his buddy. His hesitation cost him. Ramona kicked with all her strength across his jaw. The staccato snap of bones cut across the continuing buzz from the jumper cables.

The biker landed hard several yards away and lay stunned. When he sat up at last, his jaw was set at quite an odd angle to the right. He raised a hand but only gingerly touched his chin.

Ramona strutted toward him. "You said something about

the big boys," she reminded him. "They showin' up soon?"

A flicker of doubt crossed his features.

"Maybe *you'll* be practicin' that swan dive off the bridge," Ramona said.

She and Darnell stepped closer to the biker. Jen, giving the electrically live body on the floor a wide berth, circled around nervously behind them.

The biker still seemed stunned from Ramona's roundhouse kick. Rather than respond to her taunts, he spit blood onto the floor, an action that obviously caused him great pain.

Ramona stepped closer still. She didn't harbor any illusions that he and his companions would've spared her. The little she knew of the Sabbat from first the West Coast and now the East, they weren't the forgiving types. He hadn't counted on Darnell and Jen, and wasn't that just a pisser for biker boy?

But her next step was interrupted by the sound of more engines gunning nearby—cars, several of them, and coming closer.

Ramona turned back to the biker. Broken jaw and all, his face was twisted into a maddening sneer. "Better be quick," he muttered painfully, as laughter, deep in his gut like a smothered cough, began to wrack his body.

"*Whelp!*" A different voice caught Ramona's attention from behind.

She turned to see the top half of the stranger protruding from an opening in the floor where, before, a stack of crates had rested.

"*This way. Hurry!*" His voice was forceful, commanding. It lacked any sense of desperation, yet hinted that he expected no delay in obedience.

Ramona again faced the biker, who was laughing giddily now. Blood dripped from his mouth.

She sent another kick across his face. He spun and landed in a heap, unmoving, but Ramona's blood was up. She wanted to take his head off altogether.

But the stranger was waiting expectantly. The position of the opening was such that Darnell and Jen couldn't see him. Only Ramona. His gaze bore into her.

The cars that had heartened the biker were very close now. The beams of headlights streamed through the gaping hole where the bay door had been ripped away. The biker lay completely still, but the cars had to be more Sabbat. How many, Ramona didn't know. And she didn't want to find out.

"Come on," she called to Darnell and Jen. She led them to the open trapdoor. The stranger was nowhere to be seen.

"Where'd this come from?" Jen asked.

Ramona shrugged. "It was under some boxes." She paused above the opening. Who was this stranger who threatened her before and helped her now? But a car crashing through the intact bay door chased the questions from her mind. Ramona dove through the opening, and Darnell and Jen followed right behind her. Darnell had the presence of mind to pull the trapdoor shut.

They found themselves crowded into a low, narrow crawlspace lined with pipes of various sizes. The only light was the little that seeped around the edges of the trapdoor.

"Great," muttered Ramona. Her first thought was that the stranger had hopped out and run while she wasn't looking, and that now she and the others were trapped—at least until the Sabbat reinforcements turned on the lights and found the trapdoor.

Or maybe the stranger had escaped ahead of them.

Ramona crawled forward into the darkness. Her eyes were adjusting rapidly.

"Ow!" Jen hadn't kept her head down.

"Shut the fuck up!" Darnell hissed at her in a harsh whisper.

Ramona ignored them and kept crawling. She almost fell headlong into the hole that opened beneath her. She stopped so abruptly that Darnell bumped smack into her ass, and Jen into him.

"Hey...!"

"Shut the fuck up!"

Ramona crawled into the hole head-first. "This way. Down," she said over her shoulder in case they couldn't see her.

The pipes gave way to dirt and rock, but the new tunnel was no more spacious than the crawlspace. If anything, the walls closed more tightly about her. Ramona had never been underground before. She'd never had reason to suspect that claustrophobia might be a problem for her, but she could suddenly feel air growing scarce.

You don't breathe no more, bitch, she reminded herself, and crawled ahead so Darnell and Jen could follow her down.

The tunnel ahead sloped downward, and that seemed as good a direction as any. A tiny but putrid-smelling trickle of water led Ramona onward. The ceiling of the passage dropped more than the floor, and the space became tighter still. Soon Ramona was crawling with her face turned sideways, cheek pressed down in the muck. Behind, Jen whimpered and Darnell cursed under his breath. Ramona's back scraped against the ceiling, but she was already pressed as hard to the floor as she could be.

She scanned the darkness ahead. Her eyes had adjusted as much as they were going to. There was just too little light, and nothing to see but rock and dirt. She didn't want to wedge herself in, but neither did she want to try to direct Jen and Darnell back the other way to either try the other direction or reemerge into the garage. Ahead was better.

Ramona pushed forward with a little more force and popped through the tight spot. "It opens up a little up here," she let the others know. The tunnel turned downward more steeply as well. Their pace quickened in the less restrictive space, and soon they came to a rough curve. Ramona could feel fresh air on her face. Twenty yards more, and they crawled out onto the steep bank of the Hudson River, not far from the George Washington Bridge.

Ramona glanced around, but there was no sign of the stranger. She almost asked if the others had seen him but decided this was neither the time nor the place. Discussions with Darnell and Jen tended to degenerate rapidly into arguments, and Ramona wanted a bit more distance from the Sabbat, however many of those bastards were swarming around. Who knew if they might find the trapdoor, or if they had lookouts posted on or near the bridge?

"This way," Ramona said, as she started north along the river.

"Where are we going now?" Jen asked. She peeled off her outer sweatshirt, stained down the front with the sludge from the tunnel.

"Hayesburg," said Ramona. New York City was a bit too hot all of a sudden. *Just like L.A.*, she thought.

Darnell must've agreed. Otherwise he wouldn't have hesitated to argue. "Hayesburg," he repeated. "Where's that?"

"Don't know," Ramona answered. "Guess we'll have to find it." She kept her eyes peeled for any lurking Sabbat—or for the stranger, who seemed, for better or worse, to have taken an interest in her. As she quickened her trot to a run, she tried to decide what she would do if she met him again—thank him, or kick his ass? She didn't come up with an answer right away.

Sunday, 18 July 1999, 4:39 AM
Interstate 81-North
Near Roanoke, Virginia

The sun and the moon, hand in hand, in all their white brilliance were trapped within the small mirror. Ahead, the rhythmic white lines rushed forward out of the darkness, one after another after another, like beautiful swans, each unerring in the pursuit of its predecessor.

All else was darkness.

The wind of the swans' passing slapped at Leopold's face. He blinked away the crimson tears evoked by the sweet, visual cacophony of Sight and unSight. The white light of sun and moon burst forth from the mirror and shattered into a spectrum of hues, each beckoning him to lose himself in its stark purity. Rainbow bands enveloped him. Sun and moon were contained no longer. The twin orbs expanded beyond the plastic edges of the mirror and bathed Leopold in blinding light.

At the same instant, the swans, without breaking their single-file ranks, veered wildly to the right. A deep horn sounded that gripped Leopold in his bones. The noise was from behind him. He looked over his shoulder to face sun and moon, free of the rearview mirror, as they bore down on top of him.

Leopold lurched at the steering wheel, shot right, passing again the streaming swans. Sun and moon roared past. The spectral colors flashed and were gone.

The car's tires strayed from pavement and took uncertain hold of the gravel shoulder as the vehicle fish-tailed. Instincts honed by distant mortal experience took over. Leopold turned into the slide, overcompensated, turned the wheel steadily the other direction to correct the second slide. Two wheels lifted free of the ground. The car hovered at the cusp of flight for a second that stretched out toward eternity...then heavily righted itself, slid to a halt.

Leopold could see in his mind the next moment that had not come to pass—the car flipping onto its side, its roof, tumbling along the highway and into the embankment in a shower of glass and crumpled metal.

Silence calmed the swirling mix of Sight and unSight. White lines lay still upon the road where they'd taken the place of the swans in flight. Sun and moon were transformed into smaller, piercing, red lights that had come to rest a hundred yards down the interstate.

The muse's laughter, bubbling from nowhere, receded into the distance. In the confusion of the moment, Leopold had been unaware of her. Now he spun, hoping to catch a glimpse of her, but his motion sent the world hurtling again toward the shifting axes of insanity.

He laid his head back against the seat and allowed her to escape unmolested.

She would not abandon him. He was growing more confident of this fact every hour. He was her chosen one, a conduit of unguessed revelation. She still led him onward so that he might create perfection. At her urging, he had relieved that young man in Atlanta of his automobile and driven north all last night, all tonight.

The answers lay in this direction. Leopold was certain.

Even so, he realized, morning would be upon him shortly. He needed to find shelter again soon. The journey north would have to continue tomorrow night.

Footsteps. As the world settled around Leopold, he was partially aware of the man approaching from the direction of the semi that had pulled over just up the road.

"Jesus God, are you all right?" asked the trucker. "Are you drunk, or just stupid, or—dear Lord, your eye is—"

Leopold lashed out, jerked the trucker through the open window, and in the space of one heartbeat was feasting from the broken neck.

A few minutes later, Leopold pulled away from the lifeless body on the edge of I-81 and cut across the median to the empty southbound lanes.

There was a truckstop not far back, he thought. *I will persuade a driver to provide shelter for me.*

The driver would not leave during the day. Of this, Leopold felt certain.

part two:
bone

Thursday, 22 July 1999, 1:02 AM
Old Hayesburg Elementary School
Hayesburg, New York

Ramona lay on her back on the slick, hardwood floor and stared unseeing into the dim heights of the vaulted ceiling. She squeezed her eyes closed. All her will was absorbed in resisting the urge that had tempted her the entire night. The footsteps that she felt and heard coming toward her were both relief and distraction. Ramona recognized Jen without looking—the quiet approach, hesitant not stealthy.

Jen stopped a few feet away but didn't speak. Ramona opened her eyes. The only light in the cavernous room, from streetlights outside, filtered down from windows near the ceiling. Jen nodded with a nervous smile. Her lips, once pouty like a beautiful model's, Ramona imagined, were pale to the point of bluish.

"I didn't want to bother you," Jenny said. Seconds passed. She seemed increasingly uncomfortable with the silence. "I thought maybe you were—"

"Sleeping?" Ramona asked with a disdainful harumph. "Do you really sleep? Even in the daytime?"

Jen pulled up a chair and sat. The only chairs they had found in this boarded-up elementary school were child-sized—apparently all the adults had taken their chairs with them when the building was closed—and Jen, sitting there in the center of the otherwise empty gymnasium, instead of dwarfing the small seat, seemed to shrink to fit it. She looked the part of a child alone in a vast, dark space.

"No," Jen answered. "I don't *feel* like I sleep. But I do… I guess."

"Dreams?"

Jen shook her head slowly. "Not that I remember." She stared down at her feet. "It doesn't feel like being asleep. It feels like..."

"Being dead," said Ramona. The words hung in the grave-like silence of the gym.

Jen squeezed her eyes tightly shut and continued shaking her head in an attempt to deny what she had to know was the truth. Ramona knew what the girl must be feeling. Ramona had been through it herself, was still going through it to some extent, but not to the degree that Jen was. Maybe Jen had lost more with her mortal life and that made it harder.

A single crimson tear dripped from the corner of Jen's eye, betraying her inability to accept their new reality. The drop of blood struck the shiny grain of the floor. Ramona raised a finger and wiped the track of the tear from Jen's cheek, pressed her finger to her tongue.

Vampire, Ramona thought.

As she tasted the rich blood, the word stuck in her mind. *Vampire.*

Darnell was right. How could Jen pretend they had become anything else? But, Ramona also thought, badgering Jen wasn't going to bring her around. Couldn't Darnell see that? Hadn't he felt any of what Jen was laboring with? Didn't he have qualms about the monster he'd become?

I'm afraid of what I've become, Ramona thought.

"When is this going to end?" Jen whispered. Blood lined the bottom edges of her eyes.

"Don't know." Ramona closed her eyes again. She could still taste Jen's blood. Again, she felt the urge she'd been denying all night.

This is the next step, Ramona thought.

Unlike her friend, she had accepted becoming a vampire, but now she was finding out what that really meant. "Sometimes you just have to suck it up," Ramona said aloud to herself.

With Jen's sharp intake of breath, Ramona realized too late what her comment must've sounded like—a flippant dismissal of Jen's worries. Ramona sat up, intending to set the record straight, but Jen had hopped up and was already halfway across the gym. She was trying to suppress her sobs, but drops of blood marked her path.

Ramona sighed. *That girl has gotta toughen up some time*, she thought. But Ramona could've used the company tonight.

Where has Darnell got to? she wondered. He'd been rummaging around in the basement earlier, climbing over the piles of discarded furniture, searching for a sub-basement or deeper storage area that would be even farther removed from sunlight.

"You don't have to do that, you know," Ramona had told him, but he'd only grunted and kept on with what he was doing.

Both he and Jenny had reacted strangely to Ramona's most recent discovery.

They'd left New York City four nights ago. The first night they'd covered little ground. Ramona had stolen a map from a convenience store, and they'd found a condemned tenement where they'd weathered out the day.

The second night they headed north, toward Hayesburg. It was slow going initially. Sabbat killers seemed to lurk in every shadow. Even Darnell was jumpy. Ramona watched, to no effect, for signs of both the Sabbat and the mysterious stranger, who carried an air of danger but had also made possible their escape. Again, the three sought out an abandoned building to pass the day in relative safety.

The next night, however, found them much farther north and without shelter as the first pink and orange stains of morning began to spread above the horizon. Ramona and the others were on the outskirts of one of the small towns sprinkled along the Hudson River, and there was no obvious choice for a temporary haven.

"Any luck?" Ramona asked Darnell, who had just made a third sweep of the town. "Burned-out building?"

"Nothin' with a basement," he growled.

Jen picked obsessively at her fingernails and sat in anxious silence.

"Why you worried about the sun?" Darnell taunted her. "You ain't no vampire, remember?"

Ramona blocked out their bickering. She didn't have time

for it. The three, along with their other companion, Eddie, had crossed much of the country in a light-sealed van—that had been Eddie's idea—and had never lacked for a place to spend the day. Maybe, Ramona thought, they should've held on to the van longer, or gotten another. But more and more, as the weeks had passed, she'd hated being cooped up inside a vehicle of any type. The two nights of travel on foot from the city had been long, but they'd allowed Ramona and the others to be active. It would've been worse being shut inside a car, wondering if every other car that appeared carried a Sabbat hit squad. Besides, with their preternatural physical capabilities, the three had made good time.

A car's no good, Ramona decided. The night was for exploring, for smelling the breeze, for feeling the ground beneath her feet.

She looked down at the clawed extremities that her feet had become—both Darnell and Jen had noticed, she was sure, but both had had the good sense not to question her—and she dug her toes into the soil. Cool comfort enveloped her feet, as if she partook of a natural kinship with the earth itself. She dug a bit deeper, then, startlingly, her feet began gradually to sink into the ground. Unexplained and unexpected as it was, it felt right somehow; it seemed what she was meant for.

Words of her lost mortal faith came to her mind—*Ashes to ashes. Dust to dust.*

"Come here," she enjoined her friends.

Perplexed, they did so, and each took the hand that Ramona held out.

"Close your eyes. Don't think about anything," she told them.

Through her fingertips, Ramona could sense the blood that lay beneath the undead flesh she grasped. She could feel the unease with which Darnell held her hand, and the tension in Jen's every muscle. But Ramona could also feel them through the soil beneath their feet. She felt the coolness, the kinship of the earth, and, instinctively, she let that kinship spread to them. They began to slip into her trance without realizing, and the earth welcomed them also.

Ashes to ashes. Dust to dust.

"What are you—" Jen began to protest weakly beneath the weight of the trance, but Ramona gripped her hand fiercely and was met with silence.

The chill began to spread upward from her feet through her legs. She could tell somehow that the others felt it too. Abdomen, torso, were accepted by the earth. Ramona stretched out her will to calm Jen. Darnell accepted this embrace passively, if not comfortably. Their bodies sank into the ground, melded with the soil to which they should already have returned permanently.

Ramona imagined the first rays of the sun breaking through the leaves. In her mind, the leaves burst into flame. They joined the smoldering and burning of her flesh as the light touched her face. Was she burning? She had sunk too deeply into the stupor of the dead to know, to care. Regardless, the earth drank her in, extinguished the fire, encompassed every fiber of her being.

Ashes to ashes. Dust to dust.

Darkness. Cold. Safety. Oblivion.

When Ramona opened her eyes, night had fallen. The vengeful sun was again banished until the next morning. She lay on the ground in a shallow depression, as did Jen and Darnell on either side of her. The other two stirred, blinked awake as if aroused from a dream. Ramona lay still, savoring the coolness, the same chill that permeated her flesh.

I could stay there, she knew suddenly. *I could sink deep into the ground and not come back.* The thought was appealing. But what of her friends? What of Zhavon?

Jen sat and stared ahead blankly. Darnell brushed the dirt from his clothes. Neither spoke. They avoided Ramona's gaze.

Finally, Jen, her face tinged with fear, turned to Ramona. "How—"

Darnell scrambled to his feet, smacked Jen across the back of the head. "Shut up! And you…" he turned his attention and a long, accusing finger to Ramona. "Don't you *ever* do that to me again!" Then he whirled and stomped off toward the town.

Jen, too confused to be angry at Darnell, still watched Ramona like a sparrow watches the hawk.

"It just happened," Ramona answered the question Jen had

started to ask. "It just happened."

She climbed to her feet and started in the direction Darnell had gone. After a moment, she heard Jen following as well.

"I couldn't stop it," said Jen from behind.

"If you had, the sun would've got you," Ramona growled.

She didn't understand everything that was happening. How could she explain it to them if they couldn't *feel* it?

The next night, they'd arrived in Hayesburg. Ramona had known that Zhavon wasn't far away. Again, Ramona didn't know how she could tell. She just *knew*. There hadn't been time to seek out the girl right away, however, because Darnell and Jen, in a rare instance of agreement, had insisted on seeking shelter if this was where they were going to stay.

Ramona had been about to suggest that they didn't need a building for shelter any more, but she'd seen the anger in Darnell's eyes, the fear in Jen's, and decided against it. They'd found the boarded-up school and spent a day there.

Now, Ramona lay on the floor, her fingers touching the synthetic sealant that protected the natural wood, as the sound of Jen's footsteps and sobbing receded into the distance.

I let them have their way this time, Ramona thought. She'd stayed with them this past day here in the school. *But what are they afraid of?* she wondered. Sinking into the earth to escape the light of the sun had come as naturally to her as... as drinking blood. *It's another part of this... this thing that we've all become. Part that they're not ready for.*

Ramona sat upright on the slick floor, stared at her feet, curled and uncurled the gnarled, clawed toes. There were some things she wasn't ready for either. Only she didn't have a choice. Maybe there was nothing wrong with Darnell and Jenny hanging on to what they could of the days before.

I shouldn't rush them, Ramona decided. Besides, she had her own problems without making more.

All night, before Jen had approached her, Ramona had been lying there trying to pinpoint the cause of the urges she was feeling. Back in the days before the change, she had always been very conscious of her own moods and motivations. The change had brought on a whole new set of causes and effects, most of which Ramona had learned through trial and painful error. The laundry list of danger had become a mantra of sorts:

Beware the sun; it burns flesh.

Beware lack of blood; the hunger will take control.

Beware too much blood, the sight and smell; the hunger, again, will take control.

Beware your own kind; they are everywhere.

Strangely enough for Ramona, who had never been poetic, the flow of the words had evolved naturally, the rhythm emerging from some hidden place within her, from an inner song that was no longer masked by the sound of a beating heart.

Tonight, however, Ramona was struggling with a new urge. Or if not new, a compulsion much stronger than she had felt it before.

Zhavon.

Ramona knew that the girl had been sent to Hayesburg, her mother hoping that a small town would be more forgiving than the city of the kind of mistake that had almost gotten Zhavon killed— *would* have gotten Zhavon killed if it hadn't been for Ramona. The mortal girl's presence was the reason Ramona had brought her friends here. The Sabbat attack had been a useful excuse. Otherwise Darnell, at least, would've put up a struggle, not because he had any better ideas, but because that was what he did. He and Jen had followed Ramona because they were adrift in this new world of the night. Ramona, unintentionally, had stumbled upon a purpose—or rather the hint of a purpose.

Zhavon.

What was it, Ramona wondered, that attracted her to the girl, that had, so many nights, consciously or otherwise, directed Ramona's steps to that neighborhood, that fire escape, that window? She wished she knew, because again she felt drawn to the streets, and though Ramona had not yet explored in any detail this new town, she knew where—or with whom— she would end up.

As she had for the past few hours, however, Ramona denied herself and remained in the elementary school. She sat alone in the center of the gym and stared, only half-seeing, into the shadows where once children had played, exercised, probably been forced by some sadistic teacher to square dance. *Why don't I go to her?* Ramona thought. *It's why we're here— why I brought us here.*

Barely had the unavoidable thought been given voice in her mind than Ramona was outside. She instinctively shied away from the harsh glare of the streetlights. Vague thoughts tugged at her, but they were kept at an arm's length by her protective armor of hyper-alert physical senses: the chorus of crickets almost drowned out the sound of flapping bat wings around the eaves of the school building; the rich, earthy odor of lawn fertilizer mixed with the diffuse fumes of industry that hung over the town; asphalt underfoot scraped against the pads of her thick soles.

Ramona gave herself to the sensations. Her powerful muscles and keen reflexes didn't need her direction to move quickly but warily, to keep out of sight—not that anyone stirred at this hour in the sleepy town, but Ramona's exposed, monstrous feet didn't lend themselves any longer to mixing unobtrusively with mortals. She wandered without purpose but knowing full well where her meandering path would inevitably lead.

The school was no longer in sight. Several blocks away, a dog barked, began a small chain reaction as two more joined in and continued for maybe two minutes—well beyond any memory of what had started them barking. Ramona ignored the lesser urge to find one of them, to curl up beside it and enjoy the warm comfort of a beating heart and a wet tongue. She was very much like them in some ways, but she was also far different.

Eventually, Ramona found herself standing before a small, ranch-style house in a line of others, a concise rectangle of red bricks shaded near-black in the darkness. How little, Ramona realized, the people in these safe little houses would know of the type of life she'd led as a mortal, much less of the existence that now had been thrust upon her.

Zhavon's mother was right to send her here, Ramona thought. There were too many traps in the world without going looking for every danger the city had to offer.

Ramona climbed onto a low branch in the tree facing the window—*the* window. *How do I know?* she wondered briefly, but she no longer tried to answer all of those questions that confronted her. *I know.*

And as her bestial gaze parted the obscuring darkness, she knew also why she had been right to fear coming to this place.

Thursday, 22 July 1999, 2:31 AM
Meadowview Lane
Hayesburg, New York

Red, gleaming eyes haunted Zhavon's dreams, and as she crossed the threshold between sleep and wakefulness, everything else faded away, changed.

But the eyes remained.

Zhavon blinked hard. She knew that she wasn't still dreaming, but she felt less than awake. The eyes were still there, outside the window.

Shouldn't they be gone? she wondered groggily. *I'm awake. They should be gone.*

She half-heartedly thought of calling Aunt Irma—Aunt Irma was as mean as Mama and three times as big; *nobody* messed with Aunt Irma—but for Zhavon, the proximity of her aunt, the very walls of the house around them, seemed less real than those red eyes.

Watching.

Zhavon hadn't been startled awake. She didn't run screaming from the eyes beyond the window, but there was a voice deep inside her urging caution. *Get Aunt Irma,* it said. *Call the police. Do it now.*

Was that Mama's voice, or was it the voice that was always there within Zhavon, the one she usually ignored? She knew it was right this time—the hair standing up on her arms and on the back of her neck told her that much—but it was such a little voice, and every second it seemed so much farther away.

Her mind dredged up old dangers—the attack, the strange pair of shoes on the fire escape. But those had been back in the city. Back home.

Get Irma... call the police... now.

The voice was breaking up like a weak radio station. No. It wasn't static drowning out the words, she realized. Another sound. The white noise of her own blood flowing, the sound of her pulse amplified as if she held giant seashells over her ears.

Irma... now...

A sea of blood washed over the voice, dragged it far away, until only the inexorable sweep and pull of the ocean remained.

Zhavon stared through the glass, and the image before her was her own. She saw through those eyes a world tinted blood-red. She saw herself sitting in bed, slowly putting her feet to the floor, pulling her nightshirt over her head.

The voice... what was it saying?

She saw her own body, rounded, full of life. The veins were not so close to the surface, yet the deafening roar of a tidal wave filled her ears. She watched as she reached for a shirt, jeans, shoes.

The roaring wave carried her forward, obliterated the sound of her footsteps. Her vision dimmed.

Zhavon opened her eyes—had they been closed? She turned a doorknob, opened the front door, then stepped outside, into the arms of the girl from her dreams.

Thursday, 22 July 1999, 2:40 AM
Meadowview Lane
Hayesburg, New York

Ramona drew in Zhavon, clutched the girl tightly to her chest.

"I...I..." Zhavon tried to speak.

Ramona gently shushed her, stroked the tight ringlets of the girl's hair, nuzzled the hollow beneath her ear.

"I..."

"Shhh."

Ramona brushed her fingers across Zhavon's forehead, traced the line of her brow, cheek, jaw. Warmth radiated from the mortal's skin—genuine warmth, capillaries, canals of life-sustaining blood, the flow driven by a beating heart. Ramona's fingers descended along the curve of Zhavon's neck and lingered there. Beside the tensed muscles, the jugular pulsated irresistibly. Ramona slid her mouth along taut skin. Her tongue darted out and tasted the sweat of fear and anticipation. Merely a thin veneer of flesh denied her that for which she hungered.

Now her tongue felt the severe edge of canines lowered in response to her hunger.

No!

Ramona fought for control. She pulled away, but the cry of anguish she heard was not her own.

Zhavon dropped to her knees. Tears streamed down her face.

Real tears, Ramona thought. She raised her fingers to her own cheek, felt the pure moisture there— not bloody tracks— from where she had pressed against Zhavon. *Real tears.*

Ramona turned from the mortal girl and felt herself staggering away.

I can't. I can't! she thought desperately.

The spark of mortal life, the call of similar human experience, the very qualities within Zhavon that had attracted Ramona in the first place—those were what Ramona would destroy if she satisfied her hunger, and she knew that, just as she hadn't been able to curb her desire to see the girl for more than a few nights, once she began feeding, she wouldn't be able to rein in her hunger.

I can't.

Ramona's protests grew more feeble.

I've gotta get away from here.

I can't.

Ramona turned and, to her horror, saw Zhavon crawling after her.

Thursday, 22 July 1999, 2:46 AM
Meadowview Lane
Hayesburg, New York

Zhavon couldn't stop the tears that blurred her vision and ran down her face. She'd seen such pain and hunger deep in those red eyes. Such desire. Zhavon found herself crawling after the girl—not meaning to follow but unable to stop. Rational thought had long since given way to animal attraction. Her body was not hers to command.

The other girl stumbled around the corner of the house. Zhavon tried to stand. Her muscles failed her. She continued to crawl, afraid that the hungering girl would leave her behind. But when Zhavon turned the corner of the house, the lighter-skinned girl was not far ahead. In fact, she too had fallen to her knees. Her back was to Zhavon.

Zhavon closed the distance between them, vaguely noticing the strange, gnarled feet that stuck out behind the other girl. Still, the warnings in Zhavon's mind were silenced beneath the ocean that was called to the surface.

Zhavon was close enough to touch the stranger, reached out, placed her hand on the girl's shoulder.

As the girl twisted to face Zhavon, Zhavon saw the earlier confusion retreat beneath the red hunger in those animal eyes. But something... something of a retreating plea, of helplessness, reached out to Zhavon. "Ramona?" said Zhavon, unsure how she knew the name, but certain that she was right.

And with the sound of the name, the hunger took over, and the beast was on Zhavon.

Thursday, 22 July 1999, 2:52 AM
Meadowview Lane
Hayesburg, New York

Ramona heard her name, knew that the girl had named her. The animal within her knew as well. It rose up and struck to appease its hunger.

Ramona tore at the collar of Zhavon's shirt, ripped away the fabric and struck fiercely. Her fangs gouged into the base of Zhavon's neck—through skin, muscle, tendon, searching for the artery.

There!

Blood flowed into Ramona's mouth. The few, insignificant scraps of flesh she swallowed were washed down with the sweet blood, pumped in forceful bursts by Zhavon's strong heart.

The girl was knocked back by Ramona's initial blow. Zhavon cried out in pain—pain that Ramona remembered. The fangs carried simultaneously the blunt force of a hammer and the piercing agony of a thousand needles slipped under fingernails.

But then Zhavon's back arched and her pained moan shifted to something else, as the ecstasy of the feeding took control. Ramona knew that if she was gentle, in the end, it was not the pain but the pleasure that would fill Zhavon's mind.

In the end...

Ramona drank greedily. The hunger drove her onward. Her entire being reveled in the kill.

The kill...

Zhavon pressed against Ramona. The mortal's grip, her fingers digging into Ramona's bare arms, could've been the impassioned grip of a lover. Her head lolled back, and more tears ran down onto Ramona's face.

The beating of her prey's heart filled Ramona. Warmth spread through her dead limbs, crept toward her extremities. The hunger led her to take more blood. Soon, she knew, the heart would stop.

No!

Ramona paused in her feeding. A trickle of blood ran down her chin.

The attraction to Zhavon and her familiar mortal life could not hold the hunger at bay—but they must! Nostalgia and bloodlust—Ramona had known which would win out. That was why she'd stayed away much of the night.

But she'd given in to temptation.

Zhavon began to quiver in Ramona's arms. Shortly, there would no longer be enough blood in her body to support life. She would go into shock. She would die.

No... please, no.

Ramona wanted to tear herself away, to flee into the darkness, but as the next beat of Zhavon's heart pumped more blood into Ramona's mouth, a new tide of hunger washed over her. Unable to stop herself, she attacked the gaping wound again, dug deeper, tore away impeding flesh, drew as much blood as possible.

Zhavon winced, but she was captive to the rapture of the kill. She didn't struggle, but grasped Ramona more tightly, pressed their bodies together so that they were as one.

Ramona's will, too, was bent to the kill. The knowledge that Zhavon's humanity would be gone forever was not completely lost among Ramona's desires, that her own would be lessened somehow, that the next time the hunger rose, she would not manage to resist even this much.

She had lost completely the will to resist the hunger when the wooden stake slammed into her back—into her heart.

Ramona's eyes and mouth shot open. A cry of pain emerged with a gurgled spray of blood from her throat.

Zhavon whimpered piteously as she was released, and slumped to the ground.

A second wrenching of the stake forced it through the

remainder of Ramona's torso to protrude from the front. Despite the fresh blood in her body, her limbs were seized by a stiffening chill. She tried to grasp the stake, to push it back through, but her strength abandoned her before she even touched it.

As she toppled over like an up-ended statue, another figure swooped down upon Zhavon. He sniffed, momentarily, at the deep wound at the base of her neck, then licked the edges and deep into the hole. The bleeding slowed to a trickle.

Ramona watched as might a corpse at its own funeral—present but helpless to intervene.

He'll kill me now, she thought, *and then Zhavon.*

But he had no further interest in Ramona. He lifted Zhavon in his arms, and as he turned to leave, from her skewed vantage point, propped on her side by the stake, Ramona saw for an instant his monstrous left eye. It bulged as if too large for its socket, and a gelatinous ichor fizzed and bubbled around its edges.

Then he was gone—with Zhavon.

And Ramona was left paralyzed to contemplate the approaching dawn.

Thursday, 22 July 1999, 2:58 AM
Barnard College
New York City, New York

*H*add. Vengeance.

What a fortuitous turn of events, Anwar thought, *when the employment of my clan's particular skills pays for a death that any childe of Haqim would gladly bring about for free.* And he'd heard rumored that the payment for this particular *kafir* was a decanter of old and potent vitae. Old and potent. Incredibly so, if the rumors were to be believed.

Footsteps approaching. Instinctively, Anwar slipped more deeply into the shadows. He doubted that anyone could see him when he did not wish it, but he was not willing to cast caution to the winds, unless it became absolutely necessary. At times, risks were unavoidable, but to take unnecessary chances was foolish.

The footsteps belonged to a security guard, one of the mortals hired to ensure safety on the campus of this small college in the midst of such a forbidding city. It was possible, Anwar knew, that the guard might also be a pawn of the hated warlocks, and so Anwar did not test his esoteric powers of concealment. Instead, he stayed out of actual sight until the man had passed.

The campus was well lit, but Anwar found shadows easily enough. He almost laughed at the idea that street lamps and the prominently displayed emergency phones might dissuade him even a whit if he chose to take one of the young women who studied at this place. There were few enough here during the summer, and none were in evidence at this hour of the morning. Regardless, Anwar was not interested in them.

He watched the academic building across the way. Its brick

facade and the landscaped shrubbery before it were similar to the other buildings, but Anwar was sure of his instructions. His contact would emerge from that building when opportunity presented itself. No suspicions must be aroused. That concerned Anwar the most—that the contact would bungle his or her part in the mission, that Anwar would be revealed through the incompetence of a *kafir*. He would stand little chance against so many warlocks.

Strangely enough, Anwar was little concerned about treachery. It was possible, of course, that the entire mission was a set-up, that the contact would deliver him to the Tremere, but Anwar thought that unlikely. Though skilled at his craft, he harbored no illusions that his death would be a blow of any consequence to his clan, or a boon to any enemy. More deeply than his own analysis, however, he trusted the judgment of his elders. Had they seen fit to order him to a pointless end, he would go willingly and sing the praises of Haqim each step of the way.

For now, though, Anwar waited patiently. For all things under the moon and stars there would be time.

Hadd. Vengeance.

Thursday, 22 July 1999, 3:03 AM
Upstate New York

Leopold tossed the unconscious mortal into the back seat, climbed behind the wheel, and started the engine. *So close now!* he thought, as the car lurched into motion and left behind the small town, so inconsequential except for what he'd taken from it.

So close, the muse purred, echoing his thoughts. Leopold could feel her moist breath on the back of his neck.

He didn't try to whip around and catch a glimpse of her. Such rashness, he had learned, could prove quite unfortunate, as the car's various dents and the stalks of field grass stuck in the grille and bumper attested.

Leopold had gained some insight into, if not control of, the chaotic interplay of Sight and unSight. He no longer had to be on his guard every second—as long as he wasn't foolish—to avoid the topsy-turvy unfastening of his world. He recognized almost as a background the pale elements, the mundane flotsam, of his surroundings. He could make his way through that lifeless scenery that he'd always known.

So close, the muse whispered in his ear.

She lent direction to the Sight, and after practice and acclimation, he could now look at the new world without completely losing his grounding in the old.

The girl was of the new.

After days of tedious (and dangerous, as he grew accustomed to Sight) driving, the muse had directed him to the small town. Unerringly, she had led him— *along this block, and left here.*

But what is it?

Hurry, she had scolded him. *There is little time, and we are so close….*

With the help of the Eye, Leopold had come to realize the insignificance, the small-minded blandness, of his previous homes—Boston, Chicago, Atlanta— but if they were the equivalent of artistic fecal matter, this little town was less than a gnat basking in their odiferous splendor.

Yet, miracle of miracles, when Leopold had gone where the muse had led him, he'd found what would surely be the subject of his greatest work.

The girl had been in the grasp of another Cainite, one of the unwashed, but Leopold had corrected that matter.

The girl moaned, shifted her prone body on the back seat, slipped, perhaps into coma.

Leopold ventured a careful glance at her. Unlike the Cainite, the mortal resonated within the Sight. He'd known as soon as he'd made his way past the row of insubstantial houses and beheld her—her perfection of line and form, the quality with which light rebounded from her skin. She transcended the pale world.

This, Leopold was certain, was the subject for the work that would bring him true immortality.

Thank heavens I found her before it was too late, Leopold thought. *That barbarian would have destroyed her and denied her the purpose of her entire life!*

Leopold had licked the deep wound at her shoulder. His ministrations had saved her. She would live. Long enough.

So close… mmm… so close, whispered the muse.

She had led him to his subject. She would find for him a place of solitude, and she would reveal to him the proper tools.

Leopold sped north, away from the town. *I must make it as far as I can before dawn.* The steering wheel was sticky from the discharge that seeped and dripped from the Eye.

Thursday, 22 July 1999, 3:05 AM
Meadowview Lane
Hayesburg, New York

Mother fucker.

In her mind, Ramona writhed, groaned, tried to escape the constant, sharp agony that wracked her body, but the wooden stake through her heart held her completely immobile. Through the pain, she impatiently awaited the end. Her body and heart were impaled. Surely this was death to mortal or vampire. But there were the stories she'd heard....

Finish me, she thought. If the stake wasn't enough, then at least her attacker could strike the final blow and put an end to the pain. He could spare her waking another night into this hellish existence.

No, she remembered. *He's gone.*

And he had taken Zhavon.

Mother fucker.

The protective impulse, the same compulsion that had flung Ramona onto the rapists in the city, welled up within her again. She remembered her attacker's grotesque eye, pictured herself ripping it from his face.

But she lay paralyzed. Helpless. And the pain was not done with her yet. It swelled in her chest, shot through every limb, pounded in her head. Ramona's vision grew darker, faded. Darkness swept over her....

Her eyes focused again.

How long...?

The sky was noticeably lighter. Dawn was not far away. Terror gripped Ramona.

Dawn. The sun.

Her skin itched, as if already the first invisible rays licked at her, hungered for her flesh, which would crackle and burn.

She fought down the fear. Her thoughts fell together enough for her to register surprise. *Why the hell am I waking up?* she wondered.

Zhavon's kidnapper had slammed a piece of wood all the way through Ramona, but this wasn't her mortal body anymore. She wasn't dead, just immobilized.

Just.

That was all it would take. The sun would take care of the rest.

Someone could find me, take me inside before the sun rises, she thought desperately, but she knew what would be more likely to happen. If some mortals did find her, they would mistake her for dead, call the police or an ambulance, and by the time help arrived, Ramona's body would be a smoldering husk.

No. Ramona could only count on herself.

Realizing that, she tried to clear her mind, to focus all of her attention and energy on one action—she needed to reach up, grab the stake, and pull it out the front of her chest.

Otherwise, she would die. Horribly.

And although she might fantasize about an end to this curse that was her new existence, her survival instinct flowed too strongly. She couldn't bring herself simply to give in to the searing pain and death that would come with the sunrise. That grisly image, too, she blocked from her mind.

With intensely concentrated effort, she poured all her strength into her right arm, into the hand closest to the protruding stake. No other physical need mattered. The power of her blood, the full strength of her will, could be directed completely to the one task that would preserve her for another night. She visualized her hand taking hold of the stake, pulling it through so that its hold on her was destroyed. She strained with all her body and soul to make that one movement.

And, still, she couldn't so much as blink.

Realizing her failure, panic set in. The calm, rational attitude that Ramona had struggled to maintain fled and her mind filled with primeval banshee wails in the face of the encroaching sunlight. Her unrestrained, animal terror was no more useful than her concentrated effort. Both were the same to the prickling rays of the sun, just breaking through the trees.

Ramona stared straight ahead as the world was obscured by the steam that began to rise from the soft, white tissue of her eyes. She felt as if she were burning from the inside out, but then the outside, too, began to sputter as from the fire of cigarettes held against her body. Her lips began to sizzle. Exposed skin drew tight over face, neck, arms, feet. Agony and panic mingled within her, fed upon one another. The burning morning sun made the stake through her heart seem little more than a pinprick, and she lacked even the ability to struggle.

And then the stake moved.

Through the haze of pain, Ramona knew that her body had burned away, that there was no flesh remaining to hold the stake in place. That was why it moved. But such was not the case.

A hand grasped the end of the stake between her breasts. She felt herself lifted from the ground briefly as the stake was yanked loose. Its exit from her body was marked by a nauseating sound of suction, the noise of a boot being pulled from muddy ground. The gaping wound in her chest was instantly cauterized by the rays of the morning sun.

"Go deep, now!" A voice rang in her ears. A voice she'd heard before.

The face of the stranger was close to hers. His wild hair blocked the sun. He held her by the shoulders.

"Go!" he roared at her.

I don't smell you, she wanted to say. She smelled only the burning... the smoke... her own flesh.

"Go, you stupid whelp!"

Ramona turned her head. *I can move,* she thought absently.

A great drowsiness was coming over her, even with the burning. She saw the stranger again. He was next to her. She saw him sinking down into the earth.

Go deep!

Now the command struck her. Refuge against the burning.

Go deep!

And go deep she did. She sank into the ground, and the soil, a cool salve to her burning flesh, welcomed her.

Go deep.

Ashes to ashes.

Thursday, 22 July 1999, 11:06 AM
Upstate New York

Zhavon felt the pounding at her temples before anything else, like somebody was taking a hammer to her head every two or three seconds. It was a hundred times worse than the time Alvina had gotten hold of a bottle of bourbon. The pain shot from her temples down to her ears and then along her jaw, the muscles of which were tensed and cramping, even though her mouth hung open. Zhavon methodically closed and opened her mouth, worked her jaw until the muscles loosened just a little.

It took her that long to work up enough nerve to open her eyes, and a few more moments then to realize that they were open. She saw only darkness.

Nighttime, she thought. *I'm in a dark room.*

But something didn't feel right. A lot of things didn't feel right. Slowly, what her senses registered made it to her brain, and the information was filtered through the horror of the past hours.

The car, she remembered hazily. *I'm not in the car anymore.* How long had that lasted? she wondered. Minutes? Hours?

And before that had been... *the girl from my dreams.*

A dull ache radiated from the bottom of her neck. *The girl from my dreams*, Zhavon tried to recall, *she... she... took me in her arms. She...* But it all grew so fuzzy after that.

Pain. Pleasure. Zhavon remembered sucking in a breath, holding it for what seemed like forever. She remembered wanting nothing but for the feeling to continue, to go on and on and on.

Then there'd been the car. She'd felt sick but been unable to retch.

And now...? Darkness.

Needles. Tingling. Coming from her hands. They were asleep. Both her arms were asleep. Behind her. She tried to move them, couldn't very much. A different sort of pain began at her wrists. Burn. Rope burn.

Tied up, she realized, but was too weak to do anything except barely take notice. *I'm tied up. To a post, or something.* It was cold. Like concrete, or stone.

She blinked her eyes, but the darkness didn't recede. Aside from the pins and needles, she felt cold. Deep cold. Down to her bones cold. She tried to move her feet, again couldn't. *Tied too?* She thought she could feel, through her jeans, rope tied tightly around her ankles.

The pounding at her temples grew louder and drove all thought away for a while. At some point it receded. A faint breeze was chilly against Zhavon's face. She began to shiver—or realized that she was already shivering. She could see nothing, but felt that she was in a large, open space, a very large room.

An eye. She suddenly saw an image of a large, disgusting eye, floating before her in the dark. It couldn't be. Her mind must be playing tricks on her.

The pounding returned. The eye was gone, if it was ever really there.

Mama. Zhavon mouthed the word. Her dry lips stuck together for a second. No sound escaped. Quietly, she began to cry.

Thursday, 22 July 1999, 9:05 PM
Meadowview Lane
Hayesburg, New York

He was waiting for Ramona when she rose from the earth that night. "Come with me." The stranger's voice conveyed a sense of urgency but not fear. Though his sunglasses hid his eyes, occasional movements of his head indicated that he was aware of every nightsound around them.

Ramona lay unmoving on the ground. She was captivated, for the moment, by the sensation of her body separating itself from the earth beneath her. The ground had welcomed her, had taken her in and shielded her from the sun. She had been of it, and it of her.

Ashes to ashes.

Now she was again a distinct being, and something intangible was lost in the transformation—a peaceful sense of wholeness faded, was replaced by her personal needs of the moment, by the pain of her scorched body.

Ramona's throat was parched. Her eyes were so dry that her eyelids stuck when she blinked, and opened only with difficulty.

The stranger watched her carefully from where he crouched in his ragged clothes. "Come with me," he said again, but this time his words were less harsh, as if he understood the adjustment between perspectives that she was going through.

Of course, Ramona remembered. He had sunk into the ground with her. Small clumps of dirt were lodged in his tangled hair. She stared hard at him and found herself reluctantly comforted by his presence. He was so much like her, she realized, and there was none of the anxiety about him that was always so obvious with Jen and even Darnell.

With effort, Ramona licked her blistered lips. The sun had taken its toll upon her, and though the earth had protected her, it had not healed her. As she sat upright, her skin cracked and split where it stretched. She licked her lips again, tasted blood.

"Call *me* a stupid whelp," she said to the stranger. "Asshole."

He frowned at the affront but, rather than reply, turned and began to walk away.

Ramona's stiff muscles tensed as she saw him leaving. She couldn't let the stranger go! She was drawn to him—this creature, this vampire, who had sunk into the protecting arms of the earth with her. Ramona scrabbled to her feet. Sharp pain coursed through so much of her body, reminded her of the fiery demise she had nearly met that morning, but she forced her battered and blistered parts into motion.

The stranger hadn't gone far into the trees. Ramona quickly caught up. He didn't look back at her, but Ramona could tell that he'd wanted—*expected*— her to follow, and she was irritated at how easily she'd fallen into his game. But there was something about him, about his every stride—confidence, assurance. Ramona had seen men like that on the streets of L.A.; not the pimps or the more flamboyant drug dealers, but some of the others, some of the gang leaders, who walked down the street lacking any fear. Like them, the stranger carried himself with an unconscious swagger. His steps were easy, natural. His every motion indicated control. He was completely devoid of fear.

Fear.

Fear was what Ramona had lived with since the change. She, Jen, Darnell, Eddie—they had all bonded out of fear. Fear had led them to leave L.A., where so many of their kind walked the streets at night, where too many unknown dangers lurked.

Fear had remained their companion wherever they traveled. In Texas, that... *thing*—Darnell called it a werewolf; Ramona didn't know what it was, didn't care as long as she stayed away from it and its kind—had appeared out of nowhere and ripped Eddie to shreds.

In New York, the Sabbat had swooped down upon the travelers.

Last night, some bastard with an eye the size of a softball had stabbed Ramona in the back, had run her through with a wooden stake and carried off Zhavon.

And none of these nightmares even touched upon the personal fears that plagued Ramona—the suspicion, the *fear*, that some vital remnant of her mortal life was slipping away every night.

The stranger, just a few yards ahead, made his way through this wooded part of the small town as if none of those fears had ever touched him, as if he'd achieved mastery over them.

Ramona quickened her pace. Her legs faltered. She put a hand to her chest, to the jagged wound, only slightly healed over, where the stake had forced its way through her body. She almost called to the stranger to slow down, but she couldn't bring herself to so great an admission of weakness. Despite thinking that she might be able to learn from him, she resented how the stranger had treated her— confronting her and disappearing, giving her orders like she was his to boss around. His confidence, so compelling in many ways, bordered on arrogance. Ramona was not about to bow down to him.

That was only one concern, however. As she stumbled after him, the image foremost in Ramona's mind was of Zhavon being carried away by that creature with the deformed eye.

Zhavon.

Ramona's legs grew shakier with each step. "We've got to get her back," she said at last, thinking that the stranger might stop to reply, and she could rest.

He didn't stop, or even look back at her. He only grunted and continued on his way.

Ramona kept on after him. Her muscles ached after a night in the ground. Her chest and back throbbed from the damage done by the stake. Finally, as she was afraid she couldn't go on, he came to a halt.

The stranger's dark sunglasses turned to face Ramona impassively. He pointed to something in the shadows. "There," he said.

"We've got to get her back," Ramona said again, but then her gaze followed the line of his finger.

Lying in a heap among the sparse underbrush was an unconscious woman, a large, African-American woman in a flowered nightgown. Ramona wanted to yell at the stranger, to convince him to help her find Zhavon and bring her back. Instead, Ramona found herself taking tired steps toward the woman. The stranger stood and watched as Ramona dropped to her knees beside the prone figure.

"We've got to..." Ramona began, but the words stuck in her dry throat. She felt her fangs, seemingly of their own accord, lower to full extension.

The woman on the ground was unconscious but very much alive. Ramona touched a knot on the back of woman's head. She hadn't come with the stranger by choice—at least not her own choice.

For the second time in as many nights, Ramona was unable to command her muscles, but this time she was not paralyzed. Slowly, she leaned forward, lower, closer to the helpless woman. Ramona had fed from Zhavon last night but had lost much blood to the stake. The sun, too, had taken its toll. To heal, Ramona's body required blood.

She placed her hands on the woman's shoulder and head, and something about the woman's face gave Ramona pause. A blood memory tugged at her. Ramona knew this woman—or at least Zhavon, of whom Ramona had drunk, knew this woman. Ramona stared at the face, and a name drifted into her mind— *Irma. Aunt Irma.*

The world around Ramona began to spin. For a moment, it was last night again, and she was feeding on Zhavon—and she was Zhavon. Their blood mingled, mixed.

Ramona's eyes rolled back in her head as the bloodlust took hold.

Beware lack of blood; the hunger will take control.

Her fangs sank into mortal flesh, and with the blood she felt strength return to her body. Blood and strength. Strength and blood. She drank and was renewed. The heart beat, forced blood into her mouth. Its contractions grew labored, but still she drank. From far away, a voice cried out, *Irma. Aunt Irma.* The bloodlust that was Ramona drank and grew strong, drank until the heart beat no longer, until blood and life were no longer in that body.

Irma. Aunt Irma.

Ramona sat back on her haunches, stared at the body before her—the sagging flesh, the death pallor—and knew that this was what would've become of Zhavon if the creature with the eye hadn't intervened.

"Feel better?" the stranger asked from behind her.

Ramona, stunned by her fierce gluttony, turned slowly to meet his gaze.

"Tanner," he said.

"What?" Her voice was weak. She was distracted by the sensation of the blood changing her, healing her dead flesh. From the inside out, the hole from the stake filled and closed. Her burned skin regained a portion of its elasticity, but the worst of the blisters remained.

"Tanner," the stranger repeated. "My name's Tanner. Not asshole."

Ramona wanted to stand. She wanted to face him eye to eye, but she was afraid she'd fall if she tried. So she glared up at him from where she kneeled beside the rapidly cooling body. "You took this woman from that house we were next to," Ramona said.

Aunt Irma.

Ramona had never been in that house, had never seen with her own eyes the woman on the ground. Yet Ramona knew.

Tanner didn't answer her accusation. He stood; he watched.

Ramona looked away from him, but her attention fell immediately on the body, on the woman who would never get up. *Aunt Irma.*

"You're not *of* them anymore," said Tanner.

Ramona whipped around to face him. "You don't know anything about me!" But she knew she was wrong. He had joined the earth beside her. He'd brought her this woman, watched her feed. He knew more about her than she knew about herself.

"They are sustenance," said Tanner. "Nothing more."

He didn't point at the body, but Ramona knew what he was talking about. She knew *who* he was talking about.

Zhavon.

"Where is she?" Ramona asked with a sudden urgency. "Where did he take her?"

"She is nothing," Tanner said evenly. "Sustenance."

His evasion told Ramona that she was right, that he did know. Her stomach was a tight knot. Tiny droplets of bloody perspiration rose through her undead skin. All thought of learning from him of her new existence vanished, lost to the rising compulsion that was Zhavon. "You were watching me. You saw him," said Ramona.

She struggled to her feet, took a step toward him. "You've been following me since we were in the city. You saw him."

She could see her attacker, the strange eye, just like when she'd been lying on the ground with the stake through her heart. "You didn't save me right away. You followed him," she guessed. "Where'd he take her?"

Tanner folded his arms defiantly. "I didn't save you right away because you had a lesson to learn."

"Where is she?"

"You still haven't learned it. Greet the sun, and you still haven't learned."

"I don't want your lesson!" Ramona grabbed him by the shirt.

Tanner didn't move in the slightest. Though Ramona clutched his shirt, he felt as if he were stone embedded in the earth. "You have no choice," he said. "You will learn... and survive."

Ramona released him, took a step back. She saw her own puzzled expression in his black glasses.

No choice. A threat? she wondered.

But he had saved her twice—once from the Sabbat, once from the sun. Hadn't he proven himself an ally, if not a friend? Ramona regarded him warily. He was waiting impatiently, but for what? He didn't look like he was about to attack her, but he'd shown that he could move with dizzying speed.

"I know I need to keep my ass out of the sun," she said with a sneer.

Tanner remained unmoved. "You learned as much your

first night after the Embrace, whelp."

"Don't call me—!"

A slap to the jaw sent Ramona reeling. She tripped over the body behind her and landed hard on ground, but in an instant she was back on her feet and ready to defend herself.

Tanner stood with his arms crossed, as if he'd not moved. His utter calmness unnerved Ramona and chased out any brief thoughts she had of attacking.

"You're not of the mortals anymore," he said, as he pointed toward the ground at Ramona's feet.

Not at the ground, she realized, but at *her feet*, monstrous and deformed as they were. The fire dwindled within Ramona. She was suddenly self-conscious, ashamed of her deformity, of what she'd become.

"Know that you are Gangrel," said Tanner. "And that I am your sire. I made you what you are."

Ramona staggered backward as if he'd struck her again. The first words drifted away. They held little meaning for her. *Gangrel… Sire…* But his last statement…

I made you what you are.

Ramona's ears began to ring. She was acutely aware of the tightness of her skin all of a sudden—the blisters, the damage done to her by the sun that even blood had not completely healed.

I made you what you are.

The cold body lay before her, between her and this stranger, this creature so undeniably like her. A dead body of her old life, the living corpse of her new hell.

Know that you are Gangrel.

"He took the girl and drove north out of town."

Ramona thought that Tanner had spoken the words, but she looked where he'd stood and he was gone.

Thursday, 22 July 1999, 10:00 PM
Upstate New York

The Eye dragged Leopold toward consciousness sooner than he would otherwise have roused. Despite the depth of the cavern that protected him from direct exposure, his mind and body were mired in the thick lethargy that normally claimed him until the sun was fully set. He raised himself to a sitting position on the cold rock floor and wiped from his face the clear ichor that constantly drained around the Eye. The occasional discomfort was little enough price to pay for the insights he had gained.

This way, beckoned the muse.

Leopold followed. The winding tunnels were even less real than when he had arrived early that morning. The black expanses of stone faded away into nothingness. The echo of every footstep fled unhindered to the very Stygian abyss.

Leopold had lived with the eye of the artist. As a mortal, no detail had been beyond his notice. He saw not a vast desert, but every grain of sand.

After his Embrace, what before had been natural became a struggle. While the creative urge lingered beyond mortality, the capacity to fulfill that urge did not. Leopold floundered, despaired. In time, he'd come to make do, to compensate for the loss of that which he could not recapture. Obsession with detail gave way to obsession with absence—the aesthetic of the numbing void. He found a certain truth among his limitations.

Both the mortal detail and the undead loss, however, were mere facets of unSight. His greatest mortal achievement would be like a pale ghost to him now. How Leopold pitied those who were as he had been.

The Eye allowed him to see how totally insignificant was all that he'd held dear. As he made his way through the caverns, he seemed to traverse a great emptiness. Not one whit of the mountain around him was real to the Sight, and the unSight that had plagued him for the past weeks was fading as if the old memory of a youthful lover. Leopold did not care that his right eye was crusted over with the ichor. In fact, he was pleased to be rid of the limited and confusing perspective. Sight prevailed.

The change had come about sometime during the previous night—after he had achieved the girl, after he'd driven hurriedly north into the forested mountains. Had it been when he'd entered the caverns, or before that, as he'd trekked through the woods with the girl over his shoulder and the muse leading the way?

This way.

She still led him. He trusted her implicitly, she the agent of his enlightenment. He was Chosen. He would achieve such greatness that his name would be praised throughout the ages and touted more highly than that even of Toreador. Leopold would be *the* Toreador—the name no longer just the label of a clan but a title, his title, and he would be the measure of all those preceding and following.

The essence of life, of beauty... the muse purred in his ear.

Leopold cocked his head. Strange, he thought, that as the Sight became more potent and unfettered from the old vision, he still had not viewed more fully the beauty of the muse. Brief glimpses only.

Patience, she soothed his mind.

His brief doubt crumbled, indeed, as he stepped into the radiant glow of his subject. The girl was where he'd left her when he'd fled deeper into the caverns at dawn. She leaned against a twelve-foot stalagmite, her hands tied behind her. She was too weak to struggle. During the night she had evacuated her bladder. The sharp odor, a milepost of the living world, drew all of Leopold's senses into order.

Yes... life... beauty. The siren-call of the muse's words guided his thoughts.

He knew there was no reason to doubt her. Hadn't she led

him to his subject? Hadn't she brought him to this place of glorious solitude? All that remained was for her to present him with the means—the tools. At her behest, he'd left behind his hammers and chisels, instruments of unSight that they were.

He stood before the girl. She alone was real amidst the intangible surroundings of the cavern. The Sight revealed her to him—the rich tan of her skin, like freshly tilled loam; tightly curling ringlets, like creeping vines upon the face of the earth; the angle of her head leaning limply forward, a sunflower before dawn.

Bring her to fruition, the muse whispered.

"But… how?" Leopold muttered. He still didn't understand completely. How could he do what she asked?

I will show you, said the muse, as she took him by the hand.

Thursday, 22 July 1999, 10:04 PM
Meadowview Lane
Hayesburg, New York

Ramona couldn't pick up Tanner's scent, but how long had he watched her, with her catching a hint of his presence only a handful of times, and most of those only when he wanted her to know he was nearby? She didn't know what he had in mind, and she wasn't about to stick around and find out.

Silently, she made her way back to the house. Ramona kept seeing images of Aunt Irma's body lying abandoned among the trees. *Aunt Irma—she ain't* my *aunt*, Ramona reminded herself, but the pangs of conscience at leaving the body in that secluded spot, where it might not be found for several days, did not leave her. Ramona couldn't shake the uncomfortable feeling of kinship betrayed, and in a way Irma was a blood relative, for Zhavon's blood still flowed through Ramona's body. Not to mention Irma's own blood.

What about all the others? Ramona grew angry with her own potential for guilt. *Drinkin' somebody's blood don't make 'em family— else I got a damn big family.* She pushed aside these ridiculous thoughts. She couldn't take responsibility for every mortal who stumbled into her path. Not if she wanted to survive.

Sustenance. Nothing more.

Though many of the scars from the morning sun remained, Ramona's strength was mostly returned by the infusion of new blood. She slipped inside the house and found what she was looking for—the keys to the old Buick in front of Irma's house.

As she pulled away from the curb, she was full of conflicting thoughts and emotions. Twice, with Zhavon and then with her aunt, Ramona had lost control. The bloodlust had overwhelmed her. Only the unexpected attack had saved Zhavon. Irma hadn't been so lucky—if being saved by that thing with the eye could be called lucky. Ramona didn't know anything about her attacker. She couldn't explain the unnatural, bulging eye she'd seen as she'd lain in paralyzed agony. Finding Zhavon was most important to Ramona now.

Why? So you can kill her before somebody else does? she asked herself.

It was a question Ramona couldn't answer, but the same compulsion that had driven her to follow the girl, to taste her blood, drove Ramona now.

I'll control the hunger, she promised herself. She'd worry about the details later. First, she had to find Zhavon.

Tanner's words haunted her thoughts as well.

I made you what you are.

Gangrel.

He'd made her a vampire. That much seemed clear. Why? Why *her*? And what else did he know that she needed to learn? He'd said something about a lesson. But Ramona could still feel the sting of his hand against her jaw. *I ain't about to take orders from that asshole. I never asked for this.*

But he seemed to know so much more than she did.

Ramona pushed the idea from her mind. *Zhavon.* That was what she needed to concentrate on.

He took the girl and drove north out of town. That's what Tanner had said.

Ramona didn't know the roads around the area. She didn't know what was to the north except the Adirondack Mountains, but for some reason, she had the impossible feeling that she could find Zhavon.

Don't ask, girl. Just go, she told herself. Thinking too much might drive the feeling away, might leave her helpless. So she turned the car north. But another thought brought her up short.

Jen. Darnell.

What should she do about them? *They don't need to get mixed up in this,* she thought. *This is my hassle, not theirs.*

But what if they were already mixed up in this? Zhavon had been missing for an entire day. Irma would've called the police, and in a small town like this, Ramona guessed, they wouldn't make the distraught aunt wait long before they started looking. What if the police had searched the abandoned elementary school? It seemed an obvious place to hide.

Ramona turned the car around as quickly as she could without seeming too reckless. It wasn't so late that the streets were empty, and she didn't need somebody recognizing Irma's car with some strange person behind the wheel and calling the cops.

Ramona felt like she was crawling through the town toward the school, but finally she arrived. From the outside, everything looked the same as she'd left it the night before.

She made her way around behind the building and climbed through the broken window that they had found. Ramona made her way to the gym and was greeted by darkness and silence.

The basement? she wondered, but decided she didn't have time to hunt for her friends. "Guys, it's me," she called out.

She heard them coming up the stairs— Darnell's light tread, Jen's less stealthy steps—although Ramona could tell they thought they were being silent. Darnell stepped through the doorway from the stairwell and into the gymnasium but said nothing.

"Ramona!" Jen was relieved to see her friend. "The police were here during the day. We were afraid—"

"Any trouble?" Ramona cut her off.

Darnell shook his head. "They just poked around a little and left. No big deal."

Ramona knew it was more serious than that. All three were aware of how vulnerable they were during the day. Direct sunlight or no, there was no guarantee that any of them could defend themselves while the daytime sleep clung to them. Even a small group of mortals could prove fatal. But Ramona didn't want to get into all that.

"Come on," she said.

Jen started forward but then stopped when she saw that Darnell hadn't moved.

"Where to?" he asked.

Wherever he's taken Zhavon, Ramona almost said, but she stopped herself, because she could see the challenge in Darnell's eyes. What would he do if he knew the reason Ramona was so often away was a mortal?

Ramona didn't have time to answer Darnell's question.

"My God!" said Jen, as she forgot her hesitation and crossed the gym to Ramona. "What happened?" She reached toward the large bloody splotch on Ramona's chest but stopped just short of touching the stain. Not realizing she did so, Jen sniffed at the blood from a distance.

"Some bastard drove a stake through my heart, and I'm goin' after him," Ramona said, telling the truth without being completely truthful. "We don't have a lot of time." Without waiting for a response, she turned and strode out of the school. Jen's footsteps were right behind her from the start. Darnell was more reluctant, but he caught up with them by the time they reached the old Buick.

As they drove away from the school and the town, Darnell in the front next to Ramona, Jen in the backseat, Ramona told them how her attacker had snuck up behind her and jabbed the stake through her body. She told how she'd watched helplessly as he left, and of the bulging, oozing eye. That interested them enough that she sidestepped any mention of Zhavon or of Tanner.

"A stake through your heart?" Jen asked incredulously. "And you got it out? You... lived?"

"I'm here, ain't I?" said Ramona.

She was uncomfortable with misleading her friends, but she was more uncomfortable with the idea of telling them. Why, she didn't know. Something about both Zhavon and Tanner was too personal, like Ramona's own failure to control herself in the presence of blood. Her thoughts were too confused to expose to anyone else yet. Darnell and Jen didn't need to know, she decided without managing to ease her conscience.

"What's this?" Jen asked from the back seat.

"What?" Ramona asked, confused. She felt fingers touching her ear and jerked her head away from Jen. "What are you doin'?"

Ramona raised her own hand to her ear. It wasn't bleeding or anything. Then she felt what Jen must've noticed. The tip of Ramona's ear, instead of rounded as it should've been, rose to a point. The back edge, covered with short, thick hair, curled over a bit— like an animal's.

"What the...?" Ramona felt her left ear. It was the same as the right.

"Ramona?" Jen asked nervously. "Are you all right?"

"I'm fine." She could feel Darnell staring at her from the passenger's seat.

He'd said very little since they'd gotten in the car, busying himself instead with drumming his fingers on the door or shuffling his feet as he'd listened to Ramona. He was staring at her still, at her ear, but his mind, as usual, pressed on to pragmatic matters. "Do you know where we're going?" he asked.

Ramona's fingers tightened around the steering wheel. His question was another that she was trying not to think about. Last night, she'd made her way almost directly to the house where Zhavon was staying, even though Ramona had never been there or even seen it before. Tonight, she drove along unfamiliar roads. She turned when it seemed the right thing to do. "Yeah," she said, "I know."

"What's happening to you?" Jen whispered, but the words were like thunder to Ramona's primed senses.

She looked over her shoulder at her female companion, then at Darnell. The same question was unspoken on his lips. This time, Ramona answered with complete honesty. "I wish to God I knew," she said, unable to keep the uncertainty and fear from creeping into her voice.

They rode in silence for the next half hour. Midnight passed. Ramona watched the road but tried not to think about it. Picking the turns seemed easier if she didn't pay too much attention. When she consciously tried to figure out where she was going, doubts crept into her thoughts. She became convinced that she was leading her friends on a hopeless, wild goose chase, that at any moment, they would demand she turn the car around and take them back to Hayesburg, back to the relative safety of the school. After all, it had been in an equally remote area that Eddie had met his end. She cringed at the thought that she might be taking them all to their Final Deaths.

She tried to avoid those thoughts, to shove them back down whenever they surfaced. She thought instead of Zhavon—of the taste of her sweat and blood, of the scent of fear and anticipation, of how natural it had felt to hold the girl tight, to feel the ripple of her shoulder blades, the arch of her back.

Other thoughts intruded as well.

I made you what you are.

Ramona glanced out the window, saw the increasingly infrequent signs of civilization, and she wondered how Tanner had secretly followed her for so long. He'd obviously followed her in New York City, and from the city. Had he followed her before that? If he really had made her what she was, that meant he'd been in L.A. On the night of the change, he was the one who'd taken her from behind, who'd forced her head back and...

She shook her head to clear her mind. *Where you goin', girl?* she asked herself. But hadn't that always been the question?

Without warning, Ramona slammed on the brakes. Jen crashed into the back of the front seats. Darnell threw up his hands against the dashboard. Just as suddenly, Ramona threw the Buick into reverse and punched the accelerator. Jen toppled over onto the floorboard.

"What the hell...?" Darnell fought to an upright position.

The car zigzagged, almost out of control but not quite, as Ramona sped backwards down the narrow country road. The reverse lights threw all the rest of the night into pitch darkness.

"Ramona...!" Jen was climbing up the back of the driver's seat.

Ramona slammed on the brakes again. The car skidded backwards to a halt. Jen and Darnell were thrown against their seats. Ramona flicked off the lights, stared hard for a moment out the window as her friends regained their composure.

"There," she said, and threw the Buick into gear again.

She turned off the pavement and onto an uneven dirt road. Ramona hadn't really been four-wheeling before, and she suspected that the Buick hadn't either. Even in the darkness, she could see farther without the headlights, but as the car picked up speed, each sharp turn became that much more difficult to handle. They bounced over washed-out gullies. Bushes and tree branches lashed the car.

"What the hell are you doin'?" Darnell shouted.

Ramona didn't take her eyes off the dirt track. Another curve sent them fish-tailing. The back end of the car slid around, bounced off a tree, but Ramona kept going. She had the steering wheel to hold onto. Jen and Darnell ricocheted off the sides and roof of the car.

Ramona didn't fight the compulsion that propelled her and her friends along this suicidal course. *What's the point?* she wondered. She hadn't been able to stay away from Zhavon, or to keep herself from feeding on first Zhavon and then Aunt Irma. Why should this be any different? In that way, she, like Darnell and Jen, was merely along for the ride.

The Buick clipped another tree. One of the extinguished headlights shattered. A moment later, a low-hanging branch smashed into the windshield. Jagged cracks, like bolts of lightning, shot across the glass.

"*Ramona!*" Darnell was inches from her face, was yelling at the top of his lungs.

She slammed on the brakes again. The car skidded one way then the other, then, amidst a cloud of dust, came to a halt.

Silence.

Ramona stared straight ahead.

In the backseat, Jen was reverting to mortal ways—hyperventilating.

Darnell eyed Ramona angrily. "What the *fuck* are you doin'?"

Ramona stared at the car in front of them, the car that the Buick had stopped only two or three feet shy of—a dark sedan with a Georgia license plate.

Darnell saw the car now. He blinked, unbelieving. "I'll be damned."

Friday, 23 July 1999, 12:45 AM
Upstate New York

*P*atience.

But how could Leopold be patient in the face of a discovery that was the culmination of so many years of life and unlife?

Patience... or you will break her, the muse warned.

It was true, he realized distractedly. The girl passed easily out of consciousness, and though he didn't need her awake, the fruits of his labor were more sweet that way.

Does her fragility detract from her perfection as a subject? Leopold wondered.

He took a step back and focused the Sight fully upon her. As he did so, his doubts were soothed, like the cries of an infant appeased by mother's milk. Already, this work transcended by far anything he had ever before attempted, and most tellingly he was no longer fumbling along in a clumsy attempt to please the muse. This time, she had taken him by the hand, and he'd seen the *truth*. He'd felt it. It had coursed through his body more sweetly than any mortal's blood.

The essence of life. The essence of beauty.

They were his! And woe to every Toreador who had ever belittled him.

Never again! he vowed. *They will bow down before me!*

Patience, the muse reminded him, and brought him back to the task at hand.

"Yes." His whisper rose and echoed throughout the cavern.

The sound seemed to revive the girl slightly. Leopold leaned close to her. She filled his Sight. Once again, he was intent only upon revealing the essence of truth.

Friday, 23 July 1999, 1:08 AM
Upstate New York

From the car, Ramona let Darnell take the lead. Not that any of them, even Jen, couldn't have followed the trail. The kidnapper had made no apparent effort to conceal his passing. More telling even than his heavy footprints and the bent and broken branches was the path of milky green slime that led from the car and formed an intermittent trail into the woods.

Darnell sniffed at one of the piles of glop. "Fucker might as well've left a trail of used rubbers."

While Darnell led them forward, Ramona looked constantly from one side to the other. She peered into the thick underbrush.

Jen, behind Ramona, noticed. "Could there be—"

"No." Ramona knew the question that was on Jen's mind, could tell by how extra skittery Jen was and by the smell of fear that surrounded her.

"Do you think he left a false trail?" Jen asked, embarrassed by the unspoken rebuke and trying to cover the question she'd set out to ask.

Ramona shook her head. "He wasn't the sneakin' type."

"Then how'd he sneak up on you?" Jen asked.

Ramona didn't answer at first. She opened her mouth to tell them everything—about Zhavon, Tanner—but then closed it without saying a word.

They got no need to know, she thought.

Darnell seemed to have latched on to the idea of finding whoever had hurt Ramona and kicking his ass, and Jen would go along. Why confuse the issue? There'd be time to tell more later.

"I was busy," she finally said without turning to meet Jen's eyes. "Keep a close watch," Ramona added, and she could hear Jen stiffen. It wasn't a false trail Jen was worried about, Ramona knew. It was the werewolf—*werewolves;* there was more than one vampire, after all—and what had happened to Eddie. Ramona had other concerns. She didn't pretend, to herself or to the others, that she wasn't scared of those monsters. Anybody'd be crazy not to be. But worrying wouldn't save her neck. Ramona knew that out here, away from the city and even away from small towns, if there were werewolves, she and her friends would be in deep shit. But there was nothing they could do except deal with it if it happened. That or run back to the city. And leave Zhavon.

Ramona wasn't ready to do that.

It wasn't, however, those particular creatures, blurs of claws and snarling death, that Ramona watched for. She did have the uneasy feeling that she was being watched—that same feeling she'd had quite often recently, that same feeling that Zhavon must've felt when Ramona had crouched outside the girl's bedroom window. Ramona kept pace with Darnell, but her attention was set on the shadows among the trees.

Tanner.

She knew he was out there somewhere.

Is he? she wondered, beginning to doubt her intuition. *We drove for a couple hours. Could he have kept up for that long?*

The forest loomed impenetrably dark all around. The strange night sounds of the wilderness made every shadow come alive. Each insect's chirp, every leaf that quivered in the breeze, also served to remind Ramona of what had happened to her ears. They twitched; they zeroed in on every sound. They were the ears, not of a person, but of a beast.

Just as her feet were no longer human feet.

You gave in to the Beast.

Those were Tanner's words.

I made you what you are.

Tanner, who was so damned sure of himself. He seemed to know everything, could probably do anything.

I could've done it, Ramona decided at last. *I could've chased a car for a hundred miles and never been seen.* So surely Tanner could. How far had he followed her without her knowing? All the way from L.A.?

Darnell paused to sniff at the newest pile of slime. Maybe it was something about the quality of the minimal moonlight, or the effect as the light filtered through the forest canopy, but Ramona was fairly certain that many of the piles of glop had been different colors—some greenish like the first few, others much darker, almost black, some more translucent, and still others a sickly green and dark crimson, like a mix of blood and thick bile. But the foul scent was the same. Darnell confirmed that with a distasteful wrinkle of his nose.

From the car, the trail had led steadily upward into the foothills of the Adirondacks. The climb would've been tiring for a mortal, but Ramona was flushed with the vigor of fresh blood and with the knowledge that, somewhere ahead, Zhavon was in trouble.

That girl has the worst luck, thought Ramona. Would any of this have happened, she wondered, if Zhavon's mother hadn't tried to protect her daughter by sending her away from the city?

Or if I hadn't found her?

Ramona felt the weight of guilt settling onto her shoulders, but only for a moment. *But she would've been killed that night she was attacked if I hadn't been there,* she reminded herself. Ramona deftly shifted the blame back a step further to the cause of her own problems and, by extension, most of Zhavon's:

Tanner. He made me what I am—or so he says. He set all this in motion.

Ramona kept searching the deep shadows for his shape. She tried to ignore the smell of the putrid slime and sought that other familiar scent, but she didn't find it.

Is he out there?

Darnell stopped as they reached a ridge crest. He paused only briefly to sniff at the air and at the ground, then gestured down the opposite slope. "This way. We're gettin' closer."

He seemed very intent on catching his prey. Ramona wasn't sure if he was driven by the desire to avenge the injury to his friend, or if the hunt had taken hold of Darnell like sometimes it did her.

"How do you know we're closer?" Jen asked.

Darnell stood upright very stiffly and gnashed his teeth together. From many instances before, Ramona recognized his disgusted reaction to any of many things that Jen said or did. This time, however, he didn't launch into a rant. Maybe the hunt had gotten the best of him, or maybe away from the familiar landscape of the city he wasn't so sure of himself.

Whatever the reason, he spoke in a low, if strained, voice to Jen: "The scent is fresher here. We're gainin' on him. Can't you tell?"

Jen scratched around at the dirt while not meeting his gaze. "We've come a pretty long way, and dawn's getting close. Shouldn't we get back... to shelter?"

We've got all the shelter we need right here under our feet, Ramona thought, but she wasn't paying full attention to Jen.

Through a break in the trees, a long meadow was visible below to the west. The meadow ended in a steep cliff wall, and near one edge, partially hidden by a small stand of tenacious pines, was the opening to a cave.

"There," said Ramona.

"Huh?"

"What?"

"There." Ramona pointed at the cave. Darnell and Jen came to her side, followed the line of her finger. "That's where he is." Her finger began to quiver.

That's where Zhavon is.

"Why do you—"

Darnell cut Jen off. "You're sure?" he asked.

Ramona nodded. "There's a mortal with him. I wanna get her out of there."

She didn't look over at Darnell, but she could feel his pointed stare boring into her.

Haven't you felt it, Darnell? she suddenly wanted to scream. *Haven't you felt the old life—the real life—slipping away, bit by bit with every mortal you feed on? We're losing... something. And she still has it! I can't let her go.*

But Ramona stared ahead at the cave opening and said nothing.

"Let's go," said Darnell at last.

Jen was shuffling around nervously. "But what about the sunrise?"

Now it was Ramona who spoke through clenched teeth: "I won't let the sun get you."

The fair-skinned vampire wasn't relieved in the least by what Ramona had in mind, but Jen could tell that this was not a time to argue. She followed grudgingly as Darnell led the trio down the slope.

Sure enough, the trail of eye-ooze and bent shrubs led down to the meadow and straight across it.

"Wait here while I follow the trail across," Darnell said. "If it does lead to the cave, I'll signal, and you circle around."

"Fuck that," said Ramona and followed right behind him.

Jen, not about to be left by herself, followed too.

The fieldgrass, weeds, and wildflowers in the meadow stood taller than a person. Even without the ichor from the eye, Darnell could easily have followed the trail of broken stalks. As the three made their way across the meadow, Jen was constantly glancing back over her shoulder at the eastern horizon. As a result, and more irritating than her mere nervousness, which Ramona was used to by now, Jen kept stepping on Ramona's heels, or stumbling and making much more noise than Ramona and Darnell combined.

After the third or fourth time she was stepped on, Ramona whirled and growled. *"We'll kill him, and we'll stay in the cave,"* she whispered sharply. *"So watch where you're goin'!"*

Jen, despite her embarrassment, seemed somewhat relieved, and they made their way to the cave entrance without further incident. The black hole in the cliffside was larger than Ramona had realized from the ridge. Probably a large car, if it got this far, could fit through the opening. Beneath the pines that had forced their way up through the rocky soil, the wary trio paused and cocked their heads at the sound of a distant voice. Ramona could feel how close they were. She had to restrain herself from rushing ahead to Zhavon's rescue. They slipped silently through the opening.

The cave narrowed almost immediately, forcing them into single file, Darnell, Ramona, then Jen. They stepped carefully, and even Jen avoided kicking loose rocks. Probably the sound of dripping water—there must be an underground stream somewhere, Ramona thought—covered whatever slight sounds they made, but they said nothing to one another. Whether it was because of the acoustics of the cave or the potency of their hearing, the sound of that voice reached them every so often. And once, only once, Ramona heard a pained moan—a voice different from the other, a voice she recognized.

Zhavon!

Ramona again fought back the impulse to run headlong to her. *We'll do this together,* Ramona told herself. She'd brought her friends. It'd be stupid to run off by herself. But now, with every step, she waited for another moan, for Zhavon to call out. If Darnell or Jen heard the second voice, neither reacted.

Hold on, Ramona silently urged Zhavon. *Hold on.*

She thought of what this must be like for the mortal. Ramona and her friends, and the kidnapper, she guessed, could see fairly well in the dark, even the pitch black of the cave. Zhavon, though, would be blind, surrounded by the darkness, the touch of the kidnapper's hands, his fangs....

Pure rage began to well up within Ramona. She felt her own fangs slide down. Besides stabbing her with a stake, this guy had stolen her mortal.

His ass is mine! Ramona crowded Darnell, silently urged him forward.

Within a few steps, the passage opened into a much larger chamber. The ceiling rose beyond sight into the darkness.

"Yes," came the voice from ahead, much more clearly now. "Yes, my dear."

Darnell grabbed Ramona as she darted past him. He shook her by the shoulders, his eyes rebuking her, demanding caution. Ramona threw off his hands but held her place. He was right, she knew.

Together, the trio edged their way left along the cave wall. The floor was a maze of stalagmites. Slowly, Darnell led them closer to the voice.

"There... no, not quite... ah, yes."

Ramona stopped so suddenly that Jen almost ran into her again.

Blood. Ramona smelled blood. *Zhavon's blood.*

Bloodlust mingled with rage, urged Ramona forward, but she held back. She closed her eyes for a moment and took a deep, calming breath—a throwback to her mortal days. *Hold on,* she thought again, but this time the words were for her own benefit more than Zhavon's.

Darnell raised a hand to his friends, urged them to greater caution. With her next step Ramona could see, around the edge of the stalagmite in front of her, the kidnapper. His back was to them. She vaguely recognized the unkempt hair, the threadbare sweater and the old, dirty workpants. Her glimpse of him before had been so brief.

Darnell held his position, motioned for Ramona to move around farther to the left. She crept silently to the spot he'd indicated. Still, she was behind the kidnapper. He seemed to have no idea anyone was in the cave besides himself and—

He stepped back and turned just enough that his eye was visible to Ramona—that enlarged, throbbing eye. Thick trails of slime had drained down his face and body. The glop around the edges of the eye fizzled and popped as Ramona watched.

Then he took another step back and revealed...

Zhavon?

Ramona had expected it to be her bound to the large stalagmite, but instead there was some... Ramona wasn't sure *what* it was. It was vaguely human-shaped—torso, head, arms, legs. It had hair on its head and its groin, and what looked like one nippled breast, but the rest of the body was hideously deformed. The arms and fingers were bent—not broken, but twisted like clay or hot plastic—in impossible directions and— could it be?—fused somehow to the stone monolith that the creature was tied to at the ankles. As Ramona realized more fully that she *was* looking at a human form, she saw that the chest cavity was exposed. In view were a framework of ribs, lungs slowly taking in and expelling air... and a beating heart.

My God! Ramona recoiled in disgust. *How can it be alive?*

She looked away from the disfigured face, stared instead at the rope around the ankles, at the relatively untouched feet, at the discarded clothing around the feet on the cave floor.

And Ramona recognized the clothes.

She took another step back, unable to absorb what she saw.

The kidnapper, his gruesome eye focused only on the creature before him, stepped forward again. Unaware of his hidden audience, he reached a hand out to his captive's face. The creature instinctively flinched but was too weak and disoriented to resist effectively. Where the kidnapper's hand touched, the cheek sagged.

It's melting! Ramona had never seen anything like this—skin melting like wax!

The torturer drew the flesh out with his hand in a way that no skin should ever stretch. He touched the elongated cheek to the creature's shoulder, rubbed gently as skin melded to skin. He held the spot for a moment, then patted it gently. And all the while he touched her, the eye glowed an unnatural saffron, like a jaundiced, rotting egg.

"Yes, she is beautiful," he said, as if answering a question. He leaned forward and gently kissed the creature on its newly shaped cheek. "You approach perfection, my lovely. You will make me the toast of every Toreador." A giddy laugh wracked his emaciated frame. The glow receded from the eye again. "I will be the Toreador of Toreadors!"

Toreador? Ramona's mind was reeling. She couldn't make sense of what she saw or heard.

But then the creature opened its mouth—the portion that would still open—and a low, pained groan escaped its lips.

The sound drove Ramona to her knees, confirmed exactly what she'd been trying to tell herself was not, *could not*, be true.

Another agonized moan.

The scent of blood, the clothes, the voice…

Zhavon!

Ramona's vision began to cloud over with red bloodrage. Her fingers curled into claws matching those on her feet. She glanced over at Darnell. He seemed too calm. He was gesturing to her. What was he trying to tell her? Then she understood. She should go high. He'd hit low.

No sooner had she realized his meaning than she nodded once and then sprang. Darnell leapt at the same instant.

Ramona was going for the eye. As she soared through the damp cavern air, she could already feel her claw skewering the eye. She could see it pop from the socket, trailing a stream of gore and blood.

But the future she foresaw was not to be.

Darnell's low, less-arched dive brought him to the kidnapper a split second before Ramona. Darnell slammed into the Toreador's knees and he lurched violently.

Ramona landed on his shoulders, and the slash of her claw raked across the kidnapper's face—a fraction of an inch to the right of the eye. She caught a nostril, and pulled away a sizeable hunk of his nose, but his initial stumble was enough to save the eye.

All three landed roughly on the ground, Ramona on top of the Toreador, Darnell rolling away and quickly on his feet again, ready to strike.

"What...? Who are...?" The Toreador's cries of distress were cut off as Ramona wrestled him onto his back.

As she raised a hand for a blow that might well take his head off, he bared his fangs and hissed like the cornered animal that he was.

Ramona knew for certain that he was one of them.

At that same instant, however, the deformed eye seemed to bulge even larger and glowed a sickly yellow. Suddenly, the fizzing ichor around the eye sprayed into Ramona's face. She reflexively closed her eyes, but the slime burned her skin like acid, and where it struck her already blistered skin, she felt it burning through to the bone.

Ramona threw her hands to her face, burning them too, and rolled away, screaming in pain.

"Ramona!" Jen, seeing her friend hurt, sprang into action now. Ramona opened her eyes in time to see both Jen and Darnell charge the kidnapper, who was quickly on his feet.

With a swipe of his hand, the wiry kidnapper sent Jen

bloodied and sprawling. Darnell had to dive to the side to avoid her stumbling form. He landed not far from Ramona.

"Get the mortal," he growled to her. "We'll take care of this prick." With no more pause than that, he was throwing himself again at their enemy, and unlike with Jen, the kidnapper was no match for Darnell's speed and power. Darnell drove him backward and onto the ground.

Ramona shook her head trying to clear her mind. She ignored the last burning of whatever it was that had sprayed from the eye. She climbed to her feet and rushed over to Zhavon.

Zhavon? This can't be her.

Ramona couldn't bring herself to believe that it was.

No....

But one of the creature's eyes opened, and it stared into Ramona's face. The mouth opened, but only garbled sound came out. Ramona looked away. She had to force herself to turn back—and wished she hadn't. She saw the forked tongue, both tips fused to the roof of the mouth. Ramona looked again at the creature's eye—*at Zhavon's eye*—and her disgust melted away to pity.

"I'll help you..." Ramona paused, choked on the name, "Zhavon."

Zhavon nodded, then her eye closed. Her jaw and head hung limp.

Ramona turned at the sound of screams. Darnell was rolling into a crouch. He had dodged another spray from the eye, but Jen hadn't been so lucky. The shoulder and sleeve of her sweatshirt smoked and sizzled, as did the skin beneath.

Ramona turned hurriedly back to Zhavon, sliced the rope around her ankles with one deft flick of a claw. The girl's arms were a different story. There was no rope to slit or untie, only skin and stone—the skin was fused to the stalagmite behind Zhavon. And the stone would take far too long to chip away.

The melee, meanwhile, had become something of a standoff. Darnell and Jen, favoring her burnt shoulder, warily circled their prey and watched especially closely the strange eye. The kidnapper, for his part, was backing slowly toward a wall trying to prevent either of his attackers getting behind him. Having gauged his opponents, he paid closer attention to Darnell.

Ramona dithered for only a moment. She hated to inflict more suffering on the girl, but more than anything else she wanted to get poor Zhavon away from that place of torture. Ramona grasped the mortal's arm and pulled. Skin ripped away from stone, and a piercing scream filled the cavern and echoed deafeningly.

But it was not Zhavon who screamed.

The gangly kidnapper stood ramrod straight. His head jerked up. He glared beyond his immediate attackers, whom he no longer seemed to notice.

"Do not touch my masterpiece!" he bellowed, and suddenly he seemed taller than before, less emaciated. The eye shed an ominous, pale light across the chamber.

Ramona lifted Zhavon in her arms, but then froze as the eye's gaze fell upon them. That stare locked Ramona in place as the cold hatred of countless years sapped the passion from her bones. How insignificant this one mortal seemed now, how petty the urges that drove Ramona. Who was she to interfere with this monumental work of art?

Ramona's own desires washed away under the weight of ages. She dropped to bent knee and laid the mortal on the ground.

Darnell and Jen didn't understand Ramona's actions, but they saw their enemy's distraction and pounced.

Leave him alone, Ramona thought, suddenly perplexed. *Why are they bothering him?*

The eye flashed a brilliant blast of golden light, and the scene unraveled before Ramona as if in slow motion. Jen leapt at the kidnapper's side, but from the cave floor, a stalagmite erupted where before none had been. It shot upward and caught Jen in mid-air. Its jagged point ripped into her belly, knocking her upright. It tore through her body, crushing bones, splitting skin as it forced its way through her chest cavity. Emerging through her arched back and then completely piercing her neck, the stalagmite finally halted.

Jen's head, a bloody heap of bone and blonde hair, fell to the cave floor.

Darnell attacked at the same time that Jen did but, to Ramona, he too appeared as if he moved in slow motion in the flashing golden light.

The Toreador caught Darnell.

The force of Darnell's lunge should've at least knocked his target back a few steps, but the kidnapper clamped a hand on each of Darnell's shoulders and caught him without so much as flinching.

Then he squeezed. He pulled Darnell's shoulders each to the side, and as Ramona looked on in rapt horror, their enemy pulled Darnell's shoulders a foot broader. The flesh, *the bone*, stretched out beneath the kidnapper's hands.

Darnell howled as he fell to his knees. His arms hung useless at his sides. The shoulder joints and muscles were hopelessly misaligned. And then the monster with the eye reached for Darnell's face.

"Come on!"

Ramona jumped at the sound of Tanner next to her. The shock jarred her back to the moment, pried her loose from the grip of the eye.

"Let's get out of here!" he urged in a harsh whisper.

There was something strange about him, but amidst the confusion, the thought didn't fully form in Ramona's mind.

"Grab her and come on!" He gestured toward Zhavon, then turned to leave, just like he had earlier that night.

Zhavon. Blood. Jen. Could it really have been the same night?

Tanner had led her into the trees just after sunset. Now it was nearly dawn. And, again, he'd ordered her to follow and then turned to leave. Ramona looked back to where the monster was pressing his fingers into Darnell's brow. The bones gave way like clay at the hands of a sculptor. Darnell shrieked as the openings of his eyes grew smaller and smaller.

"Damn you, whelp. He'll have to fend for himself!"

Ramona looked again to Tanner. The last time he had assumed she would follow. In all his confidence he'd just kept walking. This time, he'd stopped to make sure. This time, his voice was imploring her. Staring into his eyes, Ramona knew what was different.

Fear.

His face was awash in it. He was facing something he'd rather flee from than fight.

I made you what you are.

Yet he didn't know what to do. He was afraid.

The realization struck terror into Ramona.

I am your sire, he'd said. *I made you what you are.*

She'd thought he would be the one to reveal secret knowledge to her, to show her the meaning of this new existence. But he didn't understand what was happening here. He was running away. Afraid.

Ramona lifted Zhavon once more and began to run after Tanner. Seeing her follow, he took off in earnest. Darnell's screams echoed throughout the cave. They chased Ramona down the tunnel. She ran faster and faster, but she couldn't outrun them.

And then she was out of the cave, in the meadow. Darnell's screams still echoed in her ears.

Tanner didn't slow down, but Ramona, even bearing the load of the inert Zhavon, almost caught up to him. The sky was growing light to the east. Seeing that reminded Ramona not so much of the pain she'd suffered just one sunrise ago, but instead of how Jen had worried about where they would stay—Jen, whose head lay on the cave floor at the feet of a monster. Ramona missed a step, stumbled, almost fell with Zhavon to the ground.

How much worse off is Darnell? Ramona wondered. *I should go back and save him*, she thought. *But how?*

She shook her head. *It doesn't matter. I should... be there with him... die with him.*

But there, ahead of her in the meadow, was her sire, the one who'd created her as a vampire. He seemed so much more cunning than she was. He could sneak up on her with no problem and then disappear without a trace. And *he* was running away.

That should tell you something, girl, she thought.

They crossed the meadow and began up the hill. Tanner

had pulled away when Ramona had stumbled, but she'd almost caught up with him again. He ran without pause toward the ridge. Not a leaf or twig moved with his passing. The crunch of Ramona's every footstep seemed to announce her presence to the early morning. She began to chastise herself: *I'm being as loud as...* then stopped.

Jen.

Tanner stopped halfway up the western face of the hill. "This'll do," he said. "Sun's probably already burnin' on the other side of the ridge. We'll go to ground here."

Go to ground. Of course. There was no time to find shelter. But Ramona stared at the limp figure in her arms. "I can't just leave her," she said plaintively.

Tanner looked directly at Ramona for the first time since they'd gotten out of the cave. His expression was blank. He said nothing.

"I can't leave her!" Ramona shouted at him. Her eyes were blurring with tears of blood.

"Do what you must," he said evenly.

"Fuck you!"

Tanner watched her impassively.

Ramona lowered Zhavon to the ground, stroked her hair. "I can't just..." Zhavon's face was as badly deformed as the rest of her body, maybe worse. One eye was simply gone, hidden beneath stretched flesh and bone perhaps. The nose was flattened, smashed to the side, probably no longer functional for breathing, judging by the gentle, constant panting from what remained of Zhavon's mouth. Her beautiful lips were flattened, stretched, and her head was at a sharp angle, held there by the fleshy cheek that Ramona had seen fused to the girl's shoulder.

"I can't just..."

Ramona smelled blood. It was all over her, she saw. Zhavon's arms, where they'd been torn away from the stone, were bleeding and had been the whole time Ramona was carrying her.

"Do what you must," Tanner said solemnly, and then he sank into the ground.

Ramona stared after him. She was unsure if he merely sank beneath the topsoil, or if his body actually became a part of the earth. She was unsure which would be the case with her own body when she joined him in just a few moments. She had no longer than that to decide. The last few minutes of daybreak, when the sun finally rose above the horizon, always seemed to go so quickly. Already, her skin grew warm to the touch, as if she had a fever. But only living flesh could be fevered.

Zhavon's twisted body lay at Ramona's feet. The mortal girl had been transformed into a monster as surely as Ramona had been. Except while Ramona could hunt, could find sustenance and survive, Zhavon could not go on like she was.

Ramona stroked the girl's smooth, chocolate skin—almost the only recognizable feature, except for the single eye that opened to stare at Ramona now. Zhavon couldn't speak. Even if her tongue weren't melted to the roof of her mouth, she lacked the strength.

Probably she wouldn't survive through the day, Ramona tried to tell herself. And if Zhavon did, no surgeon could correct the damage done to her.

I'd be doing her a mercy, Ramona thought. *I can't just leave her.*

The sun was rising. There was so little time.

Ramona looked into the human eye in the midst of that monstrosity of warped flesh. She wanted to say something, to comfort Zhavon, but there were no words. Tenderly, Ramona kissed what should have been a perfect, teenaged cheek. She looked one last time on Zhavon in her nakedness, and tried to see in the obscene mound the girl she had known.

Then Ramona reached down to the exposed heart, placed her hand on the beating organ. Despite the unimaginable trauma done to the body, the heart still beat, still forced Zhavon's lifeblood through that form.

As the sun began to singe her back, Ramona drank deeply. The blood was sweet, but bitterness consumed her soul. Ramona drank until the mortal fire was quenched, and then she sank into the earth.

part three:
ash

Friday, 23 July 1999, 9:09 PM
Upstate New York

A s the tide of consciousness began to tug gently but unmistakably at Ramona, she found herself sorely tempted to ignore it, to burrow more deeply into the subterranean calm she had discovered. No single reason for her reticence asserted itself; the feeling was broad and many-layered like a patchwork quilt. She saw herself nestled among the sheets and blankets on her bed, not wanting to crawl out and pack herself off to school, where nearly anything could happen. That hesitation, however, was rooted not in contentment with the present so much as dread of the future.

Slowly she grew more aware of her surroundings. She was not the young girl she had been. School was not the problem. There were no sheets, no blankets. The peace that enveloped her was that of the earth itself—soil, stone, roots, crawly creatures. She was with them; she was of them.

Is this what it's like at the very end? Ramona wondered. Could death—*real* death—be more peaceful?

She stretched out her awakening consciousness to that which surrounded her. She entwined herself among the massive sprawl of roots that anchored and nourished a great oak. She traced the roundabout twists of a groundhog's tunnels.

Maybe I'll just stay.

It would be so easy, an end to the pain.

But even as the contentment took hold, something else stirred within her—hunger. It had a firm grip on her heart, a stranglehold on her soul. For it was not her body that hungered, but the ravenous Beast within her that howled for release. Thoughts of rest, of peace, served only to heighten the fury of its ravings.

You gave in to the Beast.

Already, it had driven her for two years, just as it drove her from rest now. She had felt the hunger, many times, but she had never realized the force behind it. She had never before known how close to the surface the Beast lay.

Ramona, as well, rose closer to the surface—the surface of the life-sustaining earth. Darkness and contentment receded into distant memory. The sensation of air upon her face entered her consciousness only slowly. She stretched her fingers, her toes, forcing motion into muscle and sinew that should long ago have rotted to dust.

Ashes to ashes.

Night sounds filtered through her waning lethargy. Crickets and tree frogs reminded her that she was far from the familiar asphalt jungle in which the mortals encased themselves. The sounds reminded her, warned her.

"If you're good and ready...?"

The voice, so near, shocked Ramona fully to her senses. In less than a second, she was on her feet, crouched, ready to receive attack.

Not thirty feet away squatted Tanner, arms folded, a scowl visible on that of his face not hidden by his hair or sunglasses.

His presence brought back the most recent memories to Ramona. They swept over her like a wall of flame driven by a cruel wind. Jen was gone. The same might be true of Darnell. And Zhavon...

Zhavon!

Her name was a desperate wail. It bore witness to the Beast within Ramona. She slumped to the ground remembering her crime of the night before—how she had fed directly from the girl's beating heart until it had surrendered the last of its lifeblood. Zhavon's lifeblood.

Ramona, sitting cross-legged, head in her hands, expected tears of blood—Zhavon's blood—to overwhelm her. She waited for the tears, but they did not come. There was only a great emptiness. And across the emptiness echoed the howls of the Beast.

"Never," Tanner admonished her, "come from the ground without knowing who—or what—is there."

Ramona ignored him. He was clearly annoyed, but she didn't care. She couldn't pull herself from the morass of guilt surrounding Zhavon's death. Only recently had Ramona begun to comprehend the nature of the bond between herself and the girl—how being near the mortal kept Ramona in touch with that fading portion of humanity within herself. Except now Zhavon was gone. Dead at Ramona's own hand. She thought for a moment that she heard the baying of the Beast all around her, but it was merely the breeze playing among the leaves of the trees.

Tanner didn't move. He stared unblinking at her.

Ramona glared back at him. None of this made any sense to her. For two years she had known nothing but fear and hunger. Now before her was a person who could explain it, but he seemed more interested in ordering her around.

Well, Mr. Lincoln done freed the slaves, she thought.

Tanner had stolen her old life. He hadn't asked her if she'd wanted this existence of night and blood.

"I must go," he said at last. "I was waiting for you."

"You want me to thank you?" Ramona asked, but her defiance was undercut by the renewal of fear. He was going to leave again. Since she'd found out about him, that had been the way of things. He would appear briefly, and then he was gone—outside Ramona's window, at the garage, in the woods in Hayesburg. The only difference here was that for the first time he'd bothered to tell her before he disappeared.

"I got questions," Ramona said.

"All in good time." He didn't move. He was too calm. It was like he wasn't alive.

"I don't know about you," Ramona snapped, "but I ain't havin' a good time."

Still expressionless, Tanner stared at her. "I have to get others."

Others.

Ramona wasn't sure what he meant. Others, like Zhavon, to feed the ravenous Beast? Or by others did he mean Darnell and

Jen, who needed rescuing? Although Jen, Ramona reminded herself, was beyond rescue.

"We have to get Darnell," Ramona told Tanner.

He shook his head. "I'll get others first."

His face gave away nothing, but Ramona remembered the look of fear she'd seen in him last night. She didn't want to go back into that cave either, but she couldn't just leave Darnell.

"Darnell isn't dead...might not be dead," she insisted.

"Better for him if he is," said Tanner matter-of-factly.

Ramona wanted to argue the point but, thinking how that madman with the eye had deformed Zhavon, realized that Tanner was probably right.

"But we have to find out," she said.

Surprisingly, Tanner nodded his assent. "Yes. I will bring others, and then we'll destroy that creature."

Ramona watched him closely. His scowl was not so deep now that she wasn't arguing with him. From what he said, he held out less hope than she did that Darnell had survived this long. Tanner's interest was vengeance. She wasn't surprised. Men were like that. Tanner felt his pride had been wounded somehow, and he was going to go back and kick that creature's ass.

That creature.

All Ramona could picture was the humongous eye, pulsating, oozing. Had it really sprayed some kind of acid in her face? She ran her finger along the partially healed skin— healed thanks to Zhavon's blood—around her eyes and nose. Already the fight in the cave seemed like something from a horrible dream. It had faded to near obscurity, though the tiny acid burns on her shirt were real enough.

It was real for Jen and Darnell, Ramona thought.

And for Zhavon.

"Where's Zhavon's body?" Ramona asked suspiciously, as the last of the fog cleared from her mind, and the memories from last night grew more distinct. This was the spot where she had ended Zhavon's life, but the body was nowhere to be seen.

"I buried it," said Tanner.

"Where?" Ramona demanded. Her fingertips had formed

into claws. She flexed them at her sides.

"I must go," Tanner said, his consternation returning.

Ramona stepped toward him. "You're not goin' anywhere until I get some answers."

She knew that she shouldn't be so confrontational, that Tanner would be more likely to teach her what she needed to know to survive if she treated him respectfully, but his manner and his words drove her so quickly to aggravation without fail. Why, she wondered, should she treat him with respect if he wasn't going to do the same to her?

"I'm not asking permission, whelp."

Whelp. There was that name again. Ramona bristled at the sound of it. "We're gonna have to have words about this 'whelp' business."

Without warning, Tanner bared his fangs and let loose a demonic hiss. He snatched the glasses from his face and revealed blood-red eyes—the pupils were vertical slits like a cat's—and their gaze bore right through Ramona. She stumbled back a step.

"I will brook your insolence no more," he said through clenched teeth. "I buried the body by Table Rock, two miles that way." He pointed off into the forest. "Wait there, and I will send others. We shouldn't be so close to the cave."

He turned on his heels but paused several yards away. "Show proper deference to your elders, or you will not survive."

And with that he was gone. Ramona barely saw him move, but he was no longer there.

My God, she thought. *His eyes...*

She stood and stared at the spot where he had been standing, at the spot where those inhuman eyes had fixed their gaze on her.

Her legs were suddenly unsteady. She sat unceremoniously on the ground.

He's as bad as that Toreador thing.

And Tanner, her sire, had made her in his image.

Friday, 23 July 1999, 10:10 PM
Upstate New York

Table Rock was easy to find—two miles north, where Tanner had pointed before he disappeared. Ramona was disturbed that he could slip away from her so easily. She hadn't even been distracted; she'd been staring straight at him, and he was suddenly no longer there. Like when the biker had approached her that first night by the bridge: he'd been here... and then there. With no in between.

It was the type of thing that *she* could do to mortals.

But not at first, she realized.

Several months had passed after the change before she'd begun to understand and to control the remarkable abilities she'd gained, and months more before she'd been able to exercise those abilities with any consistency or competence, even around mortals.

Were these other vampires just more practiced than she was? Was it a matter of experience, or were they that much more powerful than her, like her compared to a mortal? Ramona couldn't think of a good way to find out. So far, Tanner hadn't proven very informative, and she doubted he would teach her something that might lessen his hold over her. He enjoyed his superiority too much to relinquish it. Ramona would have to learn what she could from him and read between the lines for the rest.

Maybe once they'd kicked this Toreador's ass— *whatever the hell a Toreador is*—Tanner would open up a little more.

"At least he better stop callin' me 'whelp,'" Ramona said aloud to herself.

There was no secret to how Table Rock had gotten its name. It was a large slab of stone, maybe thirty by forty feet Ramona guessed, its roughly square surface amazingly level. "Like a freakin' table," said Ramona to herself again, as she climbed onto the rock. "Some pioneer really stretched his imagination for this one." The sound of her own voice eased her mind, if only slightly.

Ramona was less interested in the rock, and more in the human-sized patch of freshly turned earth on the mild incline nearby.

Zhavon.

Ramona suddenly felt as if the earth had opened beneath her feet. The stone no longer seemed stable. As she stepped down to the ground, her knees buckled. She staggered. The bitterness toward Tanner that she'd been nurturing was swept away, and only emptiness remained, a great void where before had been...what?

Saving Darnell, the Toreador, Tanner, the Sabbat, survival itself—all the things that should have occupied her mind were very small and far away, unimportant, meaningless.

All that mattered were loss and guilt.

Zhavon.

Ramona dropped to her knees atop the freshly turned earth that was her condemnation. She pressed her face in the dirt and remembered the time she'd carried the injured mortal through darkened streets and returned her to her home.

You saved her life, a voice within Ramona said. *She was already living on borrowed time.*

"I killed her," sobbed Ramona, though as she wiped the dirt from her face she felt that it was dry. She should be crying. She wanted to cry. But there were no tears. She was dry and empty.

It was your right to take her, said the voice. *You saved her.*

"I killed her."

You've killed before. You'll kill again.

"Zhavon..." She choked on the name. There was no comfort in the words the voice spoke to her. There was no comfort in the world to soothe her. She could have left the girl after saving her. Ramona could have stayed away after that, denied herself. She lay sprawled on the grave remembering her attempt to flee, remembering how Zhavon had followed *her*.

She wanted you! said the voice. *She wanted you to take her blood.*

But Ramona could hear the lie hidden in the words. A mortal couldn't prevail against the hunger any more than Ramona could. She remembered the night of the change— how that figure, how *Tanner*, had taken her. She'd given in. She couldn't help but give in. She had even thought for a few moments that she wanted to give in, but there was no real choice, no free will.

She wanted you to take her blood.

"No!" Ramona rejected the lies.

Zhavon had not chosen this, had not wanted this.

Ramona hadn't chosen this.

Tanner had chosen. He had chosen for Ramona, and he had chosen for Zhavon.

Ramona dug her fingers into the dirt, clenched her claws into a fist.

"Fucking bastard." She wanted Tanner to be back. She wanted to rip open his chest, to tear out his heart and stuff it down his throat. She would feast on his blood and watch that smug look freeze into a death mask.

There is strength in his blood. It is your due.

Ramona shook her head to clear her thoughts, to chase away the voice. She again touched her own dry face and wondered why she couldn't cry. She searched for the sorrow that before had threatened to overwhelm her, but she couldn't feel it. All she found were signs of its passing, like footprints of some extinct creature—footprints of her own extinct humanity. Compassion was giving way to bitterness, hope to hatred.

She patted smooth the gouges she'd made on the grave, then dragged herself back to the rock, climbed onto it, and collapsed. She lay there not willing to look at the grave, not willing to face the resting place of a person whose blood flowed through her veins.

Ramona would not face it, but the blood knew. It knew

that, like the flower plucked from the tree, humanity reaped would soon wither and die.

Ramona lay still and cold upon the flat stone. The crickets and tree frogs took no notice of her anguish.

Friday, 23 July 1999, 10:45 PM
Chantry of the Five Boroughs
New York City, New York

Johnston Foley tested the gem one final time. The flame, transferred from match to purple candle, sputtered for a moment, then caught. His thoughts were perfectly focused as he began the incantation and gradually moved the candle nearer the tiny, quartz sphere in the open chest.

The candle was not even within two feet when the flame was extinguished, snuffed as convincingly as if unseen fingers had smothered the wick between them.

Amazing, thought Johnston.

For the past week, the ambient power had grown stronger and stronger. Johnston had never before seen the candle extinguished at such a distance. It was a simple, unsophisticated ritual, but still he couldn't help feel it was a portent of no slight significance. He would unravel the mysteries of the gem, and his superiors would undoubtedly take notice of his efficiency and skill. How could they not?

Aisling Sturbridge had returned from her council meeting in Baltimore. She told Johnston little of the goings-on there, but even she couldn't conceal her interest in the gem. When he had shown her this same ritual two nights ago, he'd seen the nearly imperceptible rise of her eyebrow—that telltale gesture that with her, he imagined, would be the only sign of any emotion from murderous rage to sexual ecstasy.

She must be kicking herself for delegating the gem to me, Johnston thought. *Surely my role in this will be made known to the Pontifex… maybe even to Meerlinda herself!*

Johnston smoothed the wrinkles from his ceremonial robe and made an effort to clear such giddy thoughts from his mind. Jacqueline had gathered the necessary items—and had done a respectable job, Johnston had to admit. Aaron, a more consistently reliable apprentice, had performed the ceremonial cleansings and invoked the appropriate protective wards around Johnston's chambers—both to prevent the unwary from interrupting the ritual, and more importantly as a precaution against anything that might be unleashed by the ritual. Johnston, ensconced within the confines of the wards, might in the larger view be expendable. The entire chantry was not.

Johnston took a step back from the stone and surveyed the paraphernalia on the work table: two eight-inch-tall, four-inch-wide, oval mirrors with polished silver rims, perfectly smooth glass and silver backing; five sticks of pine carved to the size of pencils and flawlessly sanded; a flat silver tray engraved with a *fleur-de-lis* matching the inlay on the wooden chest; seven candles of red wax melded with the entrails of a wild owl; several pieces of golden-edged parchment; an obsidian inkwell; and a particular set of ritual quills. The parchment, ink, and quills Johnston had attended to personally. The other items that Jacqueline had gathered, as well as Aaron's work, Johnston had inspected as well and been satisfied.

Now it was time.

He closed his eyes and, with an ease born of decades of repetition, cleared all extraneous concerns from his mind. Each bit of mental flotsam he tucked in its appropriate niche, until his faculties were completely unencumbered, leaving him free to turn his mind's eye inward to that place where mystical energies collected like a pool above an ever-bubbling spring. Down he dove, through the surface pool, deep into the aquifer itself, a repository to which few ever gained access.

Part of Johnston's mind was vaguely aware that time was proceeding without him, that hours were passing beyond the limits of his body. His eyes opened, but the perversity of time, the discrepancy between a physical act and the arrival of light waves carrying to an eye the sight of that act, were grown inconstant. The surface portion of his mind that was attending to external reality received stimuli that were minutes rather than nanoseconds old.

Johnston saw when he had placed the two mirrors on either side of the wooden chest containing the gem. He saw the distant moments when his hands had arranged the seven candles equidistant from one another and the chest.

Suddenly time skipped ahead, as it was wont to do. Johnston must have placed the silver tray before the chest, for there it sat. His lips were moving, as if of their own accord. He chanted words of a language far older than most linguists would have believed possible, but the time-sense of his speech was different from that of his vision. Words that would sound in the next hour mingled with sights that were already minutes old. The Tremere was less the controller and more the medium for the ritual. From the aquifer of his soul, it received shape and form.

A ripple in the pool obscured the time-sense, shifted relationships. Johnston saw now the way in which his hands would grasp the pine sticks. His eyes recorded how he would snap each stick, and how not sap but blood would drain into the silver tray.

At the snap of the final stick, the seven candles flamed to life. The smoke shone red—an illusion projected by the now glowing quartz, which burned as brightly as any flame since those that had raged at the formation of the world. The odor reminded Johnston of the comfort of his mother's womb—how many centuries had passed? Yet he was there, warm, comforted by the close swish-swish of her heart. He was become his embryo-self, connected to the greater being. From the amorphous stuff of his fledgling body, a hand took shape.

When the hand reached out, though, he felt surrounding him not the soft, forgiving flesh of his mother's protecting womb, but hard, cold stone. He tried to pull back his hand, but the stone grew like living flesh to take hold of him. Even the cord that was his connection to life wrapped around him like a noose. All about, a tempest rose. Warmth and comfort fled.

Johnston tried to scream as he was dragged down into the darkness.

Saturday, 24 July 1999, 1:17 AM
Upstate New York

Ramona didn't remember ever having fallen asleep since the night of the change—unless she counted her daily escape from the sun, but those hours seemed more like hibernation, or catatonia, than real sleep. She wasn't sure that she'd fallen asleep this night—it hardly seemed likely—but suddenly she noticed that time had passed. The night was deeper. Just like a mortal could intuitively tell morning from afternoon from evening, Ramona was sensitive to the phases of night. It was not a hard thing to learn. Now she found herself later in the night, and somehow she had missed the intervening hours.

Sleep? She didn't feel particularly rested. She hadn't dreamed, but again that was something that hadn't occurred since the change. She and Jen had talked about that not too long ago, just a couple of nights ago, although with all that had happened it seemed more like years ago. Jen was freed from her fears, and Ramona was left with no one to share her own.

Her chest ached, not from injury but from emptiness. Maybe it was the weight of her loss that had pressed her into slumber. For a few brief hours, she had been devoid of thought and memory and pain. But they were her constant companions now, and had not gone far.

What had called her back to her world of loss? For undoubtedly grief and bitterness had not yet run their course. Maybe it was the nearby scrabbling sound that was only slowly intruding upon her conscious mind.

Ramona sat bolt upright. She thought she saw the back of a man rooting around in the dirt of the fresh grave. At the sound of her movement, however, he whirled to face her. She was confronted by the rheumy eyes and bared yellowed fangs of a giant rat.

Ramona's shock quickly gave way to instinct. Within a second, she was on her feet, crouched, ready to spring.

The rat-thing gave a half-hearted hiss. Loose grave dirt fell from its twitching nose. The creature seemed as likely to flee as attack, as it edged away, putting the grave between itself and Ramona, whatever protection the small mound of earth might afford.

"You are Tanner-childe," said the rat.

Ramona stood speechless. Her shock, first at finding the creature so close to her and then seeing its face, was nothing compared to her surprise at hearing words come from those inhuman lips. Her eyes narrowed as she regarded the creature more carefully.

Its body was bent but human, covered by filthy rags that smelled of garbage and worse. Its face, though distinctly ratlike— large bulbous eyeballs set close together, twitching whiskers, protruding and grotesquely misproportioned nose, receded jaw, tiny jagged teeth—retained a vaguely human shape.

"You are Tanner-childe," the rat said again, in way of confirmation, since Ramona hadn't responded. "He said you were a stubborn one."

The rat chuckled at his own little joke, or maybe he wasn't laughing and just had something stuck in his throat. Ramona was unsure about the disturbing, coughing sound he made.

Still keeping a wary eye on Ramona, the rat began rooting at the heaped earth again. "New grave," he muttered.

Ramona leapt down from the rock and landed by the grave. She swiped at the rat and yelled: "Get away, you fuckin' rat-faced son-of-a-bitch!"

The rat ducked under her claw and almost fell over himself scuttering backward out of her reach. He hissed like a cornered animal.

"Sometimes blood still in bodies," he insisted. "Enough to share." He stretched out his neck and watched closely to see if Ramona would accept his conciliatory offer.

"Ain't nobody diggin' up this body!" Ramona took another step toward him and raised a claw. He backed away farther.

"Your blood?" the rat asked, as if that were a claim he could understand.

Ramona looked down at the grave. What difference did it make now, she wondered, what happened to the body? Zhavon was dead. Gone forever. But, still, Ramona couldn't stand the thought of this rat-thing digging up the poor girl's remains and gnawing on them.

"My blood," she said quietly. "Nobody's diggin' up this body."

The rat nodded. Apparently the matter was settled, as far as he was concerned. He edged closer to Ramona, there being no further cause for confrontation.

"What is your name, Tanner-childe?" he asked in a way that was again mostly trusting and not unfriendly.

"Ramona." She told him without really thinking. She didn't think she had anything to fear from him, as long as he stayed away from the grave.

The rat waited for a moment, as if he expected her to say something more, but Ramona was silent. So he straightened a bit and spoke: "I am Ratface. I know all the towns and cities of New York. I am smarter than the lupines, swifter than the Sabbat."

Still he looked at Ramona, as if she might have something else to say.

"That's nice," she said at last. *I didn't ask for your freakin' life story.*

They stood silently for a few minutes. Ramona watched to make sure he stayed away from the grave. Ratface sniffed around Table Rock, pointedly taking interest in everything *but* the grave.

"Your *name* is Ratface?" she asked eventually, uncomfortable with the silence, which was broken only by Ratface's gentle snorting as he rooted around. "Your mama have a burr up her butt?"

Ratface paused in his sniffing. He looked up with what might have been a glint of sadness in his eyes. "It is what I am called...now."

She didn't need to ask *why* he was called that. "I wouldn't let nobody call me Ratface," said Ramona. She couldn't help glancing down at her own monstrous feet, and thinking of her ears, and Tanner's eyes.

What'll they be callin' me? she wondered. Was she any better off than this disgusting Ratface? Was she going to keep changing and end up little more than an animal? Ramona had always thought of the night she became a vampire as *the* change, but it seemed more and more like she wasn't done changing yet.

Tanner's got some shit to answer for, she decided.

And she could faintly hear the voice from before: *There is strength in his blood.*

Ramona shook her head, shook the voice away. She watched Ratface sniffing the large rock, nearby trees, the air. Finally, he climbed up onto the rock, turned three tight circles in one spot, and then sat. He continued to sniff at the air occasionally, but for the most part seemed to wait, without need for further conversation. His presence bothered Ramona. She would've preferred to be alone at the graveside and to sort through her grief privately, or perhaps to figure out why the great emptiness inside her so outweighed her sense of loss. She couldn't understand why she felt so distanced from Zhavon's death. But every time Ramona started to get hold of one of her tangled emotions, she was invariably distracted by Ratface as he fidgeted and grunted up on the rock. Her irritation with him, however, was mixed with a sense of relief, strangely enough. She realized chances were that nothing but time would untangle her feelings, and for now there was nothing to be gained by wallowing in pity and doubt, no matter how great the urge to do just that.

"Tanner sent you?" she asked Ratface.

"Yes. He has called a Gather."

"Gather? Gathering of what?"

Ratface regarded her for a moment. Puzzlement crossed his features briefly, but then he nodded as if he'd answered some question for himself. "Of the Gangrel," he said. "There are many not far away, guarding Buffalo. Many will come. Maybe even Xaviar himself."

Gangrel.

Ratface's words sparked memories in Ramona, brought back what Tanner had said to her the night before: *Know that you are Gangrel.*

And now Ratface used the same word. *A Gather of the Gangrel.* "But what is Gangrel?" Ramona asked herself, not meaning to speak the words aloud.

Ratface chuckled again; it was the sound of an old lady trying to spit. "Gangrel is our clan. I am Gangrel. You are Gangrel. Has Tanner not taught you?"

Know that you are Gangrel, Tanner had said. *And that I am your sire. I made you what you are.*

"He's my sire," Ramona mumbled.

"Yes," Ratface nodded. "And you—his childe."

Ramona gave Ratface a hard look, squinted suspiciously. "Are you his childe?"

Ratface's eyes bulged even larger. "Me? Tanner's childe?" He laughed quite loudly this time. "Heavens no. And I wouldn't let him hear you suggest that. He's a picky one, Tanner is."

"He's an asshole is what he is."

Ratface started to laugh again but caught himself. He glanced around nervously, as if Tanner might be listening from behind the nearest tree. "I'd be careful if I were you," he said. His speech was more normal now; his initial me-Tarzan-you-Jane pidgin had given way to complete sentences, and he was proving talkative. "Tanner has Embraced before, but seldom revealed himself, as far as I know."

"Embraced?" Ramona asked. Everything Ratface said was like a riddle.

"Embraced. Taken a mortal to be one of us." Ratface was still nervous. He spoke quietly and looked around constantly. "He has Embraced others, but mostly he has left them to flounder on their own, and they perished. He must think highly of you to have revealed himself to you."

"Well, I don't think too much of him," Ramona grumbled. She could see that Ratface was amused by what she said, but he was just as obviously afraid of Tanner.

Ratface looked around again and then practically whispered to her: "Do you know why he called the Gather?"

Ratface clearly was asking about something he thought he shouldn't be. He was hunched down like he expected to be struck for uttering the words. Ramona, remembering how Tanner had hit her without warning, supposed that Ratface's manner wasn't all that unreasonable. She was tempted to tell him everything she knew, just on the off-chance that doing so would piss off Tanner. He deserved it. But the truth was that she didn't have a very clear of what had happened herself. In the end, she rejected candor for shock value.

"Because he was afraid."

Ratface's eyes grew wide again. Ramona suppressed her own laughter this time. That wasn't what Ratface was expecting to hear, but it was true. She had seen the fear in Tanner's face. She didn't feel the need to go into more detail—to tell that *she'd* been scared shitless as well, and that if Tanner hadn't hustled her out of the cave, she too, like Jen and probably Darnell, would be dead. She didn't know what to say about the Toreador. She didn't have much to compare it to. Better to let Tanner tell the story when he got back. But Ramona still had hundreds of questions, and Ratface was proving more forthcoming than Tanner ever had.

"So Gangrel is one clan," she said. "Is Sabbat another?"

Ratface shook his head. "Not exactly. Gangrel is one clan of several that make up the Camarilla—the alliance that opposes the Sabbat."

Ramona's head was spinning. Every answer Ratface gave her created two more questions. "Jesus—sire, Embrace, Gangrel, Camarilla, Sabbat—I need a fuckin' dictionary."

Ratface continued as if she hadn't interrupted him. "The Sabbat are...monsters. Very dangerous. They'd destroy the Masquerade if it were up to them."

"Masquerade?"

Ratface nodded vigorously. "Before, when you were a mortal, did you know there were those like us living among you?"

Ramona shook her head. "Not really. I mean... they were just movies and stories and shit."

"Exactly. That's the Masquerade. If the mortals knew about

us, they'd hunt us down and that would be the end."

Ramona thought about that for a moment. She and her friends had almost always tried to lie low and not to attract a lot of attention. It just seemed safer that way. They'd mostly tried to hide from other vampires as well as from mortals. It made sense... unless the Sabbat thought there were enough vampires to take on the mortals. But if that were the case, why weren't vampires in charge of everything already?

"Shh." Ratface roused her from thought. His enlarged, rodent ears were pricked up. "That way. Someone's coming."

"You always were tough to sneak up on," said a voice from the direction Ratface was peering. A moment later, a tall man strode out of the darkness and over to Table Rock.

He was taller than Ramona and Ratface, and wore sturdy hiking boots, worn jeans, and a heavy corduroy shirt, all dirty and dusty from long use but not tattered like their own clothes. The newcomer drew himself up before them. He picked a twig out of his long and unruly hair and flicked the tiny stick into the woods.

"I am Brant Edmonson," he said. "When the mortals fought among themselves for the western lands, I prowled the trails. When Elijah the Cruel was lost to the Beast, I was with mighty Xaviar as we put him down."

Ratface nodded respectfully. Ramona was caught off guard by what she considered the awkwardness of the introduction.

"I am Ratface," said Ratface. "I know all the towns and cities of New York. I am smarter than the lupines, swifter than the Sabbat."

Ramona listened to the words she'd heard before. She didn't know what to say to this Brant Edmonson. Ratface seemed to have his little spiel planned already. The new guy didn't seem to be a threat. His sudden appearance hadn't alarmed Ratface, and Ratface was skittish if anything. This close, Ramona could smell that Edmonson was like them, that the blood didn't flow naturally through his body, that it was really somebody else's blood in the first place. Without thinking, Ramona reached out and shook Brant Edmonson's hand. It seemed like the uptight, corncob-up-your-ass kind of thing that these folks might do.

"I'm Ramona," she said, then stepped back.

Brant seemed surprised and gave her a funny look, like he thought he was eating sugar but tasted salt instead. The funny look slowly faded though, and Ramona realized that his eyes weren't focused on her anymore. He was looking over her shoulder. Ratface too, she saw, was looking to the other side of Table Rock. His ears were pricked up again.

Ramona turned and saw the dark figure across the clearing. A throaty growl rumbled through the night, but the rumble was actually words: "I am Stalker-in-the-Woods. I do not run from the mortals. I catch their bullets in my teeth. I drink their blood and grind their bones to dust."

Ramona edged away so that she wasn't closest as the newest Gangrel stepped onto Table Rock. Stalker-in-the-Woods was hunched over, but still his shoulders were more than a foot higher than Ramona's head. His wild mane of hair covered him almost like a cloak; he wore no other clothes. He was all gaunt muscle and scars.

Edmonson stepped forward. He stood with his chin raised defiantly.

"I am Brant Edmonson. When the mortals fought among themselves for the western lands, I prowled the trails. When Elijah the Cruel was lost to the Beast, I was with mighty Xaviar as we put him down."

From where he stood, Ratface spoke his introduction as he had twice already. Stalker-in-the-Woods looked at him, and Ratface looked away, not meeting the creature's gaze.

The attention of Stalker-in-the-Woods shifted to Ramona. He stepped closer. Ramona suddenly felt her mouth as dry as if she hadn't drunk blood in a year. Stalker-in-the-Woods moved closer still. His eyes were yellowed and bloodshot, his face black with dried blood.

Ramona started to open her mouth, but no words came to her tongue. She wasn't tempted to shake hands with Stalker-in-the-Woods.

"She is Ramona Tanner-childe," said Ratface, at last.

Stalker-in-the-Woods ignored Ratface and stared at Ramona until she looked away. This seemed to satisfy him. He turned and moved toward Brant until the two were only a few feet apart. Edmonson held his ground. His hands were relaxed at his sides.

Ramona almost jumped when she felt Ratface next to her. She hadn't heard him move. His hand was on her elbow and he was ushering her to the side.

"He's a mean one," Ratface whispered. "We'd do best to stay out of his way."

Edmonson didn't share Ratface's opinion. He stood toe-to-toe with Stalker-in-the-Woods, and to Ramona's surprise, the smaller, more human Gangrel smiled.

There was no warning of Stalker-in-the-Woods's attack. He sprang with a ferocious snarl before Ramona even knew he was moving. Brant took the full brunt of the lunge. Stalker-in-the-Woods bowled him over backwards. The fight was quick and one-sided, but not in the way Ramona had expected in that first instant.

Edmonson went down under his larger opponent but was not surprised. He rolled as he landed, shifting his weight so that Stalker-in-the-Woods was caught off balance and tumbled off. Before the dust kicked up by Stalker-in-the-Woods's lunge had settled, it was over. Edmonson knelt by his prone attacker's side, one razor-sharp claw barely piercing the flesh of Stalker-in-the-Woods's neck. If the larger Gangrel so much as moved, Brant could rip his throat out with the flick of a wrist.

The hard stares of the two combatants met, and an unspoken acknowledgement passed between them. Brant withdrew his claw and stood, never taking his eyes from Stalker-in-the-Woods.

Ramona felt sharp pain in her hands and looked down to realize that she had dug her fingernails—her *claws*—deep into her palms. She watched Stalker-in-the-Woods, expecting him any second to leap up and fling himself at Edmonson again. But Stalker-in-the-Woods climbed slowly to his feet. He did not dust himself off; he did not speak. He stalked slowly and silently away into the darkness.

Ramona briefly felt the urge to taunt him as he left, but she knew that she wasn't the one who'd defeated him. He wasn't somebody she needed to antagonize. Probably he could make quick work of her, like she'd thought he was going to of Brant.

Edmonson was not taunting Stalker-in-the-Woods, but neither did he seem particularly worried. Unlike Ramona and Ratface, who were glancing nervously toward the deepest shadows every few seconds, he looked as if nothing had happened. The only difference was that now the dust on his clothes was fresher and billowed into small clouds when he crossed his arms.

"So you're Tanner's childe," Brant said.

Ramona nodded.

"I've learned a lot from Tanner," he added.

"Wish I could say the same," Ramona muttered without thinking, then wished she hadn't said it.

To her relief, Edmonson smiled, and not nervously like Ratface when she'd criticized Tanner earlier. She saw no fear of Tanner in Brant's eyes; she saw no fear of anything.

"Tanner is a good teacher," said Brant, "in his own time."

In his own time. His words reminded Ramona of something he'd said earlier. *When the mortals fought among themselves for the western lands, I prowled the trails.* The western lands—did he mean the West-west? Cowboys-and-Indians West? It sure sounded like that to Ramona. But that would make him over a hundred years old! No wonder they treated her like such a baby. She wanted to ask, but she didn't know if she should. There seemed to be strange customs among these Gangrel. First, the stiff, formal sort of introductions—it seemed very important to them to announce who they were, what they'd done. Second, the fight that had begun and ended in two blinks of an eye. That she thought she understood. She'd seen turf wars in L.A. Edmonson had made it clear that he stood above Stalker-in-the-Woods. But clear for how long? Ramona wondered. She kept glancing over in the direction he had gone.

Saturday, 24 July 1999, 3:32 AM
Chantry of the Five Boroughs
New York City, New York

There was no fighting the swirling darkness. It pulled Johnston down, and he was mildly surprised when he eventually found himself again. His precarious time-sense was completely subsumed beneath the burgeoning perspective that dominated his awareness, and much to Johnston's dismay, this new perspective was as fractious and chaotic as his own was orderly. He was assailed by whirling streams of contradictory thoughts, fears, needs.

Johnston sensed a consciousness that he should have been able to wrest under his control, but the consciousness was bolstered, augmented. It was slippery and strong, and before he knew it, Johnston felt tendrils of personality coiling around him. Frantically, he extracted himself from the entangling psyche. He'd recovered from his disorientation just enough to pull back. The tendrils snaked after him, but Johnston remained beyond them. With great effort, he closed himself to the maddening consciousness—to the *mad* consciousness, he realized—by latching onto a distant sensation, tangible evidence of his own identity. He did not see the quill, but he felt it in his fingers— the smooth, gently curving barrel; the downy plume. It was inextricably linked to who he was, to the ritual he performed, and it was his anchor amidst the raging storm, his shield against the *other*.

Having shored up his sense of his own consciousness and held the cyclone of the other at bay, Johnston reached out again to that perspective. He searched for sensory stimuli, for context to the madness. He searched thoroughly but quickly. His defenses appeared firm, but he might or might not have warning if they gave way. If that happened, he would be swept away by the storm.

The vision formed quickly, forcefully, and for a moment it threatened to pull Johnston back into the madness. But he was steadfast in his resolve. His finger stroked the quill. He distractedly worried that he might damage the instrument, but the alternative was far more ominous.

Johnston found himself (not himself, the other) in an open space—dark, damp, cool. Through non-existent light, he saw insubstantial walls, shimmering formations of rock, limestone. The surreal surroundings faded almost completely from view, then returned to partial reality. Johnston felt as if he was real (not he, the other), but that the parameters of the environs danced temperamentally through ever-shifting phases.

Then the hands reached forward, his hands (the other's hands), and took hold of that alone which, except for the hands themselves, was real and substantial—a young black man; Kindred, judging from the exposed fangs. Exposed because the man's lower jaw was missing. No, not missing, Johnston realized, but stretched impossibly far, so that it hung down below the man's knees. The Kindred's tongue was forked, not once but perhaps a half dozen times, and each of the resulting strands of flesh wagged and squirmed, giving the appearance that somehow the man had unhinged his jaw and was swallowing a miniature head of Medusa. His eyes rolled up into his head, but he was not yet destroyed.

As Johnston watched, the hands, long and pale with bulbous knuckles, grasped the Kindred's deformed shoulders. Flesh and bone melted and were reshaped beneath the touch. The snake-tongues wagged feverishly.

Johnston withdrew as much as he could from the vision. He had no desire to see more. Instead, he began cautiously to probe the other consciousness, the entity of which he'd been an eye. Johnston was careful not to wade again into the raging chaos of that mind; he explored from a distance. While he did so, he kept firm hold on the quill, and remembering ink and parchment, he put them to use.

Saturday, 24 July 1999, 4:05 AM
Upstate New York

For hours they kept coming, and they were all Gangrel. One at a time they wandered in, or occasionally two arrived together who had met on the way. Most had traveled east, though once near Table Rock they circled and approached from various directions. They were a wary lot. Most entered the clearing around the rock for at least a short time. Some soon edged back into the more complete darkness of the forest. Others never ventured beyond the protective cover of the trees in the first place. But Ramona knew they were out there, as was Stalker-in-the-Woods. Watching.

There was some quiet talking among them. Acquaintances separated for several years greeted one another and caught up. They told stories of their adventures, but never until after the ritualistic greetings:

"I'm Snodgrass. This scar is from a lupine I met in Central Park."

"I am Mutabo. I feasted on the blood of the slavers who brought me to this country."

"I am Renée Lightning. There are few Kindred Embraced who can match my speed."

"I am Joshua, called Bloodhound. I track through cities infested by Sabbat, or wilderness crawling with lupines. I've never failed to earn my fee."

Ramona listened to the first few introductions. She was curious about these creatures, all of whom apparently were of her clan—Gangrel. They were as different from one another as might be a group of people on a random city bus. Some, like herself, were not in their element out here in the forest, miles from the nearest city or even decent-sized town. Others seemed perfectly at ease.

None, however, appeared particularly affluent. The appearances might have been misleading, Ramona knew, but Edmonson in his worn but mostly intact attire was at the upper end of the fashion spectrum for those assembled. Many more, like Ramona, had on what they might have been wearing years ago on the night of their change—their Embrace—and they just hadn't bothered with much of a wardrobe since. Ramona knew that she had gone months at a time without any thought of what she was wearing. The weather was not really a problem anymore; wind and cold didn't bother her. And she hadn't been particularly sociable since the change. She wondered if, in a few more years, she would run around naked like Stalker-in-the-Woods, with only her hair and the night to cover her.

Ramona peered out into the darkness. Just thinking of Stalker-in-the-Woods made her nervous. He wasn't someone she wanted to stumble on unawares, or even if she was expecting it, for that matter. His eyes burned with a cold fury. Ramona, before she'd looked away, had seen the hunger within him, but it was a different hunger from what she felt. Stalker-in-the-Woods would enjoy the suffering he inflicted, whether it was on mortal or vampire—Kindred, they called one another.

Aside from being uneasy not knowing where exactly he was, Ramona was embarrassed—embarrassed and *angry*—that she had looked away. She hadn't realized at the time that Stalker-in-the-Woods was staring her down. It had just happened and she'd looked away.

She hadn't been prepared. The worst part was that she didn't know if it would've made a difference if she *had* been prepared. Stalker-in-the-Woods was so...

"Close to the Beast," Ratface had said, when Ramona asked him about the frightening Gangrel.

It was an apt description. Ramona remembered what she had felt that night the two men had attacked Zhavon. Ramona hadn't planned to rip out their throats and string their intestines across the alley. It had just happened. It had felt right...natural.

And she had enjoyed it—that scared her as much as anything. It was that kind of enjoyment that she thought she could see in Stalker-in-the-Woods.

Among the Gangrel, the dominant topics of conversation were the Sabbat and lupines. Ramona didn't take part in the discussions, but she heard bits of various stories. The tales about the Sabbat were exchanged in calm tones, as any interesting news might be related. Apparently that gang, which the Gangrel opposed—although Ramona did hear one story about a Gangrel, Korbit, who fought on the side of the Sabbat—was taking control of a great deal of territory that had belonged to the Camarilla along the East Coast. Ramona heard several cities mentioned—Atlanta, Charleston, Washington, D.C. It sounded bad, but Edmonson and the others didn't seem particularly worried.

When they spoke of the lupines, however, they did so in hushed tones. They glanced occasionally over their shoulders. Probably they denied it even to themselves, but Ramona could hear the fear in their voices. Several of the Gangrel in their litany of deeds had spoken boastfully of lupines, but uncertainty, not pride, tinged their voices as they spoke of routes of safety through lupine territory or shifting hunting grounds. Even Edmonson, as calm and confident as Tanner, spoke respectfully of such things.

It was the talk about the lupines that made Ramona begin to feel strangely detached from everything that was going on around her. The stories were all of death and dismemberment: a friend decapitated in the wilds of northern Maine; an associate crossing the Grand Tetons split open from neck to belly; another who never returned from the Everglades.

Ramona withdrew into herself. The talk moved farther and farther away, until the voices were very small. They rang in the back of her head. Certain words echoed through her mind—*lupine...Texas... werewolf...lupine*—grew closer together, finally overlapped and merged into one disquieting mass.

I saw a lupine in Texas, Ramona said. She moved her lips, but no words emerged. She didn't remember sitting, but there she was on the ground by Zhavon's grave, sifting loose dirt through her fingers.

I saw a lupine in Texas.

They had still been several hours from San Antonio. Eddie had this thing for back roads. He wouldn't drive on an interstate if he could help it, and so when they ran out of gas, they were surrounded by nothing but miles and miles of gullies, mesquite, and dust.

Jen and Darnell argued bitterly over whose fault it was they'd run out of gas. Eddie didn't seem too upset. He claimed to have an unfailing sense of direction and saw finding a shortcut through the mesquite thickets as a challenge. Ramona had asked him if his dick was a compass, but he ignored her. Too bad, they agreed, that they couldn't eat sand instead of drinking blood. Plenty of sand. No gas. No blood.

Then suddenly there was plenty of blood.

Maybe if Jen and Darnell hadn't been arguing, somebody would've heard it coming.

Lupine. The name fit the monster from Ramona's memory.

They were approaching the edge of a gully, a dry creek bed, and the lupine was there, where it hadn't been a second before. Eddie stumbled back. The left side of his face was gone. Ramona heard the first snarl as she was splattered with his blood. Before they could speak or scream, a claw ripped open his gut like a piñata full of shriveled intestines. Eddie's knees buckled, and then the monster slammed its jaws shut and took off the top of his head.

Eddie fell. His blood wetted down the dust.

Ramona and the others behind her stood in shock, mouths agape. She could feel the lupine's moist breath heavy on the dry, Texas air.

The first moment of decision arrived—the creature needed only reach out to take off Ramona's head, but instead it fell upon Eddie, burying its snout in his opened belly. Eddie whimpered as it tore him apart from the inside out.

The second moment of decision fell to Ramona, Jen, and Darnell. They could pounce on the lupine. It was fully consumed by its passion for carnage. They could strike back for Eddie, who no longer could himself. The moment hung heavy in the air, bathed in blood and the staccato crack of ribs.

As one, Ramona and the others turned and ran.

They stumbled through the mesquite. Thorns dug into their flesh, but they hardly noticed. They ran and didn't stop running until the rising sun forced them to burrow into the steep bank of a gully. They burrowed until the earth collapsed behind them, but they didn't need air. Only darkness.

I saw a lupine in Texas.

I saw a lupine in Texas.

"Ramona?"

Ratface was close to her, very close. Ramona blinked repeatedly at him. She raised a hand to wipe away Eddie's blood that had splattered on her face.

"Ramona?" Ratface's voice, too, seemed very far away, though he crouched less than a foot from her.

There were too many people here. Too many Gangrel. Ramona could see at least ten. Stalker-in- the-Woods and others were out there somewhere too.

Too many.

These were the others whom Tanner had called together. Ramona had never thought she'd want to see this many of her own kind—vampires, Kindred, Gangrel—together in one place, but if they were going back to that cave…

The thought seemed to flick a switch in her brain. *The cave… Darnell!* She'd been so caught up in her own grief and in the strangeness of the Gather that she'd almost forgotten Darnell. How long had he been in there? They had to get him out! There were plenty of Gangrel here now. Ramona scrambled to her feet.

"Where the hell is Tanner?" she asked no one in particular.

Ratface regarded her quizzically. "He is spreading word of the Gather."

"But we have to save Darnell!" Ramona suddenly couldn't stand the thought of wasting another second. They'd waited too long already. She shoved her way past Ratface and stalked over to Brant Edmonson, who was talking with Joshua.

"Let's go," she demanded. "We've got enough folks here." For the moment, she ignored the memory of Tanner's fear and convinced herself that Edmonson would be more than a match for Darnell's captor.

"Tanner has called the Gather," Edmonson said. "We'll wait for him." He spoke kindly but firmly, and didn't bother to ask what she wanted to do.

"I've been waitin' for him for too long," Ramona snarled. "I'm sick of it! There's a…a…fuckin' *thing* in a cave," she pointed toward the meadow, "and it's got one of my friends."

"We will wait for Tanner," Edmonson said again calmly. He placed a hand on her shoulder, but Ramona jerked and pushed him away.

"Don't touch me!"

Joshua moved closer. "You need to calm down."

Ramona jabbed an instantly formed claw toward his face. "Don't tell me what I need! *I* don't need anything. *We* need to rescue Darnell."

Edmonson stared at her—a harder, less friendly stare than before—but said nothing. Other Gangrel were taking notice of her outburst, of the harsh tone of her words to Edmonson and Joshua.

Ramona threw her hands in the air. "He's been there a whole day and night already. We have to get him out!" She was met with silence, which only stoked her anger. "What kind of chickenshit vampire club is this? *Any* of you fellas got any balls?" She glanced meaningfully around the clearing at the various Gangrel. "Or is that just a mortal thing?"

At that, Edmonson drew himself up to his full height and glared down at Ramona. "We will wait for Tanner," he said in short, clipped tones, and raised a finger before her face. "Until he returns, little one, you had best watch your tongue." Then he turned and walked away from her.

"Little one? *Little one!*" She took a step after Brant, but found herself restrained. Someone was holding her shoulder. She tried to jerk away again, but this time the hand held tight. She whirled, ready to attack, and to her surprise faced Ratface.

"You are not helping your friend by aggravating Edmonson," he said quietly. The strength in his hands and the earnestness in his eyes brought her up short. At the same time, a great weariness took hold of her. Her frustration and fear had flashed to anger but that, for the moment, was spent. Ratface was right, she knew. Getting her ass whipped wasn't going to help Darnell. But that knowledge did little to curb her vexation. She started to think how she'd probably alienated Brant Edmonson, but then she noticed that despite the numerous Gangrel that had already gathered, the low buzz of conversation that had waxed and waned over the past few hours had now died away completely. Even Ratface, right next to her, was looking back toward Table Rock and sniffing at the air.

Another Gangrel had arrived, and all had stopped whatever they were doing to watch him. There was not the feel of danger about him, as with Stalker- in-the-Woods. He was not even tall and confident like Brant Edmonson. Yet the gaze of every Gangrel present followed him.

"Edward Blackfeather," Ratface turned back and whispered to Ramona. "A Cherokee medicine man."

The man did have the look of an American Indian, though Ramona could never have made a guess about what tribe. He was here, so he must be Gangrel. Apparently the vampire clan cut across boundaries of gender, race, and nationality. Ramona already knew that from what she'd seen of those assembled.

Blackfeather was wiry and not tall, maybe five and a half feet, about Ramona's height. He wore what looked to be a deerskin shirt and moccasins of the same material, faded blue jeans, and a belt with a large Elvis buckle. His hair was long and white and stuck out at an awkward angle from beneath an old, felt hat, the brim of which, once round and stiff, hung limp almost down in his face. A gray and white feather hung from a string tied to his hat.

Ramona could feel the stillness that accompanied Blackfeather. It was a palpable quiet that began somewhere within him, but radiated from him as well. The Gangrel all paid him a certain deference—it didn't smell of fear exactly, but the old man's presence made the others uncomfortable.

He stepped up onto Table Rock and, acknowledging no one, began to walk slowly around the edge of the large stone. Edmonson and Joshua Bloodhound, who were sitting on the rock, eased off the opposite side to better watch what Blackfeather was doing, and from a bit more of a distance. He shuffled his feet and stared intently at the stone, not stopping until he'd completed one full circuit. Then he reached into the canvas sack he carried draped over one shoulder and pulled out a small pine bough. Using the bough like a brush or a small broom, he began to sweep the flat stone surface, starting in the center and moving in a gradually expanding spiral.

No one spoke. His sweeping must have taken at least half an hour, for he was very thorough, but none spoke and few so much as crossed or uncrossed their arms. When he was done, Blackfeather placed the pine bough in the center of the stone, where he'd started his sweeping. Then he casually stepped down from the stone and walked into the forest.

Many of the Gangrel looked to one another with questioning gazes.

"What was that all about?" Ramona asked Ratface quietly.

Ratface only shrugged, and then pointed.

Blackfeather was returning. The hushed speculation all over the clearing quickly died away. He carried an armful of sticks and small branches, which he placed near the center of the rock and then began to build into a small teepee.

He worked as silently and as deliberately at his teepee as he had at his sweeping, and for the ten minutes his construction occupied, again, no one spoke or made a sound.

At last he was done, and he placed his canvas sack on the rock next to the foot-tall teepee. From his bag he took something, but Ramona couldn't see what until he moved closer to her and stood at the edge of Table Rock. In his left hand he held a piece of white chalk—a fat piece, like a child would use to draw on a sidewalk. His hand was open and flat, perfectly still. Against his dark and deeply wrinkled skin—tanned like leather during his mortal days—the chalk looked smooth and brilliant white. With his flattened right palm, he began to press down on the chalk with a steady, circular motion. As Ramona looked on, he ground the fat piece of chalk into a fine powder using only the pressure of his hands, and not a single speck of white fell to the stone below.

As he finished and held in his hand nothing more than a pile of powdered chalk, Ramona realized that he was watching her. She had been intent on his hands and the transformation of chalk to powder, but he had been intent on her. His eyes sparkled with the mischievousness of kinship, and Ramona's startlement at noticing him watching her drained away.

For a long moment, he looked at her looking at him. Then Blackfeather turned. He knelt and began to sprinkle the chalk onto the rock, not in a haphazard manner but in a line, and as he edged backward around Table Rock he continued to spread the chalk. Not once did he look over his shoulder to check his direction as he went, but his movements were as sure as the turning of the earth.

He circled near the edge of the rock, not stopping or varying his deliberate pace until he came again to his starting point before Ramona. He stood, and then reached an open, white hand to her.

The next thing Ramona knew, she was stepping up onto Table Rock. She could see at once that the nearly completed circle Blackfeather had drawn was perfect of form, and that the teepee of sticks stood exactly in the center. For a moment, her legs nearly failed her. She could feel the weight of the trees and the sky and the stars pressing down on her, and she feared that she might be crushed against the flat stone, that she might become part of Table Rock. But Blackfeather took her hand, and the feeling passed. She stepped through the opening he had left in the circle, and with the last of the chalk he closed it behind her.

Next, Blackfeather placed his hands upon her cheeks and jaw. His touch, that of the undead, was cold, but in his eyes a mirthful fire burned. Ramona knew without seeing that the pattern of his hands was white and perfect upon her dirty face. He bade her sit, then he sat as well, across from her, on the far side of the small teepee.

The silence that had come with Blackfeather when he first appeared was thicker now, heavier. Though the quiet was not so heavy as the sky and stars, Ramona didn't know if she could speak if she tried. So she merely sat and watched.

Blackfeather, wearing a slight smile beneath his sagging felt hat, produced from his sack a silver Zippo lighter. In one motion, his long thumb flicked open the cover and spun the tiny wheel. His thumb traced a white line through the darkness, and the whirring of the metal wheel slowed to one hundred individual clicks. A six-inch flame leapt to life and pounced almost instantly on the teepee. The crackling of the dry sticks filled Ramona's ears.

The world beyond the circle was black against the dancing fire. Ramona vaguely remembered the others there—Ratface, Edmonson, Stalker-in-the- Woods—but maybe they weren't there any longer. She and Blackfeather were as alone as if they sat on the surface of the moon or at the bottom of the ocean.

Ramona tried to look at the old man's laughing eyes, at his white teeth, but her gaze was drawn to the flames that danced so close to her. She knew deep inside that she should fear the fire, just as she feared the sun. No one had ever told her as much, but she had naturally shied from fire since the change. Now it was very close. She should slide back, not sit so close, but her fear was numb and weak. She was so tired, her body, her mind…so tired.

Then she realized that Blackfeather was speaking to her. She strained to see his face through the flames and the rising smoke. Though he spoke in a low voice—he did little more than mumble under his breath—the sound carried to Ramona, but for some reason beyond her grasp, she couldn't untangle the words. They reached her ears but didn't proceed to her brain. She thought at first that he spoke a foreign tongue, maybe the language of the Cherokee, but she could fix in her mind not a single sound that he uttered. The words dissipated as soon as they touched her awareness, like smoke upon the breeze. Ramona heard, but she didn't hear.

So intent was Ramona on deciphering Blackfeather's mutterings, she didn't notice at first that he had fallen silent— the words seemed to continue with their own life, swirling upon the smoke that now clung close to the stone rather than rising skyward—or that he was calmly scooting around the fire toward her and dragging his canvas sack behind him.

The smoke, hanging low, grew thick, and shortly Ramona couldn't see much beyond the chalk circle. She tried to remember exactly what or who she expected to see beyond the smoke, but her thoughts were as elusive as Blackfeather's chant. Details of the outside world were less substantial than the gently churning smoke that almost formed a wall around Table Rock.

Blackfeather was at her side now. Reflected in his eyes, she could see the white handprints on her face glowing in the firelight. He turned his sack upside down, and one after another several small items trickled out onto the stone between them. It was an odd collection: a plastic egg, like from a child's Easter basket; a bent and rusted butter knife; a snakeskin; a small, mostly empty plastic bottle of Visine; and two sticks of chewing gum in blank, white wrappers. Blackfeather stopped the egg from rolling away, then regarded silently the former contents of his sack. He rested his chin in his hand and didn't move for several minutes.

Ramona tried to pay attention, but her mind was wrestling with the chant, which seemed still to echo from the stone, and with the smoke that obscured all beyond Table Rock.

Finally, Blackfeather shifted from his contemplative pose. He reached down and took in his hand the two pieces of gum. One he offered to Ramona. She took it and watched as he, with focused, deliberate motions, unwrapped his piece. Then, bending the gum in half, he placed it in his mouth and began to chew. The wrapper he crumpled and tossed into the fire. That done, he returned his enigmatic gaze to Ramona.

She could only guess his wishes. Slowly, she began to unwrap her piece of gum. Neither seeing nor hearing any objection from Blackfeather, she placed the gum in her mouth with the same reverence she'd once witnessed in people eating communion wafers at a Catholic mass. Ramona folded the stick exactly as Blackfeather had, and chewed. The gum was sickly sweet. Ramona grimaced. She'd grown used to the more bitter sweetness of human blood.

Blackfeather, apparently satisfied, returned his attention to the remaining items. He picked up the snakeskin, tore it in two, and handed one of the foot-and-a-half lengths to Ramona. The thin veil of brown and gray scales was rough against her skin, not slimy as she had always expected a reptile should be.

Blackfeather placed his half in the flames, still licking vigorously at the teepee. Ramona did the same with her portion and the skin was quickly consumed.

Next, Blackfeather took the tiny bottle of Visine. He held it in front of his face and squeezed so that a single drop fell to the ground before him. When he handed it to Ramona, she mimicked his actions, except when she squeezed the bottle, several drops shot out and splattered the stone. She turned the bottle upright so quickly that she fumbled with it and nearly dropped it.

Aghast at her own clumsiness, she looked warily to Blackfeather. She had no idea what kind of ceremony or spell he was performing, but she was sure she'd just ruined it. She half expected the flames from the fire to leap up and consume her, or the smoke to close in and suffocate her—never mind that she didn't breathe anymore.

But Blackfeather only shrugged and nodded toward the fire. Hesitantly, Ramona tossed the bottle into the glowing coals. The last of the liquid hissed away amidst the pungent odor of melting plastic.

Blackfeather picked up the egg next, but then he stopped and a strange expression crossed his face. Before Ramona could translate the odd pursing of his lips, he turned his head and spat his wrinkled ball of gum into the fire.

Ramona turned and did the same with hers.

"The flavor never lasts very long, does it?" said Blackfeather.

Ramona stared blankly at him and blinked. They were the first words he'd spoken since arriving, and amidst all this strangeness that he'd set in motion, he was worried about old chewing gum. Ramona opened her mouth, which despite the gum was dry and tasted of smoke, but had no idea what to say.

The old man took no notice of her befuddlement. He opened the plastic egg and took out a hard, gray mass that looked a bit like a larger version of the chewed gum. The two halves of the egg he tossed into the fire, and again the smell of melting plastic was apparent. The mass from inside the egg he handed to Ramona.

She recognized instantly the consistency and texture,

even the faint smell, of the malleable object. She squeezed and kneaded it. *Silly Putty.*

"You got a Slinky in that bag too?" she asked with a wry smile.

Blackfeather cocked his head and stared at her in complete and silent puzzlement.

"You know...." Ramona tried to explain, her smile fading. "It's fun for a girl and a boy...?"

But Blackfeather's puzzlement, if anything, grew deeper.

"Uh...sorry." Ramona held up the age-hardened mass of Silly Putty and pointed to the fire. Blackfeather nodded, so in it went.

All that remained was the rusted butter knife. Blackfeather took it and, using the crook of the bent utensil, scraped a pile of coals and ashes from the diminishing fire. Ramona instinctively cringed as he did this. She could handle sitting relatively near the fire, but reaching a hand in among the flames was a different matter altogether.

With the knife, he crushed the few coals he'd gathered that were still red. Soon, the pile consisted purely of black and gray ash. Blackfeather continued to stir the ash for some time. Finally, he raised his face and met Ramona's gaze, but where before she'd seen laughter in his eyes, now she saw only sadness.

"The Final Nights are at hand," said Blackfeather, holding Ramona's gaze despite her sudden desire to turn away, "and your road will be a difficult one."

Ramona tensed. His words spread terror through her, not because she understood them, because she did not. But she felt the truth of what he said.

Blackfeather set the knife aside and scooped two handfuls of ash. He leaned toward Ramona, raised the ash toward her face. She wanted to pull away, to run screaming from this prison of chalk and smoke. She wanted to run back to her mortal life, to the way life had been before. But none of those things were possible.

Ramona couldn't even close her eyes as Blackfeather pressed the handfuls of ash into them.

The ash, though still warm, did not burn. Ramona could

see nothing, but she could feel the Beast, like a volcano beneath the surface, rising up within her. She could feel how it filled her, how it destroyed every shred of anything else inside her. She could feel, too, that it was loose in the world as well. The hunger that dwelt within her, that dwelt within her sire, and her sire's sire, all the way back to the first spilling of human blood, that hunger was no longer contained within them. It was risen. It roamed free. And it would consume them all.

The Final Nights are at hand.

The warmth of the fire was gone. A fierce chill gripped Ramona's soul. Her very core was cold and dead.

She reached out for comfort. She fled from the cold, from the hunger. Thankfully, she found warmth, surrounded herself with it.

But still she could not completely shake the cold that gripped her.

Sunday, 25 July 1999, 12:14 AM
Barnard College
New York City, New York

On this, his fourth night of observation, the particular side
door on the academic building opened for the first time
that Anwar had seen. Instantly, he was totally alert, transcend-
ing even his normally high level of vigilance and entering the
hypersensitive state where duty and faith merged and were one.
The individual who emerged from the side door was
unimpressive. He was tall, blond, thin, and dressed casually,
as any other *kafir* might be. Anwar suspected that this was his
contact but held his place. The sign he'd been told to expect was
unreceived.

The thin man surveyed his surroundings: the trees that
could give cover; the small, well-lit mall area between buildings;
the building by which Anwar stood, cloaked in shadows both
common and preternatural.

He is looking for me, Anwar thought. *But if he is the one, why
doesn't he give the sign?* Anwar was aware of no onlookers or
obstacles that might delay contact. He, however, had the
advantage of having been secreted in that spot for several hours.
Perhaps the thin man was merely being cautious.

Then the man's scanning gaze stopped on Anwar—stopped
on and *saw!* Anwar was sure of it, though the man gave no other
indication that he had seen the lurker in the shadows. Anwar
instinctively drew more deeply into the dark as a chill ran the
length of his spine.

At the same time, the thin man held his right hand before
him, palm upward, and in the blink of an eye, a low flame

burned atop the man's hand. He'd struck no match, raised no lighter, yet a flame danced upon his open palm. Then, as quickly as the flame had appeared, it was gone, and his hand was empty again. Anwar knew that anyone else observing the brief glint of flame would doubt what he'd seen, would convince himself that he was mistaken in his impression. Anwar himself would have doubted his own eyes...had the flame not been the sign he was awaiting.

Now that the time had arrived, Anwar hesitated momentarily. His impulse was to cling to the shadows and skirt the mall area between the buildings as much as possible, yet if the contact had not made proper arrangements to ensure the success of the mission, there was little Anwar could do at this late date—little except meet his end with dignity. Though uncomfortable relying on a *kafir*, he placed his faith in his elders. Deciding against an indirect approach that could consume vital seconds, Anwar strode slowly but purposefully across the open ground. He watched for any sign of danger, of betrayal—it was not yet too late to escape should the mission fall apart or the *kafir* prove untrustworthy—but no disruption greeted him.

"I am Aaron," spoke the thin man. He did not try to hide the fact that he was of the get of Khayyin. Aaron's skin appeared delicate and pale. His fingers and face were tight and frail-looking, too much so for his apparent youth.

Anwar nodded. In the cloudy blue eyes, he saw a disturbing mix of pain and resignation. He had no knowledge of how it was that his own elders had come to hold power over this warlock, or how one of the hated Tremere would have become indebted to the children of Haqim—rumor abounded regarding the unbreakable bonds of blood among the warlocks—for Anwar had no reason beyond idle curiosity to possess such information. His earlier concern, however, remained with him—his unease over relying upon a *kafir*, especially one who had obviously given himself to despair and undertaken a foul betrayal of his clan, a deed he could not hope to survive. How could one such as that be trusted?

May Haqim smile upon me, Anwar besought the blessing of the elders' elder.

"Follow me," said the *kafir*. "Stay close."

Anwar did so. They entered through the side door and proceeded down a narrow corridor that would be out of the way for any student or faculty member of the college. Anwar suspected there might be black magics that would deflect the intentions of any mortal who wandered this way. What other Tremere spells protected this chantry? he wondered.

The corridor led to a heavy oak door with frosted glass and the painted words: ASSOCIATE DEAN OF INTERDEPARTMENTAL ACADEMIC DISCIPLINARY REVIEW. Anwar imagined that the title was vague, bureaucratic, and ominous enough that any student or professor accidentally stumbling past the Tremere defenses would be stymied by the conviction that she either had no business with this office, or earnestly desired to have no business there.

Aaron harbored no such reservations. He inserted a normal enough looking key into the lock and led Anwar inside. Anwar expected to step from the drab, collegiate environment into a stronghold of splendor and debauchery befitting the sinister genius for which Clan Tremere was known—the children of Haqim hated the vile warlocks, but did not underestimate them. Instead, the office beyond the forbidding door was as drab and nondescript as the preceding corridor. A desk, filing cabinets, and a few chairs were the only furnishings.

Aaron remained silent. Perhaps he did so for reasons of safety, or perhaps, overwhelmed by his personal despair of mysterious origin, he simply had nothing left to say. Two gray robes lay draped across the desk. Aaron took one and indicated that Anwar should don the other.

"Speak not a word beyond this point," Aaron said to Anwar when they both were robed.

Anwar nodded. He had not spoken yet. He supposed he could survive without conversation a bit longer. He took in every detail of his surroundings, but whatever Tremere defenses he might have passed through so far, they were of such a subtle nature that he could not detect them. Perhaps his elders in their wisdom, hearing his exacting description of what he saw, would unravel mysteries that were hidden to him.

But no sooner had that thought crossed his mind than he saw the first evidence of sorcery since the flame had sprung from nothingness in Aaron's hand. The warlock placed his hand upon the only other door in the tiny office and muttered a few words beneath his breath.

Anwar felt his skin tingle momentarily as the words were spoken, but he couldn't be sure if the tingle was actual or merely the power of suggestion. Aaron opened the door and revealed stairs leading downward and plain, concrete walls. Would the door, Anwar wondered, have led to a closet or another room had the warlock not exercised some spell, or was the display merely deception, completely for Anwar's benefit?

But why, Anwar wondered further, *should he guard the warlock secrets...if he truly betrays them?*

It was a question Anwar could not answer. Not yet. He kept close to Aaron as they began down the steps.

Sunday, 25 July 1999, 12:31 AM
Chantry of the Five Boroughs
New York City, New York

Johnston was unsure of the passage of time in the outer world. From deep within the trance, he experienced the alternating sensations that barely an instant had passed and that several mortal lifetimes had swept by. He was at the same time fascinated and appalled by this consciousness—the *other*—to which the gem had taken him. For however long he'd been occupied with the task, he'd explored that psyche and mapped it out in his own mind. When again he surfaced, he would possess a wealth of information, and as of yet he had barely scratched the relationship between the gem and the fractious, hopelessly insane mind. There were many other questions to be answered. Foremost among them: Why? Why had the gem led him to this being?

As Johnston had contemplated the inner workings of the discovered consciousness, his physical body had not remained idle. His fingers had taken quill and ink and rendered on parchment the physical likeness to which the consciousness was attached, a likeness that not even Johnston, himself submerged within the landscape of the mind, had beheld. But the impressions from such a thorough investigation could not be mistaken, even with the muscles directing the quill directed themselves by Johnston's subconscious mind *in absentia*. Flawlessly, he'd sketched the face of the other.

His endeavor, however, would be of little use to any except himself, would not be visible to anyone else, in fact. Such was the nature of the quill Johnston's fingers worked and the enchantments he had laid upon it. To an onlooker, his scratchings upon the parchment would appear merely that, as if the ink were nothing more than water and left no mark. It was one of the few tiny vanities Johnston afforded himself, this right of first perusal in order to modify possibly substandard results. He would present to his superiors nothing less than finished, polished work. There was no cause for his precaution this time, though. The presence of the other was so palpable, so strong—nearly overwhelming— that Johnston knew the ink would flow unerringly from the quill. His rendering of the other would be perfect.

Secure in this knowledge and still enmeshed within trance, Johnston did something that normally he would not do. While maintaining the continuous chant that, in a sense, fueled this exploration of the other, he introduced the strains of a lesser incantation, which he skillfully intertwined with the ongoing chant. The maneuver was not overly complicated; it was not so difficult that a warlock of Johnston's expertise would have trouble. And indeed, he did not. Though he did not yet see it, he knew that his handiwork was at that very moment taking visible form on the parchment beneath his hands and quill. When the ritual was over, when he withdrew from the psyche of the other, the sketch would be waiting for him. He would not need to perform the minor ritual separately later.

Johnston briefly contemplated ending his current exploration, retreating again within himself; he'd accomplished a great deal, and certainly there would be further experimentation with the gem. But a nagging question still puzzled him.

Twice while taking measure of the insanity before him, Johnston had felt something odd—that an additional presence was at hand, that he and the consciousness were not alone. Someone else, or something else, was touching the mind of the other. In both instances, Johnston had traced the strand of awareness in question, the mystic fiber of mental reality, only to follow it into a tangled thicket of tortured personality. He'd resisted entering too deeply, but still he'd had the impression that another consciousness— or perhaps the shadow of another consciousness—was present. The impression could have been caused by the echo of multiple personae within the insanity itself, Johnston knew, but he decided to poke one last time into one of the tangled masses he'd found before. Then he would emerge from the trance.

To his amazement, he not only discovered the foreign presence almost immediately, he recognized it at once. The patterns were disturbingly familiar. How could he have not seen them before? Not one of his clanmates would have failed to identify the source—the source that should not have been there, that should not have been anywhere!

Johnston's surprise, the tensing of his muscles, jolted his concentration. For the first time in many years, he faltered in his ritual. His mouth did not form the next words, which should have been automatic. Almost instantly, he regained his composure, took control of the ritual that had nearly gone astray. Rather unceremoniously, he dropped the minor incantation, the ritual of revelation he'd begun within the larger, more significant ritual, but that was no great loss.

At once, Johnston's fingers went to work with the quill. The sound of the feather's tip scratching rapidly across the parchment entered his awareness. Ink flowed without visible effect. With renewed patience and calm, he depicted that which he'd discovered. It would not take long. Then he would emerge from the trance and go straight to Sturbridge with this startling news, potentially dangerous news, that could not wait.

But something was wrong.

Johnston was slowly surfacing, but the scratching of quill against parchment no longer sounded in his ears, nor did his steady chanting. His lips still moved, he formed the arcane words of power, but no sound disturbed the air.

That was when he felt the impact of the blade. With one precise, forceful jab, it severed his spinal cord. He felt his face crash against the surface of the table. The collapse of the ritual pained him far more than the physical attack. The mystical energies he'd controlled turned on him, bore into his soul none too gently, exacting a stiff price for his having bent them to his will. The psychic anguish almost masked from him the draining of his lifeblood.

Almost. So quickly it went...quickly....

Then nothing.

The warlock, deep in trance, had no opportunity to save him-self. Anwar's ferocious thrust-wrench with the *katar* was one fluid motion, and the *kafir* struck the table like a fallen tim-ber. Anwar was on his victim and drinking deeply before the eyelids ceased their fluttering.

Sustaining, fragrant vitae.

Hadd. Vengeance.

For five centuries, the children of Haqim had languished under the curse of the Tremere, had been unable to partake fully of the Path of Blood as prescribed by the elders' elder. But now the second fortress, Tajdid, was reclaimed; there would be payment in full for each hour of each century. Anwar had struck but a single blow, had taken but a single step along the road of the *hijra.*

But how sweet the blood.

There was little time to bask in the deed. New strength flowing through his veins, Anwar glanced at Aaron. The Tremere, his discomfort apparent, gawked at the body of his clansman.

Have you no stomach for blood? Anwar wondered. Or perhaps it was the focused brutality of the act that unnerved the Tremere. But surely he had known.

Aaron had led Anwar through the labyrinthine corridors of the chantry beneath the college, pausing only occasionally to mutter an incantation or to stare intently into the air at something Anwar could not see. Anwar loathed the traitor's weakness, but he still needed him to provide safe passage out of this place. They had worn the robes that Aaron had provided, but they had passed no one else. Anwar had not removed his robe until Aaron removed the protective wards on the last door that had led to these chambers and the cramped laboratory.

Anwar had cloaked himself only in silence, as he had been taught to do. His silence had been potent, even to the point of interrupting his victim's barely audible chanting. Anwar hadn't anticipated that, but it pleased him. *He knew! Yes, he knew!* At the end, the entranced Tremere had known that his blood was forfeit. Anwar was sure of it. Else there would be no justice.

Even before the blood had flowed completely down the back of his throat, Anwar reached for the gem. He had no need of the chest, and though certainly there were other items of power in the warlock den, his directions were explicit. He wrapped the red and black stone in a cloth and tucked it within his sash. Then he pulled on the robe again and, with another nod to the skittish Aaron, they were on their way.

They retraced their steps. Of that, Anwar was sure. But Aaron stopped at points not necessarily identical to those where they'd paused on the way in. The impression made on Anwar was one of an elaborate system of mystical defenses, varying perhaps in the response each required depending on the direction from which an individual passed. There were other possibilities. Anwar didn't know if the cloak he wore contained sorcerous properties, if it was merely a ruse to deflect visual detection, or if some other variable came into play. He was at a loss to deduce the inner workings of the Tremere defenses. That being the case, and escape otherwise impossible, he remained close on the heels of the warlock Aaron.

When they ascended the steps to the drab office, Anwar was still operating on heightened guard. It was not too late for some devious trap to be sprung, for a gaggle of warlocks to swoop down upon him and carry him back into the depths of their chantry.

Walking down the corridor toward the building's side door, Anwar's heart lightened slightly—he was past the point where the *kafir* had warned him not to speak—but still he was vigilant.

They stepped out of the building at long last. The summer night air, humid and carrying the stench of the city, was refreshing nonetheless.

"Your superiors will be displeased," said Anwar, speaking to the Tremere for the first time.

"Yes," nodded Aaron glumly. "I suppose they—"

With one graceful step, Anwar maneuvered and looped his garrote over the Tremere's head. The wire dug into the warlock's neck, sliced through trachea and jugular. A sharp increase and change of direction in pressure and the head and body fell separately to the brick sidewalk.

This is likely a mercy compared to what your clansmen would have devised for you, Anwar thought. But more than mercy, it was justice.

Hadd.

Anwar slipped away into the night with the gem for which he'd been sent, and another step along the road of the *hijra* was taken.

Monday, 26 July 1999, 12:00 AM
Upstate New York

*N**ever come from the ground without knowing who— or what—is there.* That was what Tanner had told her.

Fuckin' bastard, Ramona thought. But she remembered.

Table Rock was unmistakable, and several people were nearby, most of them familiar to Ramona. She wasn't concerned. As she rose out of the ground, she remembered other things that Tanner had told her:

Know that you are Gangrel. And that I am your sire. I made you what you are.

The night air, even on the outskirts of the Adirondacks, was cool. As always, Ramona felt for a moment a distinct sense of loss, of vulnerability, as she emerged from the comforting embrace of the earth. She saw right away that she was on top of Zhavon's grave. She had been *in* Zhavon's grave. Not really in it, Ramona corrected herself, but a part of it. She felt eerily calm. It was a feeling she wasn't used to experiencing—not for years now.

Brant Edmonson was standing with Mutabo and Joshua Bloodhound. They were less than ten yards away at the edge of the woods. Ramona saw Snodgrass—she thought that was his name—approaching the group with two new faces. They must have arrived since she'd gone to ground. She glanced at her watch and was surprised to see that she hadn't risen until midnight, several hours after she was usually up and about.

Other shapes moved among the trees farther out from Table Rock. Ramona wondered about Stalker-in-the-Woods. She hadn't seen him since Edmonson had bested him. Stalker, she imagined, would be one to hold a grudge. At least it wouldn't be against her—unless he resented her witnessing his embarrassment.

He shouldn't be embarrassed about gettin' beat in a fair fight, she thought, but she had her doubts as to whether Stalker-in-the-Woods would see it that way.

Ratface was not far away. In fact, he was coming toward her. He'd been less communicative since the others started showing up. Not that he was being unfriendly. Ramona didn't feel like he was snubbing her, but he'd dutifully made the rounds and greeted each new arrival, and that hadn't left much time for him to talk with her. She supposed that for someone at the bottom of the pecking order, which as far as she could tell Ratface seemed to be, it was beneficial or maybe even expected for him to ingratiate himself to as many elder Gangrel as possible.

Ramona didn't yet have a clear idea of how all the interactions among the Gangrel worked. She did know, however, that she wasn't about to lick anybody's boots. If that's what they wanted from her, they could kiss her ass.

But then she remembered the uneasy feeling she'd gotten from being too close to Stalker-in-the-Woods, and the way Tanner had struck her before she'd even seen him move. She might not always have a choice, she realized, about how or to whom she paid respect. And she'd probably already pissed off a whole bunch of people by arguing with Edmonson.

"Ramona," said Ratface as he approached, "you are with us." He seemed relieved to see her.

Ramona just nodded. Of course she was with them. He looked at her expectantly but said nothing else. Ramona quickly grew irritated with his staring.

"What?" she asked him at last.

Curiosity instantly overwhelmed Ratface's obvious hesitancy to pry. "What happened? What did he say?" he asked, rubbing his grubby little hands together. "Everybody wants to know. You didn't surface last night. We didn't know if you were coming back."

"What?" she asked again, but this time out of genuine confusion rather than aggravation.

And it all came home to Ramona. *Blackfeather. The fire.*

She quickly looked around, but there was no sign of the old man—only scattered ashes and the remnants of a few charred sticks on Table Rock.

"He's gone," said Ratface. "He left right after you went into the ground. Didn't say a word to anybody... anybody else, that is. Only to you. That was night before last." Ratface was looking sideways at her, like he suddenly didn't know if he should trust her completely. Ramona wasn't sure if she could trust herself.

Until Ratface had asked her about it, the entire ritual, Blackfeather's very presence, had been like nothing to her, like they'd never happened. But she knew that they had. Ramona falteringly raised her fingers to her face. She touched her cheeks, her nose, her eyelids. Her fingers came away caked with hardened ashes. Ratface, still unsure how to respond to her behavior, watched intently as she brushed the ashes, and the underlayer of chalk, from her face.

"Everybody was watching," said Ratface, "but nobody really saw what happened. The smoke got thick. It was like you weren't there. It was...odd."

Odd, thought Ramona. That was one way to put it. She was afraid she didn't have a better explanation than Ratface did.

The oblivion of resting nestled in the earth seemed to cling to her still. She'd noticed before that she wasn't always at her sharpest when she rose from the earth, that sometimes the details of whatever had happened immediately before her descent the previous morning were foggy at best.

But this seemed different somehow. Ramona wasn't sure how, but it was. The whole experience with Blackfeather had been so weird. *Odd*, as Ratface put it. "That was last night," Ramona said at last, correcting Ratface's mistake.

"No," he insisted. His rodent-like nose protruded so far that the tip moved a great distance when he shook his head only slightly. "Two nights ago."

Ramona glanced down at her watch. Sure enough, the LED readout showed: *7/26 Mo.* Ratface was right. She hadn't just stayed submerged until unusually late in the night; she'd stayed submerged all through one night and then well into the next!

"What did he say?" Ratface asked nervously, prying against his better judgment, but prying nonetheless.

Ramona was stunned by how long she'd slumbered. Without thinking, she answered: "'The Final Nights are at hand.' That's what he said."

She had no idea what the old man had meant, but the words seemed to have an immediate effect on Ratface. His eyes grew wide, and he eased away from Ramona as if she'd pulled out a gun and was going to blow his head off.

"The Final Nights..." Ratface muttered.

"Hey..." Ramona was jolted back from her contemplation by Ratface's alarmed reaction. She grabbed his arm and kept him from retreating any farther. "The Final Nights—what the hell is that supposed to mean?"

Ratface stared at her, as uncomprehending as Ramona was, but his confusion was of a different manner and passed almost immediately. The light of realization softened his expression.

"I forget—it's all new to you," he said in way of explanation. "The Final Nights are when the eldest of our elders, the Antediluvians, will rise from their torpor and destroy all the rest of us, their childer."

Ramona stared back at him. "What kind of answer is that? Ante-who?" she asked. "What the hell are you talkin' about?"

Ratface grimaced at her impatience. "Antediluvians—they existed before the Great Flood. You have read the Bible?"

"Yes. Fuck you," said Ramona, annoyed at his implication that she was stupid or illiterate. The truth was she personally had read next to none of the Bible, but she knew the stories well enough.

Ratface's grimace deepened. "Do you want to learn, or do you want to argue?" he asked. "To learn, you have to listen."

Ramona turned her back on him and sat by Zhavon's grave. "You're the one who came over here askin' me what the old man said." She thought about what else Blackfeather had said: she didn't think the remark about the chewing gum was worth repeating, and the part about her road being difficult was none of Ratface's damned business anyway. But something about what Ratface was trying to explain made her uncomfortable, tugged at the tightness in the pit of her stomach. She wasn't sure that she *did* want to learn. Maybe this was something better not to know.

The Final Nights are at hand.

Ratface misinterpreted her silence and continued: "The Antediluvians were the third generation of our kind from the Dark Father. There were thirteen of them. That's what the legends say, anyhow."

"And they gonna show up and kill the rest of us?" Ramona asked.

Ratface nodded. "That's what the legends say."

"If there's only thirteen of 'em, why don't we just kick their ass when they come around?"

Ratface's mouth dropped open at the suggestion. "They're... they're like gods. They're thousands of years old. You don't just kick their ass...asses."

"Hmph," Ramona snorted. "Whatever."

The contentment she'd felt upon rising from the earth was gone without a trace, shot to hell. Ratface was telling her things that she probably needed to know, but that she felt she didn't want to know. She was sitting beside Zhavon's grave, and again the heavy weight of guilt was beginning to press down upon her. Add to all that, she'd just found out that she'd slept through an entire night—in itself not a great loss. To Ramona, some of these other Gangrel seemed way old, *hundreds* of years old, so she figured missing one night wasn't that big of a deal. But she hadn't meant to do it, hadn't even known that she'd done it, and that left her uneasy.

And what about Darnell? she thought. Not one but *two* more nights had gone by, and Tanner didn't look to be back yet. Ramona knew she should be upset that no one had done anything for Darnell, but she was so tired, too tired even to be angry. She wondered briefly if Darnell had outlived her hope for him, but mostly she was just tired. The pull of the grave, the attraction of not rising from the peaceful embrace of the earth, clung to her.

Ramona glanced back over her shoulder at Ratface, who was standing with his hands on his hips and watching her.

"Do you sleep through a whole night sometimes?" she asked, trying to sound casual, to keep the worry out of her voice. Ratface shrugged. He seemed nonplussed by her sudden change of topic. "Sometimes. Not often. Some of the elder Kindred go into torpor—a deep sleep like that. It can last for nights, or months, or years. The Antediluvians are supposed to have been in torpor for millennia."

"Supposed to have been..." Ramona muttered.

"No one knows for sure—if they are, or where their resting places are," Ratface added.

Ramona repressed a shudder. *He just won't shut up about them Antediluvians,* she thought, and she'd heard more than enough about them already. Ramona turned away from him again and sat silently. She wanted him to go away, and he'd already proven that the simplest question would just keep him talking— and probably about the damned Antediluvians. But he just stood there, pawing at the dirt and making her uncomfortable.

"Don't touch the fuckin' grave," Ramona said, without turning to see if that's what he was actually pawing at.

"There's Emil," Ratface said at last. "He must've just arrived."

Ramona heard Ratface scuttle away. She was glad to be alone again, but she felt a little guilty about driving him off like that. Of all the Gangrel she'd met, he more than any other had tried to be helpful to her. He probably deserved better treatment. But then again, Ramona deserved a hell of a lot better than what she'd gotten. Besides, she didn't want to hear any more about the damned Antediluvians.

When's Tanner gonna get back? she wondered.

She was tired of waiting. He'd said he was going to get others—a lot of others were here. Ramona could see more new arrivals whom she hadn't met or heard introduced—the two with Snodgrass, a handful of others, and those were only the ones she could see from where she sat. Probably Ratface could have filled her in on the identities of everyone gathered, if she hadn't run him off.

As Ramona looked around, she noticed that none of the other Gangrel met her gaze. Edmonson and his group looked away and pretended that they hadn't been watching her. Their conversation suddenly lagged.

They were talkin' about me, she realized.

Renée Lightning looked away as well, and others. They looked at her differently, thought of her differently, after Blackfeather's visit. They had no idea what had happened either, but they regarded Ramona with suspicion and a little fear now. She could see it in their eyes, in the way each held him or herself.

Fuck 'em, she decided. Ratface was the only one of them that had any guts. She hoped he got some brownie points for talking to her.

Ramona hugged her knees to her chest. She wished Tanner would hurry up and get back. Then they would go kick the Toreador's ass. *Maybe we can save Darnell,* she thought, but she didn't hold any real hope. She'd seen what the Toreador had done to Zhavon, and what had happened to Jen—stone that hadn't been there shooting up through her body and taking her head off. Ramona didn't see how Darnell could've held on this long. She felt guilty about that too—that she didn't know for sure that he was dead. But it wouldn't have done any good for her to go back alone, she reminded herself. She just would've gotten killed too.

She remembered the fear in Tanner's eyes. He knew that the kidnapper, the thing with the eye, was something beyond even them, and Tanner would know that a hell of a lot better than she did. She had to trust his judgment on that point.

Thinking of the kidnapper, Ramona couldn't help but picture the grotesque bulging eye. She had stared into it and almost lost herself, would've lost herself if Tanner hadn't showed up and snapped her out of it. And that was after the damn thing had sprayed her with…what, acid? She could feel the burned-out gouge on her face that hadn't healed— even with all of Zhavon's blood—and her T-shirt was falling apart and full of holes where that crap had burned through.

They're like gods, Ratface had said about the Antediluvians. *You don't just kick their ass.*

Ramona's memories tugged at the churning in her stomach like the moon pulls at the oceans. Could the Toreador be one of the Antediluvians? she wondered. She hadn't thought that anything would scare Tanner, but that thing with the eye had. But if it was one, could even all these Gangrel hope to kill it? Not according to what Ratface said. But probably others knew more than Ratface, Ramona told herself. Surely Tanner knew more than Ratface did. Her sire was just more closed-mouthed about it.

She sat by herself as the night passed and tried to get a handle on the disturbing mix of guilt and fear. Her chest began to ache like her stomach had, and not from having had a wooden stake jabbed through it—although Ramona couldn't imagine that had helped very much. The physical wound was healed completely. No sign remained.

Others were still arriving at Table Rock. How many, she didn't know. She didn't really try to keep track anymore. She vaguely heard more ritual introductions, but she didn't catch any names, and no one came to greet her. Either she was too new a Gangrel to bother with, or the paranoia of those who'd seen her with Blackfeather was contagious. Ramona didn't care. She was just as happy to be left to her worries. She sat silently beside the grave that had been her resting place the night before.

Occasionally, Ramona heard a scuffle and snarls from the woods nearby. After the first time or two, she didn't even bother to turn and look. As more Gangrel arrived, some wanted to find where they stood in the pecking order, or to challenge someone that had bested them at a previous meeting. The commotion never lasted long, and Ramona doubted any serious injuries resulted. It seemed more sensible than the gang fighting in L.A. that she'd seen, where the losers, as often as not, ended up dead.

She didn't see Stalker-in-the-Woods out there, but she could imagine him trying to kick the ass of every newcomer he couldn't stare down. And she wouldn't have been half surprised to find out he'd done it.

But neither Stalker-in-the-Woods nor any of the others Ramona had met nor any of the newcomers messed with her.

Monday, 26 July 1999, 2:18 AM
Upstate New York

Ramona was thinking about Blackfeather when she noticed that Table Rock had grown completely quiet. She was thinking about the few words the old man had spoken, and of the strange ritual he'd performed—at least she thought it was a ritual of some sort. It had seemed that way; it had *felt* that way. In fact, everything connected to Blackfeather, including Ramona's reactions to him, was grounded in *feeling*. Ramona didn't *know* anything about him, except the little Ratface had said. She didn't *know* anything about what the old Cherokee had done. Lord knows, Blackfeather hadn't explained anything. He'd just done whatever it was he was doing, and she had been drawn along by the sparkle in his eyes, or maybe it was something about the smoke or the old man's mysterious chanting that had prodded Ramona to follow his vague lead. Everything she'd done had been based on what she'd felt, not what she'd known. And now he was gone, and she was left with her feelings but didn't *know* anything more than when he'd arrived.

She thought of the casual perfection with which he'd ground and spread the chalk—not a granule falling out of place, a perfectly round circle with the fire exactly in the center. And the fire itself, the small teepee, had burned just as long as necessary without needing to be fed or tended to even once.

She thought of Blackfeather's canvas sack, of the haphazard assortment of items he'd dumped onto the stone between them. The objects looked like they'd been scooped up out of the gutter: a discarded bottle of Visine, a snakeskin, a dull, rusted knife. *Silly Putty and chewin' gum, for God's sake!* Ramona shook her head. Was it supposed to make sense?

That question was the focus of her thoughts when she vaguely realized that something was wrong. She drifted back from her remembrances to the sound of...nothing. Again, the Gangrel present—and there must've been fifteen or twenty by now—had fallen silent, as when Blackfeather had arrived. Had the old man returned? Ramona looked up hoping to see him, hoping that he might answer some of her questions.

Instead, stepping onto Table Rock were two figures, one of whom she recognized immediately—Tanner. She knew from what the gathered Gangrel had said that her sire had traversed a goodly portion of the state—many of them had come from near Buffalo—but Ramona never would've guessed that from looking at him. He didn't look tired. He stood with the same confidence and poise that Ramona remembered. Maybe he was slightly more disheveled from his significant travels; maybe his dark sweater was picked a bit more than it had been, but there was no great change in his bearing. In his left hand he held a dangling rabbit. Maybe it was a hare; Ramona didn't know the difference. It was long and, unlike the rabbits Ramona had seen in pet stores, not very furry. Tanner held the creature by the ears. The head was twisted almost completely around, and blood dripped from claw wounds in its chest.

Tanner stood a step behind another Gangrel. Ramona had never seen him before, but for some reason she connected him to a name she'd heard some of the other Gangrel whisper in near-awe—Xaviar. They had speculated that he might come, that the action would get started in earnest once he was with them.

Ramona could see that Tanner regarded Xaviar with that same reverence, and it was an attitude she was as surprised to read in her sire's posture as she had been his fear in the cave. It was jarring to see that he was afraid of anything, and almost as much of a jolt to see him pay respect to anyone. She wondered how he would react to Brant Edmonson—as an equal? And what about Stalker-in-the-Woods?

But there seemed no impetus to establish dominance, to refine the pecking order, now that Xaviar was present.

Everyone, it seemed to Ramona even in those first few instants of seeing Xaviar, knew where they stood in relation to him, and they wouldn't risk displeasing him. He stood well over six feet, and was completely in black leather—vest, long pants, boots—a costume that Ramona would've thought presumptuous on most, but there was nothing phony about Xaviar. His hairline had fully receded, but long, red hair hung to the middle of his back. The same red lined his jaw as a prickly beard, and was sprinkled along his chest. Where his skin was visible—arms, chest, neck, face, forehead—it was tanned and leathery. He seemed to have taken to piercing: a ring in his nose, a half dozen studs and hoops in his left ear, a few less in the right. Ramona's earlier resentment of Gangrel elders dribbled away weakly. She knew she wouldn't cross this man.

Tanner tossed the rabbit onto the rock, casually discarding the carcass. It landed amidst a cloud of ash from the remains of the fire. He had hunted the animal and killed it, probably without even breaking stride. It held no further interest for him.

Now Xaviar stepped forward. The dead rabbit lay at his feet. He ignored it, and his gaze fell on Ramona. For an instant, he casually took note of the grave she sat next to, but his stare came to rest on her.

Ramona slowly rose to her feet. She felt weak, awkward.

Xaviar looked down at her from Table Rock. At his feet, the rabbit's blood was mixing with ash. As Blackfeather had done the night before—*two* nights before—Xaviar acknowledged no one but her. Ramona wished that he would go talk to some of the others, or maybe kick Stalker's ass. But Xaviar's gaze bore down on her.

How long has he been around? Ramona wondered. *How many people has he killed?* She felt suddenly protective of Zhavon's grave next to her. Not that she expected Xaviar to root around and dig up the body like Ratface would have. Probably a dead mortal meant no more to Xaviar than did the rabbit at his feet.

"You have seen the thing that Tanner has told me of," Xaviar said to her. Though he didn't raise his voice, his words were strong as thunder. He stood over Ramona like a storm that, at any moment, could unleash its fury.

Ramona nodded. She could feel Tanner watching her, all the others watching her, but she couldn't take her eyes from Xaviar. "Tell me what you saw," he said.

His gaze gripped Ramona, took hold of her as surely as if he'd reached out with his hands and grasped her by the shoulders.

Tell me what you saw.

Ramona felt the words pouring from her mouth. She heard herself, as if a bystander, tell him about the cave. She heard the revulsion in her voice as she described the horrid eye, how it had sprayed acid on her, how it had entranced her, and only Tanner's intervention had saved her. She heard the heartbreak in her voice as she told of the injuries done to Zhavon, so great that the girl could not have survived. Ramona heard herself tell how the creature with the eye had twisted flesh and bone as if they were no more than hot wax, and how the very floor of the cave had attacked poor Jennifer, had mangled her body, ripped off her head.

The words poured like water through a broken dam, and in the end they left Ramona empty and sickened. The full sorrow of two years rose to fill the emptiness. She dropped to her knees and retched blood onto the dirt. Her human life had been taken from her. Jen and probably Darnell had joined Eddie in death. Her few friends, those who had shared the horror of this new existence with her, were gone. And Zhavon was gone, though her blood flowed through Ramona's veins. The mortal girl had been caught up by an unavoidable current that had swept her away, much like what Ramona had gone through.

She faced those responsible—Tanner, and now Xaviar, who had bent her to his will. Ramona tried to spit the foul taste from her mouth. They would control her if she let them…if she couldn't stop them.

She could feel when Xaviar finally looked away, turned his gaze from her. He turned to Tanner and nodded, as if confirming something they had already discussed.

Ramona wiped her mouth on her tattered sleeve and looked up at the two elders on Table Rock. "Is it an Antediluvian?" she asked weakly. The churning in her stomach had taken over while the words had flooded from her mouth. It was the same sensation, only stronger, as when Ratface had told her about the eldest of the elders, and it had driven her to that conclusion.

Xaviar looked back at her again. He seemed slightly surprised, maybe amused, that she'd spoken to him of her own volition. "No, childe," he said with his quiet-thunder voice. "And shortly it won't matter *what* it is." He turned back to Tanner and prepared to ask a question.

"He called himself 'Toreador,'" said Ramona. Her voice was stronger now. The churning was receding slightly.

Surprised laughter erupted from around the clearing, but then the Gangrel seemed to remember themselves and in whose presence they stood. The laughter quickly died away. Ramona looked around blankly, too confused by the reaction to feel annoyance or ire.

Xaviar tensed. He turned back to her and cocked his head. "He called himself...*what?*"

Ramona's blood turned to ice in her veins. Tanner's eyes grew wide for an instant, then narrowed to a cold glare. Silence stretched across the clearing, into the forest.

"Toreador," she repeated. Ramona forced herself to hold Xaviar's gaze, not to look away.

"You are sure?"

Ramona nodded. She didn't understand the reason for Xaviar's sudden vehemence. Having fought to hold his gaze, she now found that she wasn't able to look away.

"Tanner?" asked Xaviar, still not freeing Ramona from his increasingly perturbed glare.

Tanner stared at the ground. "I...I hadn't heard this," he tried to explain. "It called the stone, and the stone answered. It twisted flesh like...like a Tzimisce fiend!" Then he turned angrily to Ramona. "You didn't tell me this," he accused her.

"Did you give me a chance?" she shot back. "Did you give me a fuckin' chance to tell you anything?" Instantly, she knew she shouldn't have said it, that she wasn't *supposed* to have said it. It wasn't her place. In a way, she didn't care. Tanner deserved a good tongue-lashing, or more. But she was afraid of what Xaviar might do.

What he did was smile. But it wasn't a warm smile, or jovial. "I might have expected this from a whelp, but not from you, Tanner—to bring me here with a small army of Gangrel to destroy a lone Toreador."

Tanner was staring at the ground again. He offered no defense.

"No matter," said Xaviar, watching Ramona as if he'd been speaking to her all along. "Do you know what Toreador is?" he asked her.

She shook her head.

"Of course not," he sighed, not unsympathetically, but his expression changed rapidly, became fierce and bestial. "It is the *weakest*, the most *pathetic* clan of the children of Caine."

If Xaviar's enthusiasm for the hunt, or that of any of the other Gangrel, was at all diminished by Ramona's revelation, he didn't show it. He raised his fists into the air. Savage growls rose all around the clearing.

"It begins!" he snarled, as he leapt from Table Rock and almost directly over the cowering Ramona.

Tanner followed Xaviar's lead without hesitation, and Ramona, caught up by the ferocious snarl, was on their heels in an instant. Xaviar began southward toward the cave, but he quickly veered to the east. His forceful strides took him in a wide loop around Table Rock, and the other Gangrel fell in behind him. The air boiled with their snarls. Among the howling chorus, Ramona heard her own voice, a single strand woven together with like strands of her brethren.

They were on all fours and moving more quickly for the second loop. Ramona was not far behind Xaviar and Tanner. Brant Edmonson and Joshua Bloodhound pressed near her on either side. Their claws dug into the rocky soil, threw sparks when they struck stone. Among the pack, many Gangrel had shed their human forms altogether. Large wolves, some black as midnight, others gray as dusk's last light, wove through the trees at dizzying speeds.

During the third circuit around Table Rock, the landscape itself changed. The slopes of the foothills grew more rugged and steep, mountains in their own right. The trees became towering sculptures of gray bark and multi-hued lichen and mosses—green, blue, red, black. Ramona realized that the churning in her stomach had vanished. The rising fury of the hunt had crumbled and scattered the pain of loss that had assailed her for so long, the grief that she had not been without since her mortal days. Racing through the transformed landscape, she could not help but be transformed herself. She was a lone wolf, giant, ferocious and slavering. She was alone, yet the others were with her. They were of her, and she of them, united in their kinship—the same kinship she had seen in the sparkle of Blackfeather's eyes.

The Final Nights are at hand, and your road will be a difficult one. Blackfeather's words. But had he spoken to her as she'd been, or to her as she was now? Were the words for Ramona alone, or for the larger collection of which she was merely a part? She felt the fire he'd created burning within her. She could smell the smoke. And she, the lone great wolf, saw the world with the ghost sight he had given her. Blackfeather had pressed the ritual ashes to her eyes, and now she could see.

Alone yet never more complete, she ran through the forest primeval. There was only the hunger and the hunt. Saliva ran over her fangs, dripped from her mouth.

They completed the third loop of Table Rock. Xaviar veered south again. The Gangrel all raced after him. Ramona could feel them all around her. More than she'd thought had come. Their slaver smelled of frenzy, of carnage, of death.

Toreador. Ramona's thoughts kept time to her footfalls. *Weak. Pathetic.*

There would be blood for blood. *Jen. Darnell. Zhavon.*

Amidst the press of her clanmates, Ramona could taste vengeance, and for the first time in two years, she embraced the future with gleeful anticipation.

Monday, 26 July 1999, 3:09 AM
Upstate New York

Ramona expected Xaviar to address the Gather, to discuss plans or give out assignments. But as the assault commenced, everyone seemed to know what to do. Everyone except her.

The raucous stampede near Table Rock had quickly fallen to silence as the Gangrel approached the meadow, and the ghost sight had receded, allowing Ramona her normal view of the world. She guessed now that there were twenty-five or thirty of her clanmates involved in the attack. Some circled around either side of the meadow. Apparently, Xaviar and Tanner were among those. Ramona had lost track of them and didn't see them nearby.

She hung back with several others near the ridge opposite the cave opening across the meadow. She wasn't far from the spot where she'd gone to earth three nights before—the same spot where she'd put an end to Zhavon's life. Ratface was near. Snodgrass and Renée Lightning were there. Joshua Bloodhound and three others Ramona didn't know were off to her left. No one spoke. The entire assault seemed to be orchestrated by instinct, although Ramona was relieved to see some of the others glancing about looking for guidance as well. Following Joshua's lead, the eight concealed themselves several yards up the hill toward the ridge, with just enough elevation that they could see the cave entrance across the way.

Ramona barely had time to wonder what would happen next before she saw Tanner and four others—she recognized Emil among them—entering the meadow at the far end and edging toward the cave. She concentrated and listened for any sound of their passing. Although they were a fair distance away, she'd heard smaller disruptions from farther since her change. Already, she barely noticed the once-strange sensation of her ears pricking up as she listened. This time, however, she couldn't pick out any telltale sound. Tanner and those following him moved skillfully, silently. Ramona suspected that, had they been worried about anyone seeing them, she might never have known when they slipped into the cave. As it was, she and Ratface and the others on the ridge did see as Tanner's assault party achieved the unremarkable stand of pines at the opening, and then disappeared into the darkness.

Within moments the silence grew unbearable.

Ramona felt like she was holding her breath, not that she *breathed* anymore, but the urgency and the need for silence tapped into certain distant memories, made her feel that she was doing something she shouldn't. But then her thoughts shifted to Tanner and the four Gangrel with him. She thought of just a few nights before when she, Darnell, and Jen had snuck into that cave…and what had happened.

But this was *Tanner*, she reminded herself. He was infinitely more experienced than she was with the deadly vagaries of this world of darkness, where death was such a casual and frequent occurrence. And he was with other old-hand Gangrel. They would take care of the business that Ramona and her friends had bungled.

What would she do, she wondered, if Tanner came out with the Toreador as a captive? He'd probably want her to strike the final blow. That would be just like Tanner. And though there was no question that the Toreador had to pay for Zhavon, for Jen, Ramona didn't know if she could kill in cold blood. Since arriving at the meadow, the fury of Xaviar's run, of the loops around Table Rock, had largely evaporated, giving way to memories and fear.

Maybe Darnell's still alive, she hoped. He would rip off the Toreador's head without a second thought, and Ramona wouldn't be faced with that decision.

All the uncertainties, all the questions of two years were

penned up within Ramona. They all wanted release, as she crouched on the hill not needing to hold her breath. The screams that broke the silence were almost a relief. They echoed eerily through the entrance of the cave, then filtered through the pines and gained release to the night.

But the screams were not those of the Toreador.

Everyone around her pricked up instantly. Ramona couldn't distinguish the cries one from another—the sounds were hopelessly muddled by the time they reached her—but she recognized attack snarls abruptly cut off, cries of surprise and pain.

"My God," said Joshua Bloodhound. "What's happening?"

Ramona did not answer him—her mouth was too dry, her jaw locked; words could not pass the lump in the back of her throat—but she knew.

The chaotic screams and the muffled sounds of combat went on and on. A fight at close quarters rarely went on for more than a minute, Ramona knew. Maybe no more time than that had passed, but it seemed like forever. Like those around her, Ramona was standing, though she hadn't meant to rise from her hiding place. Uncertainty gripped them all. She could feel the others looking one to another. Should they charge the cave? Surely Tanner didn't need help. But the sounds from within…

And Ramona couldn't help but remember….

The noise of struggle was growing, if not fainter, less confused. Fewer combatants were adding their voices—their snarls, their grunts, their screams—to the cacophony. Another strain of sound joined the din, however—low, drawn-out wails, moans of those in pain, moans of the dying. Ramona's mind was racing furiously, but at the same time getting nowhere. She tried unsuccessfully to refuse the conclusions that thrust themselves upon her: If the struggle continued, the Toreador was still alive; at least some of the screams and moans must be those of Gangrel, of her clanmates.

But the moans, one by one, fell silent. First one voice then another lapsed, and almost as suddenly as it had been shattered before, silence returned. The slight breeze coming down off the ridge seemed thunderous to Ramona's straining ears.

They're stalking him, Ramona thought. *He's hurt, and they're closing in for the kill.*

But just then, a figure stumbled out of the cave and put the lie to Ramona's optimism. He grabbed hold of one of the scrawny pines at the entrance and leaned against the tree for several seconds. It was Emil, Ramona saw. He didn't rest long. He heard something, glanced back into the pitch-black tunnel, then turned and fled. He tried to run, but something was wrong with his left leg. It wasn't holding his weight. He staggered, then tumbled down the incline before the cave. As he climbed back to his feet, Ramona saw that his face was blackened and burned. She absently raised a hand to the gouged scar on her own face.

There was little time for distraction, however. Out from the cave stalked the Toreador. He looked around for a moment, as if the existence of a world beyond the subterranean tunnels and caverns surprised him. Even from across the meadow, he seemed larger than Ramona recalled. The eye, too, his left eye, seemed larger—or maybe *only* the eye was larger. It appeared to glow in the starlight. It throbbed and twitched, looking somehow like a living thing, quite separate from the rest of the body around it.

As had been the case three nights earlier, Ramona viewed the Toreador with mixed reactions. At first glance, he seemed innocuous enough—he was scrawny, and had a big nose, and could anybody with hair that bad really be dangerous? *Art fag,* ran through Ramona's mind.

But then he would turn, and the eye, that hideous eye, cast him in a different light. Suddenly he was larger than life, deadly, terrifying.

Probably the Gangrel around Ramona were struggling with similar impressions. In a way, it seemed almost laughable that this particular vampire could pose a threat. But Jen wasn't laughing.

Nor was Emil.

The Toreador's disorientation was brief. *That was our chance,* Ramona realized, but it was too late. Something terrible had happened in the cave, she knew, but perhaps the close quarters had worked to the Toreador's advantage. He couldn't know what waited for him out beyond the pines shielding the entrance. The eye fixated on Emil. Even with a distance of several yards between them, the Toreador seemed to tower over the fallen Gangrel.

Watching Emil, a paralyzing question gripped Ramona: *Where's Tanner?* He'd led the group into the cave, but so far only Emil had emerged, and him beaten and burned. Suddenly, even among the other Gangrel, Ramona felt completely alone and afraid. *Where's Tanner?* she wanted to shake Emil and shout at him. *Why did you leave him inside?*

"He's yours," said Ratface, next to Ramona, but his words were for Emil. "That's right...let him get closer...now spill his guts!"

Emil had risen to his knees, and the Toreador was indeed moving closer, but Ramona could tell that the Gangrel would not strike a blow. She could see the tension in his stance; she knew that he wanted only to flee, but he wouldn't manage even that. The eye kept Emil's will from directing his muscles, just as it had done to Ramona. Tanner had been there for her. "My God," muttered Joshua. The others stared in silent disbelief.

With a few strides the Toreador closed the distance to Emil and, without hesitation, grasped the immobile Gangrel by both sides of his head. Seconds later, Emil's head no longer existed. It melted and oozed away between the Toreador's fingers. The creature, its throbbing eye casting about more than should have been possible, stood with blood and liquid flesh dripping from its hands.

The Gangrel around Ramona were shocked beyond words. To a person, their eyes or mouths or both gaped wide in astonishment. Ramona had seen something similar before— Zhavon deformed almost beyond recognition, Darnell's arms stretched from their sockets—but even she gawked in horrified fascination. For the second time that night, she felt the need to retch, tasted blood rising in her throat. But there was no time.

"Look!" Ratface was the first of their ineffectual band to find his voice. He pointed across the meadow toward the cave. From two directions, groups of half a dozen or so Gangrel were charging from the trees and bearing down on the Toreador.

What took 'em so damned long? was Ramona's first thought. Had they, like she, watched in rapt horror as Emil had died? Or like Ratface, had they underestimated the Toreador and expected Emil to finish the affair with the single swipe of a claw?

Not until Joshua ran yelling down the hill did Ramona realize that she should help as well. She'd been expecting Tanner and the self-important elders of her clan to take care of this problem—but they didn't know what they were getting into, and now she was being dragged again into the fray.

Ramona and the others followed Joshua. They had no specific plan, but they couldn't simply stand by and watch; they sped down the incline and raced toward the Toreador. With the first step, however, Ramona felt that she was moving in slow motion, that the scene was unfolding before her, and that she was plucked from it to become merely a spectator. For the second time that night, the ghost sight descended upon her; it was an unnerving filter laid over her hyper-alert senses. Unlike before, she felt no unity with her clanmates, but was filled only with dread.

Ahead, the Toreador's back was to the cave entrance. To his right was the closest group of Gangrel, led by Stalker-in-the-Woods. His blood was up, and there was nothing about him that looked human. He propelled himself forward on all fours; his face was a monstrous, fanged snout. Frothy strings of spittle trailed from his mouth.

More Gangrel charged from the Toreador's other side. Edmonson was in the fore, with Mutabo on his heels. Their easy manner of before was gone. Murder shone in their eyes. They saw no need for stealth and cut a rapidly advancing swath through the tall meadow grass. To Ramona's shifting vision, her clanmates were blurs of motion, golden sparks trailing fiery comet tails in their wakes. No creature could stand against so many Gangrel.

Despite the odds, Ramona's sense of dread only deepened.

Your road will be a difficult one.

The three converging packs of Gangrel drew closer to the Toreador, but Ramona's knees buckled as the immensity of the ghost sight struck her full force. She stumbled, lost ground on Ratface and the others. For a moment, she thought she was blacking out, so overwhelming were the sprays of color and light. The muted blacks, blues, and grays that had come to be her darkened world were replaced with illumination brighter than that of full day. The stars in the sky above burned with the intensity of countless suns. The nearly full moon loomed almost close enough to touch.

Ramona staggered. She reeled. Firm footing eluded her. She was forced to choose each step with care. Around her, a battle was unfolding, and it was her duty to take part—she was one of the reasons it had come about. But she had to look so hard to make sense of the ghost sight. The creatures around her assumed bestial forms—some wolven, others like badgers, or mountain lions, or feral dogs. But they were her brethren; a fact reinforced when her vision flickered, and she saw them again in more human guises. Ramona touched her face, touched her eyes, and her fingers brushed over the residue of dried ash and chalk.

The Final Nights are at hand.

Ramona looked around, almost expected to see the old man Blackfeather, but the meadow was filled only with grasses and wildflowers and creatures of death. She cast her newfound vision toward the Toreador, and immediately wished she hadn't. It was all she could do to resist the urge to turn and flee.

As she watched, the Toreador grasped its protruding eye and wrenched it from its socket. A bloody, fibrous nerve from the rear of the eyeball pulled free of the socket and flailed about in the air like a blind eel. As the Toreador raised the eye above his head, the nerve continued to twist and writhe. It wound around and down his arm. At the same time, the tendril stretched and grew longer—more than a foot, two feet and on—until finally it contacted the ground and began to burrow.

It all seemed to happen very slowly. *Why aren't they on him?* Ramona wondered of the other Gangrel, but in fact they were not much closer than they'd been just before. Those of Ramona's own group were only a few steps ahead of her, though she felt she had first staggered some time ago.

Again her knees buckled, but this time, she realized, not her knees but the very *earth* was shaking. The Toreador loomed increasingly large in her sight—no, not larger, she saw but *higher.* He was rising into the air. A massive protrusion of stone, a rounded hill unto itself, thrust up from the earth and lifted him many feet above the floor of the meadow. The tendril from the Toreador's eye wriggled like a frantic leech as it bore into the stone. It turned ruddy and dark, then swelled until Ramona thought it must burst.

Stalker-in-the-Woods must have seen the erupting monolith, but he did not ease his headlong gait, nor was his murderous intent deflected. Then the Toreador turned the eye to face that closest group of Gangrel. Instantly, a stone spike shot up from the earth, and Stalker-in-the-Woods's own momentum carried him full onto the tip. Ramona flinched—images of Jen flashing through her mind—as the spike carried him off his feet. Dangling above the ground, he jerked spasmodically as blood from the tip of the spike ran down from the top of his head.

The Gangrel with him rushed past his twitching corpse. Two met a similar fate within a few steps.

With each deathblow, Ramona staggered as if the stone had struck her own body, and though Stalker-in-the-Woods was already beyond even his death twitches, she saw an ephemeral vision of him as he lifted his monstrous face to the sky and howled defiantly: *I am Stalker-in-the-Woods. I die for my clan this night!*

In the same way, from the two others who shared Stalker's fate, she saw and heard that which before would have been hidden from her:

I am Ronja. I die for my clan this night!

I am Peera Giftgiver. I die for my clan this night!

The remaining three Gangrel who'd begun with Stalker paused as a wall of rock erupted directly in their path. The first of the trio, a visibly muscled woman, launched herself onto the wall and began to scurry up it. The other two had not yet reacted when the earth fell away beneath them. Just as suddenly, the wall and the woman on its downward face toppled over into the pit. The screams were crushed out of the trio within a few

seconds, but their unvoiced final cries rang in Ramona's ears:
I am Louisa... I am Crenshaw... I am Bernard Fleetfoot... I die for my clan this night!

Ramona's steps slowed to match the tempo of the litany.

At almost the same time, nearly a dozen stone megaliths, irregularly shaped columns jutting at random angles, rose from the ground to the other side of the Toreador. Edmonson and the second collection of Gangrel, moving more cautiously than their unfortunate clanmates, wove their way among the newly sprung pillars. Mutabo was the most careful. He slowed and circled wide of the stones; he watched closely for spikes rising to claim him and megaliths toppling to crush him.

The Toreador turned his eye to those Gangrel now. His face was etched not with animosity but with a businesslike grimace. Ramona thought also that she saw madness in his normal eye. How could such an abomination *not* succumb to madness?

Ramona, strangely detached from the scene, was struck by the vivid hues of her clanmates' sacrifice— crimson blood draining along the impaling pikes, pale flesh tones of vampires drained of unlife, sickly gray skin of the Toreador, veiny orb held aloft with its gelatinous ooze and ruddy, pulsating nerve. She knew in that instant that no one else saw what she did, that no one else could. For them the night sky and the stars were as they'd always been. The impossibly bright stars, the light of day itself—these were for Ramona alone, for the ghost sight Blackfeather had imparted to her.

There was more that was hidden from the others, she realized. She saw the brilliant light of the stars mirrored in the Toreador's pulsing eye, in the throbbing nerve that connected the orb to the stone. As Ramona looked on, the megaliths themselves, a stone garden of giants, began to glow from within. Their earthy grays and whites and browns began to burn a fiery red, and more megaliths rose across the meadow. The other Gangrel did not see, could not see, the change in the stones, did not see that the megaliths grew opaque, that within them churned thick fluid-red and orange, the very stuff of the earth itself. Edmonson and Mutabo and the others still made their ways toward the Toreador. They regarded the megaliths warily, but no differently than before.

Ramona tried to call out to them, but the battle was a dream unfolding before her. She saw more clearly than they did, but she could not stop them.

The first explosion knocked her to the ground. The eardrum-shattering force shook the entire meadow. The fiery earthen magma within the erupting megalith spewed into the air.

In the next few seconds, another megalith ruptured, and then a second, and a third. Giant dollops of volcanic material erased Mutabo's head and left arm. Another Gangrel near him stared in disbelief as she fell to the very spot that, a moment before, the lower half of her body had occupied.

I am Mutabo. I die for my clan this night!

I am Lisa Strongback....

I am...

Everywhere, the megaliths were glowing red and exploding. Ramona could see the fire within each stone churn and boil, then force its way out and across the sky in a blazing streak. All around her, Gangrel died. Their burnt and mangled bodies flew into the air and landed, to move no more. But the fallen called out in silent voice, and the litany of the dead grew longer:

I am Aileen Brock-childe....

I am... I am...

I am Brant Edmonson. I die for my clan this night!

Their cries were of defiance. Even in Final Death they did not yield to the enemy.

Ratface and those who'd begun on the far hillside were close to the Toreador now. Renée Lightning outpaced the rest. Hundreds of droplets of magma splattered against her, ate through her flesh. A megalith ruptured, spewing lava in magnificent arcs. Snodgrass disappeared on the far side.

Ramona stumbled. She couldn't keep up. Her hair smoldered in the heat. Each step was a struggle of will in the face of all that she saw—*all that she shouldn't see.* The ghost sight revealed too much; it might as well have blinded her. It liberated her and shackled her. She could see their approaching doom but could not negotiate reality well enough to save them.

I am Renée Lightning....
I am Snodgrass....
Ramona dropped to her knees. She was so tired. The knowledge that she had failed her clanmates drew away her strength. She'd been given the means to save them, maybe to lead them to victory, but she could not wield the ghost sight. She knew she should have been able to do something. *Damn Blackfeather,* she thought, more in resignation than in anger, as she sat numbly and waited for the spray of molten rock that would bring her painful life beyond death to a close.

Smoke hung heavy across the meadow, but through the haze Ramona saw the Toreador atop his small mountain of stone, with his eye and its obscene, throbbing nerve. He seemed heartened by the destruction of the Gangrel, and he seemed also to orchestrate the carnage with his gruesome eye. He held it in his hand still, and every direction he turned it, a megalith annihilated another Gangrel, or a pit opened beneath one of Ramona's clanmates.

I am Jacob One-ear....
I am Nadia....
The monster with the eye was not all-seeing, though. He didn't see Xaviar spring from the steep hillside above the cave entrance. The leather-clad body was a meteor of hope to Ramona; his red hair trailed behind like a tail of the spewing magma. Ramona had sudden premonitions of victory: She saw the Toreador fall beneath Xaviar; she saw the grotesque eye dashed to the stone and smashed in a spray of foul pus and fleshy matter.

But Ramona's brief vision was of hope, not of the ghost sight, and reality did not bear it out.

Xaviar did strike the Toreador square from behind, but the Toreador stood solid, as if he were embedded into the very rock beneath his feet, as if he were an extension of it. Xaviar, expecting his target to give way beneath him, fell roughly to the stone.

Land on the nerve! Ramona hoped. *Yank the eye out of his hand!*
But then an explosion jarred the ground beneath Ramona's feet. One second she was witnessing the duel between Xaviar

and the Toreador, the next she saw only a blur of motion and flashing streaks of fiery magma. Everything went black.

Distant stars.

The next Ramona knew, she was staring at the night sky. It took her a moment to realize she was lying on her back. She'd been struck by the explosion and knocked to the ground. Almost relieved that consciousness must surely fade, she reached down to learn what part of her body had been ripped or burned away. To her surprise, she was fairly intact. She'd been struck, not by molten rock, but by Ratface. He stared up at her blankly. Smoke rose from the edges of the gaping hole in his chest, and blood and tissue still sizzled from the heat.

I am Ratface. I die for my clan this night!

Ramona eased out from beneath him and lowered his body gently to the ground. More than any of these other Gangrel, Ratface had tried to be a friend to her, but there was nothing she could do for him now. She expected to join him in Final Death at any moment. His name among those of the litany was jarring to Ramona. She'd become aware of the chant with the onset of the ghost sight. The litany continued, yet the ghost sight, she realized, was gone. The night sky was again the night sky: the stars burned as they should; the moon, bright but unremarkable, was low on the horizon. The ghost sight was gone.

Ramona wasn't sure how long she'd blacked out. She looked back to the mound of stone where Xaviar and the Toreador battled, and whatever stubborn vestige of hope that might have survived this long withered within her. Xaviar was still upright, but at a very odd angle—the reason was readily apparent. Stone spikes, called from the surface of the mound, pierced him. They held him aloft. One spike protruded from the top of his right knee. Another had caught him through the biceps; his left arm was raised uselessly in the air. One foot barely touched the surface of the mound. He couldn't free himself. The Toreador, only a few feet away, moved closer to the helpless Xaviar.

Ramona slumped back down to the charred ground. The tall grass that had covered the meadow was mostly burned away. The few remaining Gangrel had long since broken ranks—although the entire battle couldn't have taken more than a few minutes—and were running, but the rupturing stones still spewed deadly lava into the air. Another explosion sent tremors across the meadow. Joshua Bloodhound lost his footing and stumbled headlong into one of the pools of molten rock that were growing numerous.

I am Joshua....

But above the litany spoke another voice: *Get up Ramona. Keep going.*

Ramona collapsed onto her back. She wanted nothing more than to stare at the stars until the rising lava closed over her, but the voice would not leave her alone. It was soft, pleading. *You have to get up, Ramona. Get up. Keep going.*

She raised her head and saw a dim figure standing very close to her amidst the acrid smoke and mist. Her eyes were watering heavily, but she thought she saw... "Jen?"

Ramona rose to her elbows. The smoke grew thicker and crowded down nearly to the ground. There was a figure before her, but it was no longer Jen.

Lying down when some bug-eyed mother needs his ass kicked?

Darnell, Ramona thought. He was there when he couldn't be, whole of body, just as Jen had been. They were taking their place among the litany of the dead.

Ramona began to climb to her feet. "I don't recall *you* kickin' his ass," she muttered at Darnell, but Darnell was no longer with her.

Don't give up, Ramona.

Ramona froze halfway up. She touched a hand to the ground to steady herself. Something stirred within her, some part of her that wanted to answer the voice, that wanted to answer Zhavon.

Don't give up.

The girl stood before Ramona, beautiful, unmarred. She spoke again, and her voice was less gentle. She practically scolded Ramona: *Don't you give up.*

Ramona smiled and rose to her full height, only to find herself alone by Ratface's smoldering body. Fresh pangs of loss tugged at her, but she had regained her bearings, and the situation did not allow her to mourn.

The megaliths had stopped rising at last, so the explosions were fewer and more predictable, but the meadow was rapidly becoming a pool of lava, as more magma blurped up from the ground. Soon the blazing sludge would cover the entire expanse between the hills. There were still many oases of solid ground, like the slight rise on which Ramona stood beside Ratface's corpse, but as the red lake slowly rose, the islands were becoming fewer and farther between.

On the mound, the Toreador remained beyond the reach of Xaviar's flailing right hand and the claws that could yet prove fatal. Then suddenly to Ramona's amazement, the creature abandoned his caution and stepped closer. Only now did Ramona realize that the Toreador was no longer holding the eye in his hand; the pulsing orb was back in its socket, more or less. She wondered for a split second if their enemy had actually taken hold of the eye—or was Ramona's seeing that way a trick of the ghost sight? But there was no time to consider the question. The Toreador stepped closer to Xaviar.

"Kill him!" Ramona screamed at Xaviar, and was startled by the sound of her own voice cutting through the dense smoke and echoing from the exposed stone. "Kill him!"

Xaviar was more than close enough, but he could no more defy the will of the eye than had Emil, or had Ramona. The Toreador grasped Xaviar's pinned arm and began to exert pressure. The limb bent and kept bending—not at the elbow or wrist or shoulder where it should, but in the middle of the forearm. The Toreador pressed slowly and steadily, meeting less and less resistance. The arm twisted like flimsy pipe cleaner.

Xaviar grimaced in pain. He clamped his teeth together until blood trickled from his mouth, but he didn't cry out.

Having found her own voice, Ramona finally felt volition return to her body, but she was separated from the Toreador and Xaviar by a moat of lava that was too wide for even her to leap. She pawed at the ground, advanced to the edge of the molten river, but there was no crossing.

The smoke and steam were so thick now she could only make out figures on the mound, but if she couldn't aid Xaviar, maybe it was better not to see. The Toreador would kill

Xaviar—melt away his skull, or pick the limbs from his body—or maybe the monster would merely toy with Xaviar, like a cat with a wounded bird.

And if the magma didn't claim her, the end would be the same for Ramona. Behind her a lone, crippled Gangrel, a dark-skinned woman, crawled toward the edge of the meadow, but every avenue of escape was now cut off by the bubbling inferno. Distorting ripples of heat played games with the smoke. Megaliths, no longer rupturing, stood like giant tombstones. Ramona turned back to the mound, ready to meet her end at last.

The Toreador wrapped his fingers around Xaviar's neck. Ramona waited for Xaviar's flesh to melt away, for his head to loll at an impossible angle. But instead, the Toreador *lifted* Xaviar—lifted him with such strength that Xaviar slid up along the spikes. The sound of bone grating against stone sent chills down Ramona's spine.

The Toreador lifted Xaviar free of the spike and held him aloft by the neck. The fight was gone from the Gangrel leader, or perhaps he was still mesmerized by the eye. He hung limply in the Toreador's grasp.

Ramona watched helplessly for the final blow, but then suddenly the Toreador flung Xaviar like a ragdoll. His body appeared weightless as it sailed airborne over the pools of lava; it never should have gone so far—Ramona couldn't imagine the strength of the throw—but finally Xaviar crashed to the solid earth not far away. She ran to his side. He gazed at her, confused. He looked down at his mangled arm and leg, then up at Ramona, as if questioning how he'd gotten to this state.

Ramona turned toward the Toreador, prepared to shout her defiance at it—*I am Ramona. I die for my clan this night!*—but just then, the smoke cleared. Not all over, but enough that Ramona could see the Toreador clearly—and he her. Viscous fluid dripped from the eye and streamed down his face. The final cry caught in her throat, as the eye took possession of her will. There was no Tanner to save her this time. There was no one. There was only the eye, and it was forcing her...*to run.*

Ramona turned and ran. She immediately fell over Xaviar.

Almost without missing a step, she slung him onto her back and continued her headlong flight.

She had failed her clanmates, she'd resigned herself to death, but she couldn't stop her legs from carrying her away from that eye. It was sending her away, discounting her as a worthy opponent, and she was of no mind to argue. Without slowing, she cast a fearful glance over her shoulder. The eye had turned from her as the Toreador surveyed its victory. Then the smoke closed in again, and all that was visible was a vague shape on the mound—and a glow radiating from the eye through the gloom.

Ramona caught up with the woman she'd seen crawling before. There was nowhere for her to go. Bubbling, molten rock blocked every avenue of escape. But as Ramona closed to within a few yards, the woman, much of her body covered with burns, jumped out over the rising lava. Ramona stopped in her tracks.

Suicide, she thought—not a far-fetched idea at this point.

But then Ramona saw the arc of the Gangrel's leap and the small islet among the magma where she would land—close enough to the edge of the meadow that a second jump might lead to freedom.

When the Gangrel landed, however, her feet and legs punched through the topsoil, revealing the islet to be a flimsy coagulation of dirt and weeds that had been raised up rather than covered over by the lava.

The woman was too shocked to scream, but the pain was clear on her face as she sank to her knees in the magma. The illusory island was broken apart by the force of her landing.

Ramona could think only of the woman's flesh and bones melting from the bottom up. Her thighs sank under. Xaviar moaned; his mouth was mere inches from Ramona's ear. There would be no escape. For any of them.

But the silent woman caught Ramona's eye, and unspoken understanding passed between them. Without hesitation—if she'd thought, she'd have faltered—Ramona leapt.

The fumes from the lava burned as she passed over. If she'd miscalculated even a few inches or badly compensated for Xaviar's weight, it would all be over quickly. Ramona seemed to hang in the air, to move more slowly than physics would allow.

She crashed down onto the shoulders of the other Gangrel. Her impact drove the woman down to her chest. Ramona paused only a fraction of a second to regain her balance, then jumped again.

She sailed over the magma, and when she and Xaviar landed, it was on the solid earth where the meadow began to rise—not far from where she'd crouched with Ratface and the others, what seemed impossibly long ago.

Ramona looked back one last time, but the woman was gone, pushed under by Ramona's second leap.

I am Maria Evernorth. I die for my clan this night!

Ramona shifted Xaviar's weight, then turned toward the hill and ran.

Even after she'd crossed the nearest ridge and was beyond the reach of the moans of the dying and the odor of smoke and charred flesh, Ramona couldn't keep from her mind the images of carnage she'd seen that night. No matter how hard she ran, she couldn't outdistance the likenesses of burned and mangled bodies. With each step, Xaviar's weight was more a burden. She stumbled through the forest as if blind. The darkness surrounded her, thick and heavy. Her normal night vision seemed to have fled like the ghost sight before it. No light from above penetrated the canopy, and she imagined that each tree, each dark shape, was a megalith pregnant with hellfire, having thrust its way to the surface. Every sound was the Toreador tracking her down. But the eye, if it were near, would cast its sickly light.

Fatigue, as well as darkness, enveloped her. Her run slowed to a labored jog, then to a staggering gait. The Toreador could have her if he caught her, she decided. The exhaustion was of spirit as much as of body. She had emerged from the slaughter—but even her state of relative wellbeing was torment. It was proof that she had failed her clanmates, else how could they be dead while they survived? First Eddie, then Jen, Darnell, and now...how many others? Even Xaviar, who survived, was crippled. Ramona had only a rough idea of how many Gangrel had gathered, and how many had died. She didn't remember seeing any others escape, but the meadow had been so full of smoke and fire and death....

She continued on aimlessly, with no goal in mind more

significant than avoiding the nearest tree. Initially heading east over the ridge, she must have veered to the north, because her steps soon carried her to a familiar locale.

Ramona wasn't sure how many minutes she'd been standing and staring at Table Rock before her mind registered where she was. She laid Xaviar on the flat stone. It was noticeably cool after the hellish inferno they'd just escaped. He lay there, stunned and beaten, moving only to cover his face. His skin was splotchy with burns, but most telling was the left arm that hung useless at his side. Already, some of the damage done by the spike had begun to heal, though Ramona wondered if even the power of blood could repair completely that jagged wound. It was horrible to look upon, but less so than what remained of the lower portion of his arm. Below the elbow, his forearm turned in several impossible angles, not broken and shattered like the wound above, but *reshaped*—whole, yet bent one way and then another back on itself in a crude semblance of an S-curve.

Ramona didn't know if any other Gangrel had escaped. She thought that all those she'd met were dead. But there might be a few others who'd managed to get away. She guessed that they might return here if they could. There had been no instruction to that effect, but there had been no instructions about much of anything that she could remember. The Gangrel seemed to function through instinct more than order, and it seemed a natural thing to come back to Table Rock. *Is that why I'm here?* she wondered. *Instinct?* She hadn't meant to come there; she hadn't meant to go anywhere.

Fighting the pounding at her temples, Ramona walked over to the heaped dirt just beyond Table Rock. She stood above Zhavon's final resting place and reached within for the pain of that loss. But she couldn't feel it. All she saw was a heap of dirt. Ramona tried to picture Zhavon's face as she'd seen it in her vision before, to remember the sensation of holding the girl to her chest, but the Gangrel could see only a throbbing, malevolent eye. She could feel only the hollow spot on her cheek where the acid had burned deeply.

Ramona had seen her dead. The ghost sight had accomplished that, if nothing else. But did that mean that she was free of the pain of their loss, or robbed of it? The feelings that should have been there were fading and growing foreign to her. *Zhavon.* She could say the name, but she could not climb from the pit of numbing indifference. Ramona pawed at the dirt with a monstrous clawed foot. What was the death of one mortal girl compared to the horrors she'd seen tonight, to the horror her existence had become?

The pounding at her temples grew stronger. It took on the aspect of rhythmic drumming, not too unlike what would once have been the beating of her heart. Ramona clamped her palms to her head, but the pounding continued, grew louder. Hammers striking her skull, until she could stand it no longer. Then quickly order emerged from the din. And Ramona recognized the litany demanding release.

"I am Eddie," she said weakly. "I die for my clan this night.

"I am Jen. I die for my clan this night."

From somewhere miles behind her, Xaviar moaned, but her voice grew stronger.

"I am Darnell. I die for my clan this night!

"I am Stalker-in-the-Woods. I die for my clan this night!"

Xaviar moaned again. He growled. Ramona turned and saw the anger in his face, but she was not silenced.

"I am Ronja... I am Peera Giftgiver... I am Louisa. I die for my clan this night!"

"*Silence!*" Xaviar commanded her through teeth clenched in pain. With his one good arm, he dragged himself across the rock. "Stop, damn you."

"I am Bernard Fleetfoot... I am Crenshaw. I die for my clan this night!" Ramona saw Xaviar's pain and fury. Each name struck him as an accusation of his failure. *Weak and pathetic Toreador, my ass!* he was hearing. He could not face the destruction of his people, not yet. Ramona paused, but the litany still clamored for release. Couldn't Xaviar, so much older and more powerful than her, feel this? Surely Blackfeather would have understood.

Xaviar clawed his way closer, snarling with each inch. "I'll teach you to disobey me, you damn whelp."

Ramona stiffened. She took a step back from her elder, and her voice rang out stronger than ever. "I am Mutabo... I am Lisa

Strongback..." Name after name she recited. One after another, she released their spirits to the night.

"I am Brant Edmonson. I die for my clan this night!"

Xaviar pursued her. His intent was clear. But he could not catch her.

"I am Ratface. I die for my clan this night!"

Finally, Xaviar collapsed. His fury faded, and his strength was long since spent.

Ramona raised her voice to the heavens. She defied her elder's pride. She defied the terrible eye, wherever it was at this moment.

"I am Joshua Bloodhound. I die for my clan this night!

"I am Maria Evernorth. I die for my clan this night!" With this final declaration, Ramona fell to her knees, not three feet from Xaviar. He lay motionless, as if staked, but his gaze burned into her.

"Go away from here," Xaviar said. He raised his face; it looked much older and more haggard than before. Ramona watched him lying there, broken. She pitied him—and she hated him. He possessed the same arrogance that Tanner had—that self-assurance that they thought gave them the right to push around everyone else, to make decisions for everyone else. Tanner had brought Ramona into this gruesome world of darkness, but it might as well have been Xaviar that had done it. And what of Tanner? she found herself wondering. His name had not come to her as part of the litany; she had not seen him with her dead.

"Get out of here!" Xaviar bellowed, and interrupted her thoughts. "I will bring the seven clans to deal with this beast. You are no longer needed. Begone!" Ramona could feel the vitriol in his words. She was a reminder of his failure, of his most terrible defeat, and he wanted no part of her. She doubted he could catch her, not in his current condition. But he wouldn't always be in this condition.

Ramona found herself running again, her fatigue overcome by hatred, her body fueled by fear. She ran not from Xaviar, though leaving him was not, she guessed, unwise. It wasn't even the throbbing eye she ran from anymore. She ran from the emptiness that had taken root within her, that threatened to annihilate all that she'd ever been, and she feared that she'd never escape it..

About the Author

Gherbod Fleming was born behind the Iron Curtain to a Dutch expatriate and a Russian stenographer. The stenographer's husband took exception to the situation and promptly shot and killed Fleming's father. More recently, Fleming authored the Vampire: The Masquerade Trilogy of the *Blood Curse: The Devil's Advocate, The Winnowing,* and *Dark Prophecy*

Curious about other Crossroad Press books?
Stop by our site:
http://store.crossroadpress.com
We offer quality writing
in digital, audio, and print formats.

Printed in Great Britain
by Amazon